A SUNDERED LAND

Maeve Creber

First published in 2006 by

Livres Printemps
13 Russell Terrace
Exeter
EX4 4HX

ISBN 0-9551618-0-0

Cover Design by Aideen Netherway ©Aideen Netherway

Printed and bound in Great Britain by
The Cromwell Press, Trowbridge, Wiltshire.

Dedicated to the memory of Nick Hampson

Written for Jane Marcus

In the 1850s a serious, and for some, calamitous change was taking place in the Border Country. Families were tearing up their roots and leaving their centuries old traditions to find what they believed would be wealth and a better way of life. Many sought work in the shipyards of the Wear. This is the story of one such family. It is a true story, and their grandchildren and great grandchildren still live in the Sundered Land.

PREFACE

By CHRIS MULLIN
Member of Parliament for Sunderland South

My home is an early Victorian Terrace in the centre of Sunderland which, in the 19th Century, housed some of the most prosperous people in the town. It is situated a few hundred yards from the Victoria Hall, scene of the great catastrophe touched upon so movingly in this book. For more than sixty years my house was inhabited by John Doxford and his wife Mary. He was a minor member of the big shipbuilding family, the Doxfords.

Having learned of this I thought to myself, 'any family who have lived in my house for sixty years deserve to have their picture hanging on the wall'. A local antiquarian, Doug Smith, was persuaded to search through a pile of glass plates from a long defunct High Street photographer's and duly came across one labelled 'John Doxford'. It was taken to a local photographer and developed. Sure enough, out of the darkness into which he had receded more than a hundred years ago, emerged a bewhiskered Victorian gentleman in a stiff collar. Mr. John Doxford, no less.

Encouraged by this success, I began to search for a picture of his wife, Mary. After months of painstaking detective work, which succeeded only in establishing that the family had died out in the mid-1970's, I wrote an article in The Daily Telegraph describing my researches. Incredibly, this resulted in a letter from a woman in London who, as a child, had lived next door to one of the Doxford grand-children from who she had acquired sepia prints, taken in the 1890's, of John and Mary Doxford surrounded by their young grand-children. Those pictures now adorn the wall of my hallway, along with the portrait of John Doxford.

I then wrote another article in The Daily Telegraph and this produced a letter from a woman in the South West saying that her grandfather had worked as a pilot in Doxford's shipyard and that, as a young girl, her mother had visited my house to play the piano for old Mrs. Doxford; on one occasion, which she described in detail to attend a birthday party for one of the Doxford grandchildren. What's more, her mother (then aged 101) was still alive and had a clear recollection of her visit to the Doxford house and of one incident in particular.

The letter came from Maeve Creber, the author of this remarkable book. Based on her own researches and her mother's memories, and making brilliant use of local dialect, she has produced this vivid portrait of 19th Century working class life in the North East of England. It rivals anything produced by Catherine Cookson. I hope it will be widely read.

CHRIS MULLIN

1811
PROLOGUE

IN WHICH A CERTAIN MR. MACKENZIE MEETS A SMALL GIRL OF NO IMPORTANCE AT ALL ON THE SANDS OF SPITTAL.

'The peasantry of the North East part of England can bear considerable fatigue. They are a hardy race, of tolerable height, well-formed and stout. Their dress is plain and decent and they wear clogs on working days with wooden soles to resist the dampness and keep the feet within their natural warmth.'

With these words I intend to begin my work which I have entitled 'A Historical and Descriptive View of the County of Northumberland with Berwick upon Tweed and Other Places on the Scottish Border.' It is right that I should also state clearly before my reader advances further into my text, the consideration that to be ignorant of low life is a mark of imprudence or the meanest sort of pride in a gentleman and almost of criminality in the statesman, the legislator and the magistrate.

'The seamen are a most hardy and active race of men. The hard labour which they perform braces the sinews and gives them an unequalled degree of strength and they are accustomed to every kind of danger, their voyages being often hazardous and rapid.' *

Indeed I have also noted the following, that the celebrated Captain Cook began his naval career in the very waters entered by the Tweed which we now survey. However, in men of this kind whose lives are spent at sea there is a thoughtless prodigality and they have clung to many a superstitious fear and many an observance, which, though they be the boldest men on earth admits to an unhappy flaw in character. Nowhere is this more remarked than in the men of the village and community of Spittal, on the South side of the Tweed in the township of Tweedmouth which is under the authority of the County of Durham and within the boundaries of that area we know as Islandshire. The sanctity of that land, of Holy Island itself, of the revered spirit of St.Cuthbert, of the Gospels of Lindisfarne, seems not to have pervaded the awareness of the population of Spittal, who have no Church, save a loft above a stable, from whence noxious odours rise to affront the nostrils of the worshippers of whom there be some one hundred and thirty and they are crowded and pressed together in an unseemly closeness seeing that most are unwashed. This is no place to consider oneself in the Presence of the Lord, since the foul smell of stale sweat cannot be ignored. Moreover the accommodation of these unfortunate folk is wretched and the Common land that forms their boundary is the place of congregation for vagabonds and smugglers of whom it is said there are not a few within the village itself together with women of a certain kind who ply their ancient trade wherever there are landings for ships and men and of whom we need not speak. The beauties of the landscape, the variegated colourings of nature succeeding to cultivation lie in apparent confusion and not infrequently the whole is obscured and enveloped by an unwholesome sea vapour or mist.

It was as I had noted down these observations in the little book I keep in my inner pocket, in readiness to enlarge upon at a time of greater opportunity such as is afforded by the undisturbed environs of my Study, that I met a child carrying a sack of coals upon her back. Her age I estimated to be about eleven years or thereabouts for she could not be exactly sure herself and had no notion of the year in which she had been born. Her feet were unshod and her hair was a pale colour caught in the watery sunlight by gleams of auburn. Her skin was fair but freckled as is often the case with folk of this kind who spend much time out of doors and I could not help but remark, albeit to myself, that her frame was slender and though not ill nourished, yet not at all robust considering the nature of her task.

The people of these parts take pride, as I have discovered, in their ancestry which they like to think of as Viking, proclaimed in their light hair and skin and their blue eyes but I doubt that they have any clear idea of the true nature and history of those plundering marauders, for if they did they would not be so anxious to suggest their association with rape and pillage!

"What is your name, child?" I asked.

"Ma name is Kate, sir," she said.

"Kate who?" said I, "what is your family name, child?"

"They ca' me Kate," she whispered, her eyes downcast as if in shame.

"Yet I am sure, Kate, that you have another name, the name of your mother and father. What, pray, is that?"

"They is me Mam and Da, sir, though some calls me Da, Tatun."

"Your father then is Mister Tatun," I said, though I guessed the name to be Tathum which is common in these parts.

"It may be, sir," she said, "though ah have ne'er heard him to be called Mister, only Tatun."

"Are you baptised, child?" I asked, stooping to catch her words, directed as they were to the sand which seeped up between her toes now curling and pressing into that soft floor.

"Ah dinna ken, sir," said she.

"It is a bad thing to be unbaptised," I said, raising my forefinger. At this she looked up, and gazing into my eyes with greater confidence she said, "ah dinna remember for mysel' sir, but ma wee brither were ta'en to the Minister and he spake them words, and ca'ed him Robert, and spilt a wee drop a' water on his heed, and that ah ken for ah was there."

"Why, that is good, child," I said, "for now I am sure that if Robert was baptised then so were you, and it is certain that you are not Kate, but Catherine."

" Aye, sir."

"Catherine is a name to bear with pride. It has been the name of many an English Queen," I said, smiling down upon the child.

"Me Mam says tha' we folk are not o' the English blood, and we knows nought of English queens, sir, and what be their names, nor if there bees any Scots ladies Catherine so called, for we are neither Scots nor English born."

"Then Catherine, what are you?"

"Why sir, we are Spittal folk, and tha' is all."

"And have you been to school, Catherine?" I asked, for I was intrigued by the little maid.

"Nay sir, schooling is no for me nor for ma sisters neither, for we may not be idle, but ma brithers hae bin there an they dae write and read some letters on a page if it be put before them."

"Then I fear Catherine, that you will not be able to read the book that I am writing about this part of the country, though perhaps your brothers may be able to read it to you when they are older. I intend that it shall also have pictures of scenery and fine buildings."

"Are ye a buik writer, sir?"

"That I am."

"Ah hae seen a buik, sir, but I ne'er did see a buik writer before. Ah'm the first of ma kin to see a buik writer, for ma father e'en, though he be a canny seaman an must study in a buik, ah'm sure I ne'er heerd him tell o' seeing the man who put his pen to them."

"Well now, Catherine, go on your way," I said, smiling at the maid who now regarded me with an unveiled amazement which had I been a younger man might have discomforted me with the blushes of inexperienced pleasure.

"Remember to be a good girl always, so that the Lord will bless you, Catherine," I said, and I watched her moving across the strand close to the water's edge until she was out of sight in the sea mist and then I observed her slender figure emerging as if from a cloud as she made her way inland towards the miserable hovel that I supposed to be her dwelling.

I mention this encounter, though it has no significance within the wider purposes of my work, quite simply to illustrate the innocence and lack of guile of any child, even a child of these Spittal people, who later as we know, are polluted by a low cunning often applied to oppose the Excise which operates for the benefit of all law-abiding folk in this land. Indeed I have heard it rumoured that one of their number has constructed a series of tunnels and passages between all the dwellings, miserable though they are, so that contraband may be concealed and the criminals, for that is what they are, may escape with ease from one house to another on the arrival of the Excise.

I continue, now with the substance of my work:

"Berwick upon Tweed is as fine a town as one could wish to see. Its magnificent Town Hall with Assembly Rooms, as well appointed as any in the Kingdom, has an upper storey which is a common gaol. It is most healthy and pleasant, affording the unfortunates there detained, fine views of the town, Bamborough Castle and Holy Island itself. There is a long gallery in which they may perambulate and prisoners whose offences are not grave can walk in the free fresh air on the roof. Many have retrieved their fortunes in those extensive and beautiful surroundings. There are six

Free Schools belonging to the Corporation. One has no fewer than five spacious rooms, one for mathematics, one for writing and three reading schools. There is also a Grammar School for the teaching of the Classics, and education for the poor but hard working families of labourers is encouraged. Nor are the Arts forgotten, for there is a fine theatre, built by Stephen Kemble himself, the esteemed Manager of the theatre in Newcastle upon Tyne and there one may see the finest of entertainments............."

My mind, at this point, refusing all my entreaties to continue with the above text, the fruit of my researches over a considerable period of time, regardless of its value to the scholar, traveller or historian of the future, creeps back like a furtive wastrel against my will and wishes, to the remembrance of that pale creature who will be of no significance at all to any of the above, and who, in one hundred or more years' time will be as forgotten as if she had never lived.

Eneas Mackenzie

March 1811

*A Historical and Descriptive View of the County of Northumberland with Berwick upon Tweed and other Places on the Scottish Border Pub. Mackenzie and Dent (1811)

BERWICK-ON-TWEED
FEBRUARY 1837

CHAPTER ONE

Ralph Laidler, Linen Draper and Mercer, proprietor of the most patronised shop in Berwick for the purchase of fine cloth, stands behind his substantial mahogany counter, balancing the weight of his upper body on the flattened palms of his hands which press down against the glowing patina of the wood. These are capable hands, hands that know their business and can be trusted and as a shopkeeper, though now surely something more than that, he is justly proud of himself, his clientele, and of the quality of his goods, for he knows that ladies of gentility and good taste come to his establishment in their carriages to select the material for their gowns and household linens. Silks imported from the Orient as well as more humble muslins, delicately printed cottons and the latest stuffs fashionable in London and Edinburgh are stacked in carefully assorted layers which display their brilliance, their subtlety of texture, and their intricacy of design to the very best advantage. Here and there, seemingly at random a swathe of apricot silk or deep crimson velvet escapes its roll and lies open and profligate, to be fingered and held rapturously against the sensitive cheek of a lady, and from the shelves behind the counter, in apparently wanton abandon, a drape of apple green slipper satin shimmers in the Northern sunlight reflected by the uneven panes of glass in the bow window of the shop.

Ralph Laidler is a man of standing in the town. He dines on occasions with the Mayor and other members of the Corporation and whereas his father and grandfather understood dinner to be a main meal eaten at one o'clock midday, he himself has had the benefit of enlightenment that association with a more cultured society bestows and he and his good wife, though in ordinary domestic circumstances adhering to the long held practices of their forebears, in public, as one may say, dine at eight and do not sup at all except for a bowl of bread soaked in milk with a little sugar before bedtime.

Naturally, the high esteem in which he is held by the Gentility, meaning in this instance the English gentlefolk, does not permit him to aspire to associate with them on a social level, though it has to be said that things are somewhat different with that rougher breed, the Scottish nobility who are less discerning in the company they encourage, but whose more unfettered manners earn them no great respect from Mister Laidler, for he knows his place and his station and expects others to know and understand theirs. This apparent social inequality is in fact no such thing. It is a perfectly formulated system that allows each individual to interact with his fellows in confidence and decorum. It is the way the world works, and Ralph Laidler has no time or patience to spare for those whose discontented rumblings threaten to disturb the smooth running of the social fabric.

The portentous clang of the shop bell announces the arrival of a customer and the heavy door with its solid brass hinges and appurtenances is pushed open by a person who has arrived on foot, for no carriage has clattered to an unsteady halt on the cobbles of the street adjacent to the shop. His customer, well known to the proprietor since she was a child and he a young man of twenty years or so, and just taking over his father's business, is Mistress Hogarth of Spittal.

"Good morning to ye, Missis Hogarth," says Ralph Laidler,"and what brings ye across the water to the town?"

"My Margaret is ti be wed," she says.

"It's decided then is it, Missis?"

"As good as. If he hasna spake the words o' askin' yet, it'll no be lang, an dinna look doon yer nose, Rafe Laidler fer ti be sure she is ti wed wi' a kinsman o' yer own."

"Indeed, that I know, though John Laidlaw is but a very distant relation."

"He is your Granda's son's son, an on your mither's side o' ye family he is your Granda's daughter's nephew for he is related ti ye on twa sides."

"Well, never mind that, I am sure he is a fine young man."

"Aye, fine, an weel set ti be a Master Mariner. Ma lassie is but sixteen years of age an she wullna' wed until eighteen, but tis a guid thing to be makin' o' the quilt."

Useless it would be for Ralph Laidler to point out that he and his good wife have long sought to separate themselves from those branches of the family that in former times were known as limmer rogues, smugglers and reivers and still now when opportunity arises engage themselves in unlawful activities that set them at odds with His Majesty's Excise. To that end he has changed the spelling of his name to make it appear more English and to disguise its association with Border words such as 'law' for vale, which suggest nothing more than uncivilised tribes who spend their law-less days in stealing each other's sheep and womenfolk and not infrequently killing one another. In any case such an observation would make little impression on his customer since it is well known that she can neither read nor write and the significance of a deviation in spelling, when the name is pronounced the same no matter how it is spelled would be entirely lost on her. The white fishing having been good this year he has no doubt that she has money to spend, and a customer is a customer no matter who they are or how they spell their name.

"Wull ye show me yeer cotton sateen then, Mister Laidler. I need twa colours for a quilt. Ma lassie wull need a guid warm quilt for her bed.

"Ha! aye that she will, Kate, for tha' laddie'ull nae be wantin' a cauld fish in's bed."

"An hwat de ye mean by tha' Rafe Laidler? Fer I kens that look ye hae. "

"I mean nothing by it, Kate, except that the winters are cold and the blessings of a good padded quilt such as ye and your womenfolk make are not to be scorned by anyone," says Ralph Laidler preferring now the English mode of speaking in which ignoble thoughts are impossible.

"Then I wull tak five yards o' the light blue, yonder, fer the underside, an I'll tak a seat in yer shop an rest ma feet for a while an think aboot the top side stuff."

"Aye you're welcome and maybe you'll drink a cup o' tea with me, for I'm about to take some refreshment myself, Kate."

Ralph Laidler calls to his shop boy in the back room to boil up the kettle and bring tea for himself and Mistress Hogarth. He sits down in the chair beside her, for it is always pleasant to have a wee crack with a nice looking woman, even if she be no more than a Spittal lass.

Catherine Hogarth sits comfortably in the spindle back chair so thoughtfully provided by the proprietor for his customers, though she knows that for a lady of breeding Ralph Laidler will bring out a plush velvet upholstered spoon-back from his own quarters at the back of the shop. If the lady is expected, the spoon-back will be placed ready so that she may believe that furniture of such quality is an everyday matter of no special consequence to the proprietor. Mistress Hogarth also knows from experience the turn that the conversation will now take, for Ralph Laidler is a man who can never resist the opportunity to emphasise his own importance when the timing is propitious. All too often such a felicitous moment does not arrive, since it would be unsuitable to speak of oneself in terms of accomplishment in the company of one's betters, but the advantage of converse with lower folk is that it creates an inner ease which makes the enjoyment of such a conversation, possible. It is not so much the case that he intends to impress his disadvantaged listener as that he needs from time to time to impress himself.

Ralph Laidler eases himself onto the chair beside his customer and sighs.

"Ach,aye!" he says, reverting to the comfort of the vernacular as he begins to sink into the pleasure of the anticipation of his tale,"did I ever tell ye, Kate, that I was put into a buik?"

"An when was tha' then, Mister?"

"Some time ago now, mind, but twas a buik of great renown. Aye that it was!"

He pauses, hoping that Mistress Hogarth will prompt him with a further question. As if to remind her of her cue he sighs again.

"Aye!" he says.

She waits to allow him to endure the silence of her failure to respond for just a little longer. Then she says,"Wha' kind of a buik was tha' then, Mister?"

"Twas a book of learning about the County of Northumbria and other adjacent places."

"An wha' were ye in the buik, then?"

"My ain name and profession were put, along wi' those of lairds and their ladies and others of high standing, magistrates and judges and the like."

"An fishmongers an candle makers an a' tha' too?"

"Folk of full respectability, Kate."

"An how was they put inta a buik, then, Mister?"

"They was all chosen, like myself, to be subscribers to that book of learning."

"Wha's they, then?"

"Wha's they? They is gentlefolk chosen to give money to make a book."

"Tae gif money, ye say?"

"Aye."

Ralph Laidler leans back in his chair. His chest expands,"Aye, Kate, folks of means, of standing, folks chosen."

There is silence, whilst Mistress Hogarth digests the information.

"An did ye ever ken the mon tha' made the buik, Mister Laidler?"

"No personally, though I heard tell of him, and he was a most learned and worthy gentleman as I believe."

"Is tha' so?"

"Aye, and eminent, so they say. Renowned in Edinburgh and London too."

"Weel! Weel!"

"Aye." He rests back in his chair, content to let the moment lie on the air between them, heavy with import and not to be passed over. Mistress Hogarth sighs, and also settles more comfortably. She allows the silence to continue and then as if she has only just thought of it, she says,"Ah kenned him."

He looks up sharply."Nay, now Kate, how could ye ken that man? Ye canna even read his buik."

"Ah kenned him a' the same."

Ralph Laidler smiles,"No doubt ye've met with many a learned man then Kate?"

"Nay, Mister Laidler tha' I hae not an weel ye knas it, but tha' one I hae met wi'.Twas he tol' me tha' ma name wasna Kate but Catherine, which is a lady's name, and mony a fine burd is named so, an no shame in it. Fer did ye kna' tha' Catherine is a name o' Queens?"

"What Queens?"

"English Queens an tha."

"English Queens?"

"Aye, though we folk knas nothing o' English kings an queens, 'cept that wight Edward who did so batter the toon and put the Wallace to shame, as is telled."

The proprietor sits up more firmly in his chair. He is aware of a need to reclaim the initiative and direction of the conversation for to tell the truth he has but a puny knowledge of history. He strains to remember his schooldays and the mention of the particular Edward who had an association with Berwick. That there have been many battles fought between the English and the Scots he is in no doubt, but in his knowledge of the details he finds himself to be largely ignorant.

"Ach aye, he were a limmer rogue that Wallace," he ventures.

"Nay, Mister Laidler, he were nay limmer, twas t' ither mon, tha' Edward twas he was a rogue, ye remember."

"Ach aye, we all knows that, Kate, but in my mind, in my judgment, twas both."

"Both mister?"

"Aye, both. Both of them was traitors and knaves."

"The Wallace wa' nay traitor."

"Well, never mind he Kate, we must always bear in mind that these historical figures did not live in our times."

"Nay, as ye'll ken they was in Berwick in the twelve hundred and nineties as ah believe."

Ralph Laidler never could hold a date of history in his head, but he gives a solemn nod to signify wisdom and affirmation.

"Aye," he says firmly as if about to pronounce a judgment,"they did not have the advantages of these modern days, as we know, and therefore we must view the sorry events of long ago with the eyes of charity and understanding. We must employ the retrospective of hindsight. Aye."

"Wha' retrospective is tha' then, Mister, an wha' is they advantages?"

"Many, Kate."

"Ah canna think o' many. Can ye give us an example noo?"

"Plenty. Too numerous to mention."

"Wha'? Too wha', Mister?"

"Numerous, Kate. It means we must not question these things."

"Is tha' wha' education tells us if we hae it, Mister, tha' we best no ask a few questions?"

"Education teaches us things of importance and we must learn them, not waste our time in idle speculation. Our teachers are wise folk who tell us what is best for us to know, and that we cannot judge for ourselves. That is what education is."

"Ah, the likes o' me hae none, so we's still askin. "

Ralph Laidler shakes his head as if in sorrow and changes the subject.

"Where did ye meet this famous man, the buik writer Kate? In the grand salons of Edinburgh, or the palaces of scholarship maybe, where ye are wont to go of an afternoon?

"Nay, Mister Laidler, dinna mak fun o' me fer ah met wi' the gentleman truly on the sands o' Spittal when he were composing of his buik."

"Aye well, so it may be, but I myself have doubts that the gentleman you met was the same one that made the buik, for what learned gentleman and scholar would be composing a work of authority upon the sands of Spittal?" Ralph Laidler gives a benevolent and indulgent smile.

"Twas he fo' sure."

"Well now, Kate, we will not disagree though I am afraid that you are mistaken." He leans towards the counter and pulls open a heavy mahogany drawer, then standing he uses both hands to lift out the book."Volume one, Kate. Tis a work in two volumes." He eases himself back into his chair."Let me read you the dedication."

"Wha's tha' then, Mister?"

"That is the tribute to the person for whom the book is written. I think when you hear it you will realize that whatever gentleman you met on Spittal sands, it was not he who wrote this buik." He clears his throat again and reads: " 'May it please your Lordship, having made arrangements for publishing an Historical and Descriptive View of Northumberland it was impossible that your Lordship, the heir of the noble and illustrious House of Percy —' "

"Mony a rogue an a rebel in they Percies, as is telled," interrupts Mistress Hogarth.

Clicking his tongue in irritation, Ralph Laidler gives her a sour look and returns to the book."'Noble and illustrious House of Percy impossible that it should not occur to our minds in selecting a patron, under whose auspices we should present to the public a work in which the virtues and heroism of your immortal ancestors —' "

"They is no immortal, Ralph, they is deeyed, like arl them tha' went before."

" ' and the unparalleled patriotism and liberality of your dignified Father, constitute so prominent and interesting a part.' " He pauses,"Aye, indeed," he says, then he continues reading, 'At the very commencement of your public career your Lordship justified the expectations that were formed from your high rank and splendid extraction, and in opposing a barbarous, impolitic, and loathsome system of slavery, so disgraceful to the British Empire, displayed a rectitude of principle, liberality of spirit and ingenuous goodness of heart, which matured by experience, must form a great and estimable character. This presage is further strengthened by your steady and correct conduct at an age when dissipation is scarcely supposed to deserve censure.' "   Ralph Laidlaw sighs and shakes his head to show agreement here, then he continues,"'That your Lordship may long live to emulate the princely munificence of your noble Father and to render important services to your country and that the ancient House of Percy may preserve its honours unfaded to the latest age is the sincere wish of your Lordship's obliged and obedient servants, the Publishers.' "

He looks up,"A dedication, Kate, to his Lordship and his noble House of Percy."

"Wull ye read tha' bit again aboot the emulating and tha.' "

"He says he hopes that his Lordship will 'long live to emulate the princely munificence of his noble Father. That means, Kate — "

"Aye, ah knas wha' it means, Ralph, an well may it be wished, for they Percies wha' fought against the king in ancient times as ah've heerd, they rebel Percies hae well moneyed their sels. They well seen tae tha'. Ye'll no hae they Percies tae come inta yeer shop an beg fer a bit stuff."

"They are noble, Kate. You and I are not." Ralph Laidler certainly believes this to be true in the case of the woman he now addresses whose irreverent comments prove her disastrous lack of respect and breeding. In his own case, though he knows himself to be less than the nobility, he yet hopes to make himself acceptable in their company. He closes the book and puts it reverently on the counter.

"Now, seeing that it is a kinsman of mine that your Margaret is marrying I will let ye have three yards of good stuff for the quilt for nothing. "

"Tha' is a guid emulatin' o' munificence, Mister Laidler," she says,"but t'would be a better emulatin' if 'twere five yard."

Ralph Laidler, forgetting the carefully cultivated English that he now aspires to speak, reaches for the vernacular with all the force of its expression.

"Aw ye jade, ye brasent limmer! Wad ye say sich thing! Tak wha' ye're gift noo an be on yeer way fer ah haf mony matters ti attend ti this day. Di ye think tha' ahm a wealthy mon to be gien awa' ma stock ti ahl tha' wants it? Off wi' ye noo,an tak wha' ye're gift! An' dinna forget ti pay me fer the other! An as fer meetin' wi' scholars an them o' learnin' on yon sands, dinna gie me sich blather."

"An ah'll be needin' cotton wadding as weel, Mister Laidler, will ye no let us hae a little on account maybe? If ah had yeer grand education an yeer canny emulatin' ah wad hae nay need ti ask fer yer kindness, but ye knaws tha' when the boat comes in ye shall be paid in full."

When the transaction is complete, though not entirely to the satisfaction of either party, Ralph Laidler opens the heavy door and watches the departing figure of Mistress Hogarth.

"They're nay but beggarly folk, they Spittalers," he thinks,"an tis a great shame that one of mine is to be associated wi' them. That Margaret is nae more than a brasent strumpet, fer all tha' she can dance an guile us wi' her charms. But wha' can one expect from ignorance. Weel, ma kinsman has nay asked fer her yet, an there's mony a slip, as the saying goes!"

Slowly and carefully he pulls open the mahogany drawer. Lovingly he handles the leather of the volume and dusts it over with his sleeve. Then he opens it again to the title page.

"A Historical and Descriptive View of the County of Northumberland with Berwick upon Tweed and Other Places on the Scottish Border" he reads aloud."Carefully collected from personal Research, Original Communication, and Works of Undoubted Authority. Published by Mackenzie, aye, there it is." He reads on"Sold also by Craddock and Joy, London, and by all the respectable booksellers in the North of England." He turns the pages of introduction until he reaches the page headed Subscribers. His finger runs down the list, pausing every now and then,"The Right Honourable Lord Algernon Percy" he murmurs,"The Right Honourable Lady Elizabeth Percy, The Right Honourable Lady Julia Percy, The Right Honourable Lady Agnes Percy and here he is, Hugh Earl Percy himself." He turns the pages and finally the roving fore- finger stops, triumphant."Ralph Laidler, Linen Drap. Berwick. Ach aye, there it is, plain enough for anyone to see." He flicks through the remaining pages."Tis a serious volume, nay mention here of any

Edwards or them that fought wi' them. Wha' twaddlin' nonsense is spake by them Spittalers." Solemnly he replaces the book in its drawer and calls for the shop boy to clear the teacups.

"Spittal folk is nought but sounding brass and tinkling cymbals, boy," he says.

"Hwhat's they?" asks the boy.

"They's in the Bible, ye should knaw tha.'"

"Spittal folk is in the Bible?"

"Nay, ye ignoran' rogue, ahm speakin' of the sounding brass and tha.' "

"Ah!" The boy gathers up the empty cups and hurries into the back room leaving Ralph Laidler to shake his head despairingly,"nay benefit of their education, nay application to their studies in the young folk of today. Like is said in the book, tis nought but an age o' dissipation wi'out the censure. Ach Aye!"

CHAPTER TWO

The hiring of servants takes place twice yearly in the town of Berwick upon Tweed. It is a long practiced tradition and one not wholly approved of by Ralph Laidler, Linen Draper, for it permits many low and common folk to congregate in the town and in particular the Market place which is proximate to his establishment. Such an opportunity is relished by those who take satisfaction in lewd behaviour and vulgar speech and manners, and all of this is accompanied by clamour and ear splitting noise which is hardly to be born for half an hour, much less a whole day, in which it must be endured until long after the sun goes down. If it were not for the fact that business of a sort is brisk Ralph Laidler would close down his shop and board up his window with the wooden shutters but the truth is that many of the farming folk come into town on that day, whole families in their carts, to buy their spring or autumn needs of cloth; serge, cotton, muslin, and cambric to supply their households and servants.

Ralph Laidler has no liking for the general hubbub, which, for his wife, if she is obliged to stay in the town on that day, will cause her to retire to bed with a migrainous headache lasting for a week and entailing the taking of meals in the privacy of her chamber where the curtains may be closed in a futile attempt to prevent the entrance of daylight and noise.

The gentry, whose patronage he enjoys and has been fortunate enough to cultivate, will not honour him with their custom on such days for they are not to be seen in the town except for the occasional curious young wife well chaperoned by her husband who will direct her eyes away from scenes of ribaldry that might offend her more delicate sensibility. Such young women are known to possess a desire to observe the behaviour of the common people which they mistakenly regard as quaint, but the gentlefolk and landowners are more properly represented by their estate managers and bailiffs whose responsibility it is to oversee the business of servant hiring. The spectacle must be endured of young maids and men standing in the market place to be examined and gawped at as if they were horses. The girls hold a green twig or flower in their hand to signify that they seek a position and the young men, likewise, fix a green branch in their hats. When a prospective employer approaches one of these would-be hirelings, what does he find? Is it a young person anxious to appear obliging and ready to carry the burden of the tasks that will be required of him or her? Far from it! Ralph Laidler has noted that young people nowadays are argumentative and even disrespectful in their manners. They think they have the right to question their employers about conditions of work and terms of employment! They are suspicious of what they consider to be attempts to undervalue their labour, and such bickering and haggling, not infrequently leading to threats of blows, and the hurling of insults ensues, to make the street quite unsuitable for passage by decent and respectable folk. In days gone past but still remembered, the young did not dare to rebuke their elders and had a proper understanding of who their betters were. Their manners were more refined and they had a natural sense of the seemly, now entirely lost. In those days a lass, sometimes no more than twelve or thirteen years old did not stare openly into an employer's face, but cast her eyes downward, blushing with decorous modesty if he should stop to raise her maidenly chin with his forefinger or riding crop the better to judge the likelihood of her demeanour in his wife's parlour, bed chamber, kitchen, or his own dairy. Nowadays she is more likely to present him with a brazen countenance which intends to impress with her defiance rather than her complaisance. All this is to be blamed upon a general lowering and laxity in moral values which is the scourge and the affliction of our present times. This is certainly the informed opinion of Ralph Laidler. One can only fear and wonder where this is leading to for future generations.

This same moral laxity becomes even more distressingly apparent as the day wears on. The Public Houses, all too interested in their opportunity to attract trade no matter of what ribald nature that may be, open their windows and encourage musicians, if vulgar fiddlers and pipers can be so called. Gone are the pleasant and harmonious airs of yesteryear, for such is the cacophony and caterwauling that they make from the screeching of bow on string and drone of pipes that it cannot be recognised as music in Ralph Laidlers's ears. They seat themselves close by inside and strike up to inflame the senses and raise the excitements of passion in the young and foolish people there assembled whose elders appear to exercise no control over them. When the hiring is over the girls and the men separate, the men to gawp in little groups and the girls to parade themselves shamelessly as if in innocent girlish chatter, but in truth to do nothing more or less than to attract an admirer in the most blatant fashion, even lifting the hem to display the intimacies of the ankle when neither the weather nor the condition of the pavement require it.

Then, in couples, man and girl, they enter the Public House, a place where no lady of any respectability would set foot, even if accompanied by a gentleman, and there, openly and unashamedly they drink Punch or ale, or hot ale and brandy. It is not unusual for couples to spend between two shillings and sixpence and five shillings on this intemperance, more than a week's or even a month's wages, money they can ill afford and which should be put to better and more sober use, or saved, that they might aspire to raise themselves and their offspring above their menial state. But as Ralph Laidler has observed, the youth of today think only of today and its vanities and take no thought of the morrow.

Worse is to follow. As the influence of the beverage takes hold, they and their partners move on, to a room that has been set aside and prepared by the landlord for dancing and here are exhibited scenes of great indelicacy, most unpleasant to the eye of any peaceable observer, as is Ralph Laidler. For whereas in the Halls of country houses occasional dancing does take place but always in harmony with mans' finer instincts, the old style minuet perhaps, or in some pleasant rustic barn amongst the honest labourers of the field, a country dance of long tradition may be enjoyed, but here are performed, to a wild frenzy of fiddling, common jigs and reels interspersed with the wailing of Northumbrian pipes which lack that healthy pride and vigour of the Scottish kind. Moreover, one couple at a time takes the floor whilst a dozen others wait their turn and as each couple leaves the floor there is such raucous applause and such egging on of the next pair that the noise gets louder and louder as one after another the couples demonstrate their skills in the open debauchery of this so-called dancing. Never is such swirling and lifting of skirts, such displays of ankles and even of knees, or such swinging of hips seen as in these depraved procedures. Eventually, the assembly being now in an uproar, everyone including the musicians gets up onto the benches to shout, stamp their feet to the rhythm of the music (since we must call it such), and half intoxicated as they are the men begin to hurl abuse at one another and all too often to fight over some trollop, and even the women can and do fight like tigers.

That is not the end. Ralph Laidler has seen that at the finish of each dance and in particular, at the end of the night's entertainment the fiddler gives a shrill and raucous squeak across his strings with the bow and this is the signal for hearty and improper kisses to be exchanged such as would be blushed at even within the privacy of the marital chamber! These are scenes that remind of nothing so much as the ways of foreigners, Catholic Spaniards, Frenchies, or even the godless Red Indian savages who know no better. All this Ralph Laidler has been obliged to observe unwillingly in order to safeguard the decency of his house and the decorum of his wife's chamber behind its firmly closed doors.

§

Johnny Laidlaw (Ralph Laidler would have you note the small but significant difference in spelling of the family name) stands in the corner of the room, tallest by far of the group of young sea-farers who are his companions and near to the door leading to the bar-room, as if his presence amongst the dancers and musicians is accidental and cannot be taken for granted. At any moment, it seems, he may withdraw himself and be the cause of disappointment in many a young lass's heart, who hopes that he will notice her that night. At one and twenty years, Johnny Laidlaw has circumnavigated the world and has witnessed many of its ways even if he has been largely an observer rather than a participator despite much encouragement from his ship-mates.

From a distance his dark brows appear to overshadow his eyes giving them the appearance of being deep set and accentuating his high cheek bones but on drawing nearer one cannot but remark the blueness of these same eyes, a very pale and yet startling blue, of one habituated to straining into the distance over an expanse of ocean and protecting them from the brilliance of light from sea and sky that is now permanently reflected in them. He turns his head neither to the right nor the left and does not smile or display any pleasure or interest in what he sees, yet with those narrowed eyes he projects a concentration which remains fixed on the spectacle before him.

A girl of not more than sixteen years so slight of figure that it seems she could be lost entirely in the throng, is jostled by the press of people near the bar room door and brushes against him as if by accident. Her fair hair tinged with auburn is tied back in an unruly knot and without looking up at him (which she disdains to do, as other girls, who flutter their lashes and make cow eyes) she says in a confident voice that all may hear, "wi' ye dance wi' me then Johnny?"

"Nay, thou knaws ah dinna dance."

"Some says ye de."

"Ah sayed ah dinna, no I canna. "

"As ye please."

Several of the young lasses who hear this interchange begin to titter behind their hands. Margaret Hogarth is too forward in her manners and they are glad to see her brought a little lower, for the truth is that there is hardly a young female in the room who would not be brought to near fainting if she had the good fortune to be smiled upon by Johnny Laidlaw far less to be chosen by him as a dancing partner. The girl takes the arm of Jimmy Mendham and together they push their way to the floor to excite the spectators in the rendering of a reel which is soon accompanied by the enthusiastic applause of the whole assembly and the piercing shrieks and whoops of the young men. Johnny Laidlaw appears to be unmoved as he leans back against the doorway. His eyes which never leave the dancing couple remain without expression except for the fixedness of their gaze and his arms which are folded in front of him betray no interest in the seductive intensity of the rhythm. Then the fiddlers temporarily exhausted from their exertions call for ale and it is brought in large earthenware pitchers and poured into the tankards of the musicians who wipe the sweat from their brows and out of their eyes with their neckerchiefs. Gradually a call goes up which starts as a low murmur but grows in volume as it is caught up by the crowd, "where's Jamie? Where's Jamie Strength?" The cry is carried by those in the public bar, "Jamie, come on ma bonny lad, ye' re wanted within." From his seat on the settle in the corner not too far from the fire, an old man raises his arm. His companions lean towards him to help him rise but he pushes them away and eases himself into a standing position and even though his body is now twisted with age and aching, it is still the body of a man of formidable size, the most extraordinary feature of his appearance being his hands which with their long and bony fingers are of such great size as to be out of proportion to his frame.

Jamie Strength, whose real name is James Stuart, named for the Pretender with whom he claims direct kinship, is reputed to be nigh on one hundred and fourteen years old. He is the son of General John Stuart and the grandson of the Lady of Airlie who was disgracefully murdered by members of the Clan Campbell whose villainous deeds and treachery whate'er side they be on are known by all. He was present on the field at Culloden and was an officer in General Wolfe's army witnessing the death of that great leader at Quebec. To this day he is clad in the uniform of a British Ensign and though faded, its scarlet lapels and brass buttons proclaim the pride with which he wears it. It is said that he has married five times and has some twenty-seven children, ten of whom have been killed fighting for their country. He has obtained the name by which he is known throughout the region on account of his extraordinary strength which though now failing because of his years, at one time enabled him to carry a cart loaded with one ton and a half of hay. Slowly he makes his way unaided through the throng in the public bar and a passage is cleared for him into the dancing room. There one of the fiddlers gives him his instrument and a stool is brought for him at the edge of the floor. But Jamie Strength is not yet ready to strike up a tune. He looks around the assembly and asks for an oak table to be brought into the middle of the room. "Hwat wi' ye gie us, Jamie?" asks one of the younger men.

"Ah"ll gie ye nay Scots nor English jigs thus time," he answers in a voice still powerful to be heard, "nay," and he signals to the other musicians who begin to take their places around him, "bring up tha' bra' lad they ca' Jawnny Laidlaw, an him an me, the auld an the young'll tigither show ye how they dance a reel in the fair land across the Western sea, o' Ireland."

Then all eyes turn to Johnny Laidlaw as he unfolds his arms and strides down towards the centre of the dancing room and with one leap is standing on the oaken table, so that he towers above the heads of the spectators.

"Are ye fit like, Jawnny?" calls the fiddler.

"Aye, tha' ah am, Jamie lad."

"Then awa' we go."

Jamie Strength draws the bow powerfully across the strings in a long and screeching opening chord which is accompanied by shouts of encouragement from the crowd now joined by a press of folk from the public bar who have followed Jamie into the dancing room. Johnny Laidlaw stands tall, erect, unmoving, with his arms almost stiff and straight down by his sides, his palms turned outwards, and then the sound of Jamie's lone fiddle strikes through the hubbub in the room with the spell-binding beating rhythm of the Irish Reel. It seems that not a muscle moves on the lone dancer's body, his arms remain by his side and his face looks straight ahead and then as the rhythm takes hold, his feet catch it and as if independent of the still and rigid body they take up intricate patterns of movement to beat out a sharp counterpoint and the hard leather tipped with steel of sole and heel clacks down upon the wooden table top. The cries of encouragement die down, and even those at the edges of the scene who were chattering idly, fall to silence and turn to watch this spectacle of skill, drawn into the spell of the fast moving precision of the feet. The other fiddlers who have gathered around old Jamie take up the accelerating beat of bow, leather and metal on wood. Now the erect body, dramatic in its stillness that contrasts with the ever quickening precision of the feet, revolves to face the opposite side of the room and though the music swells, the accompanying pounding rhythm of sole and heel is always louder. The audience is stunned to silence and admiration. Then Jeanie Macdonald runs forward and scrambles up onto the table opposite Johnny Laidlaw. He smiles and without breaking the sequence of music and beat, his feet tap out a phrase or pattern of rhythm and then pause, inviting his young partner to imitate with her own. She tries and the spectators, finding their voices shout, "Weel done, Jeannie, lass." Johnny Laidlaw now challenges her to copy a more complicated step as he pauses again, but this one is too difficult for the girl who cannot follow it. She scrambles down off the table, laughing and is applauded by the onlookers. In a flash another girl has leapt up onto the table to confront the dancer. It is Margaret Hogarth, whose eyes blaze with defiance as she stares straight into the pale blue of Johnny Laidlaw's eyes. His gaze is steady as he holds hers as if the two of them were locked in some mortal combat. She waits, her body erect, her arms straight down by her sides. He pauses for a moment and then his feet beat out a pattern of steps so intricate that the spectators gasp. Without removing her gaze from his face, Margaret accepts the challenge and repeats the steps with perfect accuracy. The crowd gasps again. Johnny offers another sequence with accelerated rhythm, Margaret copies it, pauses and offers Johnny a sequence of her own inserting a crossed feet leap into the middle. Johnny takes it, repeating it with a double crossed feet leap. Margaret performs it with ease and circles to face back to the fiddlers again as she does so, so that she is now back to back with Johnny. He circles in one leap so that they are side by side, and now as if by some unspoken but understood agreement, they cross their arms and link them behind their backs and together their feet clack down upon the table in perfect synchronization. The audience begin to cheer and clap in rhythm with the beat of the reel and the couple, still linked, circle on the spot, as if they were one body with a shared but secret language expressed in the rapid, matching movement of their feet. Faster and faster they turn and turn again and the crowd are in an uproar. Then one of the fiddlers stops playing, then another, and another, then a fourth and a fifth, until only the clear notes of Jamie Strength's instrument can be heard, which grow softer and softer, and the feet on the table strike down still with precision but with a gentler grace. The crowd goes quiet again as they witness the winding down of the dance and then Jamie ends with one last pull on the bow over the strings, a ear-splitting scream from the fiddle, accompanied by a final leap high into the air from the dancers whose arms are still linked, which releases the audience into a frenzy of wild applause and screams of "Johnny! Johnny! Maggie! Maggie Hogarth! Jamie! Jamie lad!"

Jamie Strength falls forward dropping the fiddle and the bow, but many anxious hands catch him and hold him as he gradually straightens, breathing deeply. They wipe his face where the sweat runs in little grooves.

"Ye ahright, Jamie?" asks one of the fiddlers.

"Aye, fer a moment then ah thought ah mus' bi takin' the road ti ma Maker, no bifore ma time, mind, but he wullna' have us yet, it seems."

"Ye's no afeard then Jamie, afeard o meeting Him?"

"Afeard! Nay lad, afeard to gan where arl ma kith an ma companions's gan ahready? Ye'll nay see auld folk shaking in their boots for fear o deeth, like them as is gan ti hang i' the morn. We's seen it ahl, laddie, an tis nay big thing."

They help him back to his settle, and this time he accepts the guidance of their arms. "Ach aye," he says, "tis nay big thing this deeth." He leans forward again. "Bring us a wee drop o' the bonny Scots liquor, lads. Noo, ah'll ask ye arl ti raise yeer glasses wi' me fer a Toast." The crowd applauds and turn one to another, "Raise glasses wi' Jamie, for the Toast"

The old man is helped to his feet again, and he strains against breathlessness to raise his voice so that all may hear.

"God bless the King, ah mean the faith's defender.

God bless – no harm in blessing – the Pretender.

But who Pretender is and who the King

God bless ma soul! Ach aye, me lads! Tha's quite anither thing!"

He is helped back into the settle whilst the crowd applauds again. "Well said, Jamie, lad."

Ralph Laidler is caught up in the enthusiasm for the Toast, and finds himself cheering with everyone else though his applause dies in his throat as he notices the approach of Kate Hogarth.

"Weel noo, Mister Laidler," she says,"ah never took ye fer a Jacobite. Wad ye nay be loyal ti the Crown o' England, then? Ah ne'er took ye fer a Papist, Rafe!"

"Gan awa' woman, dinna question yeer betters. Ye knaws nothin' o' the matter." He turns away. Is there no end to this interfering woman's prattle on matters of history which do not concern her?

The two dancers are surrounded by an admiring crowd of spectators. Ralph Laidler watches as they are slapped upon the back, though some like Jimmy Mendham and Jeannie MacDonald do not appear to be so pleased as other folk.

"An hwat are ye gapin' a', Mr. Laidler?" calls Margaret Hogarth , "wull ah gie ye a big kiss?"

"Gan awa' wi' ye, ye cheekin' limmer! Hae some respect, wull ye. Ah'm auld eno' ti bi yeer granda. "

"Aye that ah see!"

Ralph Laidler, about to pronounce the sharp retort rising to the tip of his tongue, is prevented by an urgent tapping on his shoulder.

"Wi' ye come noo, Mr Laidler" says the shop boy, "fer yer wife is took very sick wi the noise, an is gan ti her bed an asks fer ye."

"Ah'll come fer ah have nay desire ti linger wi this riffraff ."

Johnny Laidlaw pushes his way now out into the street to get some fresh air, though he is still holding the hand of Margaret Hogarth who he pulls along behind him. It is dark except for the light from a few lamps throwing little circles of misty yellow light on to the cobbles.

"Ye've bin practising since ah taught ye them steps then, Margaret."

"Aye, a wee bit."

"More than a wee bit. Night an day more like."

"Gan awa' John, ah dinna have the time, wha' wi the boat an the fishin' an helpin' Mam an goin' fer a farm servant ti Mister Richardson."

"Ye'll nay gan there. Ye'll nay gan ti Richardson."

"Aye, ah wull. Ahm chosen tae gan."

Johnny Laidlaw frowns. "Them steps ye bin practising," he says.

"A wee bit, as I told ye. Nay mair than a wee bit."

"We's a guid match then, lass."

"Didna ye kna' tha' then?

Johnny Laidlaw says nothing. The girl waits, but then turns away from him to go back inside.

"Wull ah speak ti yer Da, then, Margaret?"

She turns back to face him.

"An ye'll nay gan ti Richardson!"

"Ah canna uf ah'm spoken for elsewhere. Ah must obey ma man, they says, an maybe ah wull, an maybe ah willna."

"Ah'll speak ti yer Da, an then we'll see who's tae di the obeying, lass."

"Aye, me Da's bin telled ti expect ye, Johnny lad, an he's bin telled to say ye "Aye" when ye ask."

On this day of early Spring, year of Our Lord eighteen hundred and thirty seven, a betrothal is arranged between Johnny Laidlaw, bachelor and Mariner, son of John and Marjorie Laidlaw of Spittal, and Margaret Hogarth, spinster and House Servant, daughter of John and Catherine Hogarth she also of Spittal, and many young hearts, both of maids and men, are left to ache forever which is until the Autumn Hirings in Berwick upon Tweed.

CHAPTER THREE

The softwood quilting frame is laid along the table in the one downstairs room that serves as a kitchen and general living place of the cottage in Gibson's Row, Spittal. Every activity on which the household depends takes place here, from washing in the tin bath, cooking over the fire and the cutting up of fish, to the romps and gambols of the younger children who cannot go out of doors when the sea fret obscures the long stretch of sand or the wind turns unshod feet blue with biting cold. In the corner a short flight of stairs is hidden from view by a rough curtain and above, a space not big enough to stand up in is divided into two sleeping areas by a thin wooden partition. The door of the lower room opens directly onto the cobbled lane but though the icy Northern winds burst in like maddened beasts when the door is opened the fire that is kept burning in the huge fireplace defies the cold and keeps the occupants in close confined intimacy. The setting up of a quilting frame, then, is not something that can be lightly undertaken for it occupies the entire room with place sufficient only for a wooden chair at each end and a bench running the length of the table on each side.

The frame itself was made at least a century ago by a Spittal carpenter and though light, it is still cumbersome and must be taken down and propped against the unplastered stone wall of the room. The unfinished quilt must also be detached from the stretchers and rolled up in a clean sheet until the whole thing can be set up again. For this reason and to avoid unnecessary labour, the women spend as much time as possible throughout a quilting day at their task and can sometimes finish a quilt for a double bed within a week. Their menfolk cannot be said to be happy when a quilt is on the frame for quite apart from having their living quarters entirely taken up by the cloth, the cotton wadding, which must be unrolled and stretched and the frame itself, there is also seated around the table what appears to be the entire female population of the village old and young together with several of their bairns who sprawl and crawl and scramble over the floor and under the table, their feet bare and their noses oozing the thick yellow mucous of the continuous cold from which they all suffer, creating unrest and mayhem but who must yet be controlled sufficiently to discourage their fingers with which they wipe their running noses, from touching or soiling the fabric. As if this were not enough, the fire, source of heat and comfort, on which a kettle is kept continuously boiling, is quite obscured and a man may not take his ease on a spindle chair beside it with a pipe of tobacco until the women are gone and the table is cleared. As for his victuals, the women have little time left to see to them with the usual care that is their duty and he must make-do with warmed up left-overs and bread and cheese.

The womens' crack is unceasing, and no man can edge in even a single word. Every item of news or gossip is pursued and pressed until the subject matter is dry whilst the young girl for whom the quilt is being made is beset on all sides with tales of marital woe, and the wearisome lot that is a woman's what with childbearing and the unreasonable conjugal demands of men. Every older member of the female assembly knows that the pleasures of the marriage bed, if they ever existed, will cease when they become the relentless obligation of the wife with the inevitable consequence of being burdened with more bairns to feed and clothe.

"Ye mind wee Rhona Henderson?" says Mary Levenson. "Ye mind yon wee lassie. She was wed tae Michael MacDonner as ye'll recall, an she nay mair than sixteen years of age, like yersel' Maggie Hogarth."

"Aye, poor wee lassie," the women sigh.

"Tha' Michael MacDonner was forty five years of age, an tha' I kna, fer he was wi' me brother a'the schooling, though he was learnt nought, fer he was thick as twa shor' planks a' wood."

"Aye he was nay scholar, tha' Michael," the women agree.

"He wad shout a' wee Rhona in the kitchen, 'get ye up here wifey, get ye up, mak haste noo, be sharp. Ah've a desire o' nature upon me. Whad ye doin' woman, yeer husban' calls ye tae perform yeer duties.' Ah've heard it mesel', an the poor wee body wad answer 'ah've the washin' tae do, Michael.' An then he wad shout, 'get ye up, tha' washin' ye can dae later, get ye up an look sharp an tend tae the first duty of a wifey.'

Nae sooner was tha' Michael relieved an wee Rhona back doon in the washhouse, than he'd be calling out again, 'get ye up here, woman, ah've anither desire of nature come upon me. Ye have na' satisfied me enow, get ye up an di ye're duty."

"Tha' mon was a beast."

"Nay, he wasna fer the beasts dae na' mak sich demands as he."

"Aye, poor wee lassie, an she was a quiet body, nae bigger than a child of ten or twelve."

"An wha' became of wee Rhona then?" asks Margaret Hogarth.

"Ah! Weel ye may ask it, lass. She deeyed within one yeer wi' tha' Michael."

"Was it in chil'birth then?

"Nay, she miscarried thrice in tha' one yeer, an then the poor lassie deeyed, worn oot by his practices." Mary Levenson lowers her voice and the women lean forward to hear, "his practices which were unnatural an worse than his ain dog." The women groan and shake their heads.

"An' did he grieve fer his young bride? Nay he didna fer within a month he'd taen her cousin, Mollie, an she but a chil' also, fer wife. An ah ken he said tae her on the weddin' night, 'weel, ye're cousin Rhona had nae the will tae receive me as a wifey should. Ahm a mon o' great desires, an these, wifey, ye shall hae in arl their force.' "

"An wha' happened wi' tha' lassie, then?"

"Why ye knaws her. Missis MacDonner, o'er West Edge way. She wi' three bairns an three gone. Widow woman. Aye, fer the Lord had mercy on wee Mollie."

"Ha's tha' then?" asks Margaret.

"He deeyed. He was callin' oot, 'wi' ye leave yeer travail, wife and get ye up tae me, fer ah'm wi' a great desire o' nature on me' an when wee Mollie gan up tae he, fer she darenat disobey tha' monster, he sat up on the bed an roared 'come ye here, tae me arms an perform thy duties, an relieve me of the desires, be sharp,' an then he roared fer she were nay sharp enough in comin' tae him, an then he fell back like a greet stone, and was gone, his greet desire still on him an plain an stiff enow fer arl tae see at the laying oot. Twas a stroke, twas a stroke o' the Lord who had mercy on poor Mollie. Twas her cousin Rhona in heaven who called tae him 'come ye here, mon, fer ah've a great desire upon me tae see ye here before ye gans doon tae the ither place. Be sharp!' "

The activity around the quilting frame ceases while the women shake with laughter.

"Sae, be warned Margaret, fer men is arl the same, an marriage tames a craw!"

"Ma Johnny'ull nay be like tha."

"Wull he nat! Ye'll see, then lassie," says Mary Levenson.

The decisions to be made about the quilt itself are never easy to come upon as each woman, since the days when she played beneath the quilting table herself and before she could walk or talk, considers herself an expert in the craft and Margaret Hogarth has already stated that when the women gather to make her quilt, which must be soon, she wishes for no second rate workmanship, no 'it'll do' talk, for her marriage quilt must be of the finest quality. She will not have Mary Levenson to draw the traditional patterns freehand from memory nor will she permit her mother to trace them in chalk around a well-worn template. No, she has made up her mind and Margaret has always been sure of her own mind, that she will have the great Joseph Hedley, itinerant quilter to come to the cottage himself and draw the patterns professionally with his blue crayon. Then there will be not two or three motifs, but many, and the stitchers will follow the intricate and delicate lines of fans and ferns, feathers and stars, in-filled with lovers' knots, diamonds, plaits, sea waves and Boozy Bettys. Nor is she content with an old wool blanket for padding, as served well enough in her Ganny's day for Margaret must have the best cotton wadding that her mother can persuade old Laidler to part with on tick and even that must be warmed first and then picked over to remove the spleety.

"Ah'll no accept to tak second best, Mam," she says, "my mon, John, is nay second best an if I wadna have him I wadna accept anither, but wad remain a spinster ti ma dying day."

"H'away lass! Dinna talk sich clavers. Tis nought but claggy crowdy and pappy puddin'!" says Mistress Hogarth.

"It's nay pappy puddin', Mam. I'll no accept a marriage quilt tha' isna' executed ti the best. Ah willna have Mistress Levenson putting her marks all over the stuff jus' where she wills an no regard for wha' it should be by rights."

"So, ye will hae Joe Hedley, an who will be paying for tha' quilting mon to visit here?"

"So will I, Mam."

"An wi' what, lass?"

"Ah will help ma Da in bringin' in the nets for nay reward an he will use wha' he owes me ti pay Joe Quilter."

"An hae ye spoke ti your Da on this, girl?"

"Aye."

"An wha' di' he say?"

"He di' say tha' wad do."

"Yer Da's a soft headed fool, then. He owes ye no pay fer wha' ye dae, except yeer keep, an tha' ye kens."

Mistress Levenson, her own skills having been rejected and being none too pleased about it, awaits her moment. A moment handed to her by Fate and her own good judgment in persisting with the rudiments of literacy which will enable her to drop a veritable rock of granite to crush the pride of a silly girl, no more than an ignorant Spittal wench who does not know her station.

"An tell me, when did ye las' hear o' Joe Quilter visitin' these parts?" she says.

"Twas when he was come ti draw a quilt fer the Mayor," says Margaret.

"An hwhat mayor wad tha' be then?"

"Twas nat the Mayor that is noo, but maybe the one tha' was before tha'." Margaret turns to her mother, "Was tha' no right, Mam?"

"Ah dinna ken, lass. Ah ken tha' Joe Quilter was ti come but whether he did or no, ah canna say."

"Aye," says Mary Levenson, now ready to astound the company with her news, "twas just after he comed tae draw fer the mayor, nat this mayor, nor the one afore, but the one afore tha' ah'll have ye knaw, tha' he was merdred."

"Nay! Mary. Not merdred, surely," says Kate Hogarth.

"Aye, merdred fer sure, an ahm surprised tha' ye all are ignoran' of tha' fact, fer tis well known, twas in all the sheets of news, twas read by everyone an twas more than ten years gone. Ahm shocked tha' ye didna ken wha' happened tae tha' poor body."

Mary Levenson enjoys every moment of her triumph, which is two-fold. Not only is she now uplifted in terms of moral probity, she is also fully aware that as none of the quilting women can read, she has placed them firmly into that strata of ignorance and humility from which they will no longer presume to reject her own talents as a freehand pattern liner of quilts and this all the more so because she can read and write a little and this is conveyed to them quite clearly as they are all aware, since even the most uneducated of female kind has a deep understanding of these things and more.

"Ten years, Mistress? Nay, surely, it canna be!"

"Aye, tha' it is. Twas in twenty six. Yeer Margaret there who is sae grand an wants nane but he for her quilt, mus' ask in heaven, where tha' poor body doubtless dwells the noo. She was but a bairn when poor Joe Quilter died, merdred, til he was deeyed!"

"An wull ye tell us how it comed about, Mistress?" asks Kate Hogarth.

Mary Levenson sighs as one who will now endeavour to speak of things almost too painful to be thought of, but who will try, for the sake of the ignorant folk who now look at her so eager for her tale.

"Aye, some folks was passin' by his wee cottage in the winter time it was, an wha' did they see but marks o' blood in the snaw and when they folks went inside the hoose, it bein' arl open wha' do ye think they found?"

"A blooded corps!" said Mistress Hogarth.

"Nay, they didna."

"Wha' then?"

"A guid quilt set up in a frame, and there in the middle, the print of a hand, ahl dripping wi' blood!"

"Never!"

"Aye".

"An were it the Mayor's quilt?"

Mistress Levenson has no information on that matter but she is unwilling to lose the momentum of her story by being led off down a back alley of doubt and speculation.

"Aye, that it was," she says, as one who knows more, much more, but whose discretion forbids further disclosure. "Aye,"she says and sighs again to give the impression of one too weary of the gruesome tale to proceed further.

"An where was tha' poor body, where did they find he?"

"He had ran from his dwelling, poor mon, ti escape his foul killer, who caught him and merdred him."

The women gasp. "How was it done, Mistress?"

"His throat were cut, an' he were stabbed sixteen times."

"Never!"

"Aye, he were."

"Án who did it, d'ye think?"

"Ahl who knew him is under suspicion it sayed in the broadsheet, and ahl must look at his neighbour to see if merdrer is writ in his countenance. That's wha' it sayed."

The women fall silent.

"Weel, it wasna me!" says Margaret Hogarth, "an it be a sorry thing indeed tha' he canna draw me quilt."

"An can ye say nay mair than that, lass?" asks her mother.

"Wha' can ah say, Mam ? Ah sayed tha' ah was sorry for it. But since he is deeyed anyway an ah canna help him, tis nay a blessin' tha' tha' merdrer did get ti him before he got ti ma quilt."

"Why were it done, Mistress Levenson, d'ye think."

"Fer robbery. Twas thought the poor old body had money an quantities of it hid in his cottage, but he didna tha's for sure. His neighbours sayed tha' he was on the Parish an had been tha' for some time. How would the awld body have money when folks like ye wad be makkin' him wait fer his pay, an then giein it to him in fish more like, than guid coin!"

"Tha's nay right, Mary Levenson!" says Kate Hogarth, "We always pays our debt in full."

"Aye, if a body can wait tha' long, Kate."

There is silence and Mistress Levenson's rebuke hangs in the air.

"An dinna ye want to knaw who the murderer was thought to be?" she asks.

"They dinna know, ye sayed."

"They dinna know, but the magistrate can speculate like."

"Weel then! Wha's this speculation?"

"Twas a beggar or a young vagrant, one o' they that wanders in these parts, an does nay work, an lays about ahl day, such as is seen on Spittal Common."

"Aye, an tis getting worse. A body canna go out at neet wi'out fear for their lives. Tis not now like it used ti be in days gone by. Ye gies them money an they spends it on the drink til they dinna know wha' they does or where they be."

The women sigh and shake their heads. Mistress Levenson has told her tale, and there is an atmosphere of satisfied agreement amongst them.

"Ah willna be a Spittal lass forever, Mam," says Margaret, "Ah likes fine things, and Johnny an me will have some real crocks an plates, an a carpet on the floor, an a clock, Mam, a noble clock upstanding from the floor fer us ti tell the time."

"Will ye indeed, hinny. Weel, I hope it may be so fer ye," says Kate.

"An we wull live where there are nay merders an nay merdrers an nay Mary Levensons neither, who is rejoicin' tha' ah canna hae me quilt as I wish, an Johnny an me'll live in a gran' hoose wi' money in our pockets tae do as we pleases."

"Weel, tha'll be a gran' life, then, hinny."

" It wull!"

§

Ralph Laidler lays the newspaper on the counter and smooths it with his hand."Aye," he says to the shop boy who is lifting and stacking some bales of cloth, "it is to be hoped, lad, that one day ye may take an interest in the wise writings of clever men in the weekly journals."

"Ah hae nay time, Mister Laidler, ah'm tae busy in yeer shoppie. These bales has weight in 'em."

Ralph Laidler senses that another opportunity to read aloud to a less adequate person is presenting itself, as it often does, since so many do not read or write. It is an opportunity that he never lets pass him by, reasoning that it is always for their benefit and for the general struggle against ignorance that must be constantly theirs.

"In that case, lad, I will oblige ye by reading to ye from this paper. Mind ye listen, now, and mind ye get them bales stacked." He takes up the journal, disregarding the anguished face of his shop boy.

"'The Northern peasant placed beside an enlivening fire repairs his tools, his instruments of husbandry, or his nets, if his travail be upon the waters of the sea, while his wife prepares a warm and nutritious supper and his daughters from the age of eight years old spin, knit or sew. Whilst the tempest blows they are thus engaged in harmonious industry, or they entertain each other, making music on simple instruments or singing the traditional songs of plain, hardworking folk. Thus they take no heed of the tempest which may do its worst, but will never disturb their loyal hearts. Compare their honest toil and manners to those of the French peasant, who when cold or lacking in fuel stays in bed in a state of torpor consuming what little earnings he has, and indulging in unbridled pleasures of the flesh at the least of encouragements.' "

"Wha's they pleasures, Mister Laidler? That they Frenchies gets up ti, wha's they?"

"We do not know, boy, we are English and we know nothing of they pleasures. You uneducated folk are all the same, ye willna listen to wha's wise an guid in writing, an must ask foolish questions where none should be. Now listen." He continues to read, " 'and you will understand that your Northern peasant is as good and as worthy a creature as any in England. The same cannot be said with such assurance about the peasantry of Spittal.' Wha' hae I always telled ye about they folk? Here tis written, 'who persist in regarding themselves neither as English nor Scots and therefore lack the guidance and confidence that a clear sense of nationhood endows. Their often febrile and unstable nature may in no small part be brought about by their association with malt liquor, for though they drink a quantity of tea they are addicted to the former which is unwholesome and leads them into the misery of sottish habits and not infrequently into conflict with the laws of this land for which behaviour they have often paid a heavy price. They may believe themselves to be beyond the limits of the law but they have learned to their cost from time to time, that this is not so. It has been noted, however, that certain of these Spittal folk have endeavoured to raise themselves, and have requested that a place of worship other than the rude stable where they presently congregate, be built for them. It is most devoutly hoped that money can be found for they lack the means to find it themselves, and in the hiatus thus formed some preachers of the Methodist connection have operated with industrious zeal upon the minds of the vulgar, and their efforts have been attended with considerable success. It is even rumoured that some of these ignorant Spittal folk, who can neither read nor write, may be beguiled into following the leaders of the Primitive Methodist Movement.' " He puts down the journal, and looks at his struggling shop boy.

"So dinna be beguiled into tha' form of religion, boy. See tha' ye dinna wed a Spittal jade or strumpet like ma poor kinsman is soon tae do, fer they goes frae one thing ti another, they Spittal folk. Frae the arms o' the devil into the arms o' they Primmies."

"Ah'm no like ti hae the time fer arl tha' nor the strength neither, frae workin' in yeer shop, Mister Laidler." The boy groans as he lifts a heavy bale of cotton sateen. Then he sets it down again, "Ah'll ne'er meet a jade o' any sort, nor a strumpet neither, fer ah hae nay time nor strength, an tha's tha."

§

42

It seems that the Primitive Methodism fell on ground that was if not fertile, at least not barren when the Mission Camp first arrived in Spittal in the year 1830. It is unlikely that the slant of the Message held a more particular appeal to the unfortunates who inhabit that southern shore of the Tweed since they are well known for unbridled behaviour and a great addiction to the pleasures of tobacco and strong drink. The hold which this iniquitous branch of Methodism appeared to have over them can be attributed, surely, to the fact that when Mister William Clough arrived in Berwick in 1829 he made a point of setting up his first camp meeting in Spittal, thus allowing the inhabitants to believe that in spite of centuries of evidence to the contrary, they were of some significance.

"Remember the Sabbath Day to keep it Holy!" the Minister's voice roars out over the assembled group who sit in lines on hard wooden benches in the College Place Chapel, Berwick upon Tweed.

"Nay loud talk, nay toiling, nay hauling in of nets, nay bad language, nay running, ye bairns, nay merriment, for all these things are most displeasing to the Lord who watches over ye on the Sabbath."

"Will ye tell us Minister hwat we may be doin' on a Sunday?" calls out Donal McKay.

"Ye may be reading from the Holy Book."

"Weel noo, Minister, tha's a difficulty, fer nay many o' us hae the reading."

"Then ye must gather at the dwelling of one who does and let him read to ye, Donal."

"Aye, an with hwat else may we employ oursels?"

"With contemplating the gravity of your sins, and praising the Lord for all his benefits."

"Wad tha' tak all the hours of the day, Minister?"

"Certainly we all have sins to think on sufficient for many days, Donal."

"An hwat wid the women be doin', Minister?" calls out Marie Armstrong.

"Same as the men, lassie."

"An the sewin'?

"Nay sewing if it be for gain."

"An hwat aboot the victuals, Minister. Ma mon likes his Sunday dinner."

The Minister pauses. He himself enjoys a Sunday Roast which is put before him at one o' clock sharp without fail, by his good wife and truth to tell he has never quite questioned by what means it arrives on his table, or what honest toil is involved in its preparation.

"In so far as the nourishment can be prepared on the day preceding it should be done," he says.

Marie Armstrong turns to Mistress Levenson and whispers so that all can hear, "Did ye ever hear of a guid Yorkshire being made on the day preceding, Missis? There isna goin' ti be tui mony hours fer the women to be thinkin' on their sins."

"Wha' sins does women hae the time fer, Missis?" Mistress Levenson replies.

"Cleanse me with hyssop and I shall be clean. Wash me and I shall be whiter than snow," roars the Minister. This, he feels draws the debate on Sunday activity to a firm and fitting conclusion.

Margaret Hogarth and her sister Ann, soon to be married to Mary Levenson's son Will, are endeavouring to concentrate on the preacher's words for does it not behove them as girls soon to become wives and mothers to apply themselves to serious matters and in any case the Mission Hall, though dark and somewhat austere with its unmistakable smell of damp and cheerlessness that will permanently associate itself in the minds of some with the Christian message, offers a Sunday refuge which is in contrast to the room above the stable where the smells and snorting sounds of animals disrupt the Holy proceedings and even cause irreverent smirks and echoing snorts and farts from some of the boys. The benches are hard however and Margaret begins to reflect on the pleasant softness of the straw which serves as the seating in the stable, though of course proper wooden benches must be more pleasing to God than the make-shift arrangements of ignorant folk.

"Wha' do it mean?" she whispers to Anne.

"It be from the Bible."

"Aye, but wha' do it mean? Wha' be hyssop, for I never heard o' it before."

" Tis a thing God uses to wash folks wi."

"Wha' sort of a thing?"

"Ah telled ye."

Margaret is silent. In her mind she sees a vast wash-house. God, sleeves rolled up pounds and scrubs the folk of Spittal who stand heads bowed, in lines of tubs, yet try as she may she cannot see what He is using to cleanse them so vigorously.

"Ann!"

"Wi' ye be silent, girl, an listen wha' he says!"

"If tis good fer cleanin' will we get some after from the preacher?"

"Tis no fer tha' kind o' cleanin'. Dinna show folks yer ignorance."

At night the sisters huddle together for warmth in the bed they have shared since they were no more than babies and where they have battled with the kicking and restless feet of brothers added yearly to the other end of the mattress, disturbing many a night's sleep.

In a deep voice that mimics that of the preacher, Ann intones into her sister's ear, "Nay sleepin."

Margaret lets out a muffled giggle from beneath the covers.

"Nay laughin, " the deep voice continues.

"Nay makin' others ti laugh," says Margaret in a similar deep voice.

"Nay dancin,' "

"Nay fornicatin'. "

"Nay thinkin' even o' Johnny Laidlaw an Wull Levenson on a Sunday."

The girls' arms and legs flay about all over the bed as their laughter escapes the bed coverings.

"Ah'm thinkin' tha' ma sins is too scarlet for takin' up wi' the Prims," says Margaret.

"Aye t'wad tak up too mony Sabbaths to think on them arl."

"An mi Da, he'd be fer havin' ti think of tha' wee space beneath the earth o' the kitchen floor where there's a wee bit gin hidin.' "

"Aye, an a wee bit malt whiskey."

"Aye, an a wee bit baccy."

"Aye, an he'd have ti be tellin' the gaugers aboot wha's down there."

"Aye, an aboot tha' lugger from the Dutch lands wi' a cargo wha' he helps ti get ashore by night."

"An aboot wha' me Mam carries 'neath her skirt into Berwick toon from

Lamberton Toll."

"Aye, an he'd bi takked ti prison."

"Aye, an washed all over wi —"

"Hyssop!" The girls burst into unrestrained laughter.

"Margaret," whispers Ann, "Wull an me is decidin' not ti stay."

"Not ti stay? Not ti stay in Spittal?"

"We'll be going. The fishin' is very well fer some, but the bringin' in o' the liquor an arl tis too dangerous noo. Wull telled me o' Dickie Mendham, Jim's Auld-fella who built them cottages wi' secret rooms an passages for the hidin' o' the contraband, an made a guid livin' fer the Mendhams and the Hogarths and mony another too, but then he were discovered by the gaugers who was watching him an he were hanged at Jedburgh."

"Never!"

"'Tis true. Wull an me is goin' where there be ither work fer folks, maybe even Americky."

"Nay, Ann, dinna go lass, dinna leave us.

"Johnny an ye can come wi'us, lass."

"Ah'll no leave ma Mam, Ann, ti break her heart here wi'out us. Dinna go."

"Maybe no Americky, then, but we's leaving Spittal fer sure."

"Where wi' ye go, then?"

"Where they's building ships, lass. Ships is always guid. Guid work an guid pay fer the menfolk. Tha's wha' Wull says, an ships is always needed. There's gran' ships bein' made noo, an Wull says tha' the day wull come when ships wull be made of iron, no wood."

"Then Wull Levinson is daft, Ann, fer iron ships wad sink ti the bottom of the ocean, tis well known an arl."

"Nay, Wull says they willna an there'll never be ony time when ships is oot o' fashion, Wull says. An he willna hae wains tha' is unlairn'd, like there is here in Spittal. We wull go where's there's lairnin' for bairns. His Mam hae lairn'd the readin' when she was a wain."

"Did Mistress Levenson gan ti school then, Ann?"

"Aye tha' she did. Though she thinks shame ti say it, fer she was raised in the Poor House an made ti lairn. She willna tell ony person tha' she was raised there."

"Will ye nay miss us, Ann? Will ye nay miss the great ocean tha' stretches out afore us towards them Northern lands, an the long sands, an the runnin' and laughin' on them sands, an the fireside of a neet, an arl the family gathered aroon', an —"

"Tha' miserable preacher of a Sunday? Ah'l nay miss it. We's gannin' ti a better place wi guid wages an hooses, an fer sure ahl the folks we knaws is gannin' there too, an ahl hae nay mair 'nays' from Primmy Preacher, fer tha' mon hae so mony nays I reckon he bees hiding a merdrous past."

"Aye, maybe twas he that did fer poor awld Joe Quilter in Hexham."

"Aye, an he bees arl washed up wi' tha' hyssop ti get them stains o' blood oot"

The sisters muffle the sounds of their talk beneath the covers of the bed. Kate Hogarth lying behind the wooden partition, is fearful for her daughters. The world that is not Spittal, that lies beyond, even beyond seas, the world that she herself has never seen, will it be a better world? Will human nature as she has long observed it be kinder and softer than Spittal nature? And what will Spittal be without her girls? She lies on her back and looks up, for upwards is the dwelling place of the God she knows. Some old words she learnt long ago come to her mind, "Care fer me lasses, Lord, an dinna let the Adversary Devil as a roarin' lion who walketh aboot seekin' whom he may devour, come upon them. An let them resist that Adversary, steadfast in the Faith, an if they canna resist, hae mercy on me girls."

CHAPTER FOUR

"We are now living in an age when dissipation is scarcely supposed to deserve censure, and at no time is this to be observed more clearly than on the fifth Sunday of Lent, or as it is generally known by the more refined and God-fearing sort of persons, Passion Sunday, surely a day meant for quiet contemplation of the suffering and sacrifice of Our Lord, yet transformed by the vulgar into an opportunity for visiting the Ale-house. Their name for this Holy Day is Carling Sunday, when they may spend their carling groats on a dish of grey pease or carlings which have been steeped in water to soften them, fried in plenty of butter by the land-lord and liberally sprinkled with pepper. This day gives way to Easter Sunday on which the decorating and rolling of paste eggs takes precedence over all religious observances, followed by the pagan practices of Midsummer, when fires are lit on top of the hills and there is licentiousness and dancing by young and old throughout the night." *

Ralph Laidler puts Mr. Mackenzie's book down carefully on the counter, "there's wisdom in this buik," he thinks, "which could never have been put if it were no but for right-minded citizens like mysel' who gift the money, aye, the subscribers, the God-fearin' folk livin' here among the heathen or as that learned man says, them that's suffering from the dissipation." He puts on his coat and opens the shop door. He takes a single step out into the street and pauses. Lord knows, he thinks, but he has no wish to be wasting his time at marriages especially espousals of Spittal strumpets, but Johnny Laidlaw is a kinsman and it is very much to be regretted that he has entered into this union with one of the Hogarths. Nevertheless, his wife being incapacitated and having not left her room for the past two days, Ralph Laidler is determined to make the sacrifice and endure the wedding. He will add a tad of refinement to the proceedings and present a solemn face to remind of the gravity of the vows when all the riff-raffetty will be grinning and snivelling and thinking of the wedding night and the bride's deflowering, though God knows, with these folk, most of them lost their virginity well before the wedding night and then there will be the unbridled lusts of the guests. Ralph Laidlaw holds onto the brass handle of his shop door to steady himself against a momentary contemplation of these lusts, then he places his top hat resolutely on his head and strides out towards the river.

§

As was only to be expected of folk like the Spittallers, the wedding breakfast and the Bride Cake had been set out on planks of wood supported by barrels in the very stable loft used as a church on Sundays. Notwithstanding the unpleasant smells from the animals below, the Bride Cake had been broken and the guests, if a riff-raff of these people can be honoured with such a title had eaten and with the exception of the bride, her sisters and mother, already repaired to the Ale House though it was not yet mid-day, the very same ale-house that was the scene of Dickie Mendham's disgrace in former years. There Ralph Laidler discovers the company advanced in merriment, unafflicted by any sense of shame concerning the executed landlord and lifting their glasses in his memory as if he were a hero. To his credit, however, the groom stands apart, leaning in the doorway, his sea worn blue eyes appearing to focus on something far away.

"Well, kinsman," says Ralph Laidlaw, approaching him where he stands, "so yeer ti be wed this day."

"Aye."

"An ti a Hogarth lassie then."

"Aye."

Ralph Laidlaw shakes his head solemnly. "Ah'll wish ye weel then, kinsman. A Hogarth lassie!" he clicks his tongue and shakes his head again.

"If yeer come ti witness, Rafe Laidler, ye'll keep yeer sentiments ti yersel.'"

"Ah sayed ah wish ye weel, lad."

"Aye." Johnny Laidlaw presses his elbow against the door frame to turn away.

The bride's father, John Hogarth takes his arm and leads him into the company,"Ye'll accept a glass of port, Mister Laidler, for on this day our family is ti be honoured wi' a linkage ti yeer ain."

" Indeed. Tha's very true, there's nay denyin' it, an ah'll accept a wee glass fom yeer hand, Hogarth."

He sits down carefully. The truth certainly cannot be denied. An honour is about to be bestowed on the Hogarth family, undeserving as they may be, and is he not the respectable outward symbol of that honour, the representative, as one might say, for to tell the truth the Groom's parents, though kinsman and woman on both sides are but white fisherfolk who know nothing and after all, is it not a very pleasant and comfortable thing to be sipping a wee tumbler of port before that honour descends. The conversation around him is as one would expect from ribald company before such a wedding. Who will be the one to pluck off the Bride's garter and wave it around in triumph during the ceremony? Only these ignorant and ill-bred Spittallers would hold with such a pagan custom, thinks Ralph Laidler, though he suspects that Mistress Hogarth, the bride's mother will have a spare garter at the door, ready unloosed to give to such a one in order to satisfy custom without shame.

At noon the company departs for the wedding procession and the Minister of Religion, a Scottish Presbyterian such as is licensed to conduct marriages in stable lofts, waits for the couple to arrive. Ralph Laidler feeling more agreeably inclined towards the proceedings as a result of maybe twa wee glasses, notes that the reverend gentleman imparts a tone of greater dignity, a much needed gravitas such as is exemplified by his own presence, indeed. As the bridal procession enters, Ralph Laidler allows himself to take a professional interest in their apparel. Not of course that very much can be expected of these folk, particularly as many of his own customers are of an upper class kind of person who purchase silks of the highest quality, satin piping and sashes, finest silk gauze and all complimented with ankle length feather tippets and swansdown muffs, or for out of doors, cashmere shawls for warmth and beauty. The bride's mother, Mistress Kate Hogarth, wears on this occasion a frilled lawn tucker over a stout flannel petticoat and a full skirted muslin of indeterminate colour in the style of the last century before the obsession with semi-nudity in dress became the fashion and stays and petticoats abandoned. Her bonnet is of wire edged straw over a frilled muslin cap which cannot conceal one or two strands of the pale auburn hair she has always had and which is so unfashionable. Altogether her costume is favourable to her age and figure though undoubtedly it has seen better days for the edges of the cuffs are worn. As for the bride, she like all the other silly young women of her generation is wearing a sprigged white muslin dress that reminds rather more of a shroud than a wedding gown, cut, probably by herself to an extremely slender shape, and with a waist positioned just below the bosom which is far too revealing and in which she may catch her death of cold. This is topped with a high crowned bonnet decorated with what is intended to be a plume, but which in actuality is probably a dyed goose or pheasant feather. Her sister is similarly arrayed only with a Gypsy straw bonnet tied around with a ribbon of pink silk. Both girls display immodest white stockinged ankles without even a blush. Of course all of this was the fashion of fifteen or twenty years ago in London or Edinburgh, where ladies are now enjoying all the benefits of lacing and stays and full skirts once more and the printed muslin of this bride's dress was certainly not purchased at Ralph Laidler's establishment for it is of the cheaper quality where the dye from the print is not good, and should it rain the colours will run. Not of course that any of these sad attempts at high fashion will signify because the Northumbrian weather requires that thick woollen shawls must at all times be wrapped around the whole lot and bonnets be they of silk or straw must be clutched to the head if they are not to be the playthings of the raging winds.

Ralph Laidler notes that the groom is admirably turned out, having changed his clothes before his arrival. He wears a dark grey topcoat with a white stock and black waistcoat and if it were not for the brown and weathered look of his skin and the blueness of his eyes, he might be taken for a gentleman.

After the ceremony, the stable loft having been cleared of all the apparatus of a church, it becomes once again the centre of merrymaking and drinking to the health of Bride and Groom. Then the pipers arrive and Ralph Laidler must endure the wailing of the Northumbrian pipes followed by the devilish sound of the fiddlers. The newly married couple take the floor to perform a new fangled horn-pipe and the dancing goes on well into the night. Then the entire company along with the musicians scramble their way back to the Bride's house to put the couple to bed, after which one of them emerges triumphantly from the house to throw the bride's stocking high into the air with many whoops and great applause from the inebriated assembly.

Ralph Laidler, discovering himself to be a little unsteady after the day's responsibilities as the representative of good society and respectability, sinks quietly to the ground beside the timbers of an old boat, his fine high hat over his eyes and thus sheltered from the wind, sleeps until it is light enough to make his way back home.

The young newly weds, feeling themselves to be under some pressure to consummate their marriage more or less under the public gaze, and the bride having been quite literally undressed and placed in her own bed which she used to share with her sister, have decided in urgent whispers to wait for a quieter and less public occasion and to tell the truth there will be no surprises in the act for either of them, which is why the bride has reason to be secretly thankful that the union is now legal. In any case she has urgent matters to bring up with her new husband.

"Johnny, lad, there is nay reason now fer ye ti be at sea, nay reason at arl, lad. We can gan wi arl the rest ti Americky an them places, an be rich wi' gold an arl."

"Ye may gan where ye likes, wifey, but ah'm no gannin' an ah'm no quittin' the life o' the sea."

"Fer me, Johnny. Di ye love tha' fickle sea tha' is so perilous, di ye love it mair'n me?"

"Dinna ask sich questions, burd, ye knaws well enough tha' ah canna leave the sea, no fer ye, Margaret, no fer anyone."

"An wull we always hae ti live wi me Mam and Da then?"

"Tis best fer when ah'm awa."

He gets up and moves to the door at the head of the wooden stairs and shouts to the company below.

"Noo, gan awa' arl of ye. Quit yeer blatherin' an arl yeer noise an let ma wife an me hae some peace. Gan back ti yeer ain hearths, arl on ye." He turns back to his new wife, "but on this ah gie ye ma word, lass. Ahl be a guid husband ti ye, an ye shall hae victuals in plenty fer yersel' an arl them bairns that'll come, aye, an what is mair, lass, ye shall hae a grand clock, maybe a waggetty clock as they brings from Americky, an ye shall ne'er want, lass, as lang as ah'm yeer mon."

*Adapted from A Historical View of the County of Northumberland
Eneas Mackenzie Revised Ed. 1835

CHAPTER FIVE

"The present spring is likely to be remarkable in this district for the large numbers of persons emigrating to America. Already several persons have taken their departure and many others are preparing to leave at the approaching term of Whitsunday. The emigrants are not confined to one class of tradesmen and operatives, nor are they solely young adventurers. Some who have traded, and to all appearance properly too, for a quarter of a century and upwards, are about to sever themselves from cherished associations and commence the formation of new ties in a foreign country. On Monday morning one of those exciting scenes of departure was witnessed at the Ayton railway station. Twenty eight male members of the artisan population of that Parish surrounded by their friends and associates, waited the arrival of the seven o' clock train from Berwick. The scene was a tumultuous one, as amid the cheers of their male friends and the audible sobbing and crying of the females, the emigrants bid adieu to the place of their birth. On Sunday evening the Rev. Daniel Cameron of Ayton delivered a very appropriate address to those who were about to leave the land of their nativity. The chapel was densely crowded, and throughout the course of the address the grief at parting with so many dear friends was visibly portrayed on the countenance of almost all present."

Berwick Advertiser 12/4/1851

A group of women are gathered outside their cottages to listen as Mary Levenson, struggling and hesitating over some of the longer words, reads to them from the newspaper. As she finishes she carefully rolls up the sheet of paper and holds it reverently by her side, her head lowered and unwilling to meet the blankness of a despair which they do not properly comprehend in the eyes of her listeners who are silent. This is the silence of those too numb to speak, as each of the women realises that the world, so familiar, even so under-appreciated because of the limitations that nonetheless provided a framework of security and ease, is slipping away forever. With each family that leaves, with each group of brothers or friends, the life of the area, stable and reassuring life as it has been, where each person has known his place in the order of things and known the others around him for generations before, tears a piece that is like living flesh from those left behind. That it is happening cannot be denied, but why it is happening is less clear. Suddenly it seems that the way of life, of fishing and sea-faring and farming, that has satisfied their forebears, is no longer enough and a great tidal wave of change and movement threatens to drown the ordered centuries.

§

In the Autumn of 1858 the ground around the Church of St. Bartholomew and St. Boisil at Tweedmouth is heavy with the moisture of the decaying leaves and the path to the church is treacherously slippery. In the mist of early Autumn the air is absorbing the sweet smell, that mixture of ripeness and decay that on a rare day without a salt wind from the sea to disperse it, announces another dying in that grave-yard, the slow slipping away of the year, towards a long winter. The sturdy granite stones surrounding the church in ordered lines, leaning only very slightly under decades of unrelenting persuasion from the wind, are the people of Spittal from recent times and centuries past, now equal and shoulder to shoulder at their great meeting, joined by blood and kinship, common dust though separated in life by the irrelevance of time. The church, not in Spittal itself, has long been the Parish Church for the area and St. Bartholomew who watches over his granite flock is their own patron, for the leper community which gave Spittal its name was founded in ancient times and named for that saint and Apostle.

Kate Hogarth, now fifty eight years of age or thereabouts as she believes, moves slowly amongst the grave-stones, touching one here and tracing the name with a soft and reverent finger, then stooping to look more closely at another; each is an old friend whose face she remembers and though she cannot read, she knows the inscriptions by heart and that light touch of her finger is a caress, an acknowledgment of the strong but invisible link between the living and the dead. Upon the apex of St.Bartholomew and St Boisil's tower flies a golden fish, a great weather vane in the likeness of a salmon, twisting, turning, his scales glinting as if he now slips through the skies as he once slid through the waters of the Estuary. As in their lives, so he remains the icon of the stone assembly.

Now Kate stoops to part the long grass that threatens to obscure a name as familiar to her as her own. Here lies James Stuart, descended from James Stuart, called The Pretender, but as some would say, the rightful King of England, better known as Jamie Strength. Catherine strokes the old man's name with her gentle hand. It had seemed that Jamie and his music would never die but in the end even he has capitulated and lies with his friends and the many children he fathered who went long before him. She moves on to the newer more opulent stone that is inscribed with the name of her son-in-law's kinsman, Ralph Laidler. There is space below for the lettering of his wife's name, for she is living still, and some say merrily with a young man who was her husband's shop boy in his time, but folks gossip and not all should be believed. "Ah, ye awld rascallywag, Rafe Laidler," says Kate aloud, "so ye's come ti the same place, noo, as arl the rest o' us. Weel, God bless yeer soul, fer ye were never a bad mon in yeer heart, an many's the time ye've helped us wi' the stuff fer quilts an the like." Almost completely obscured by the grass are the little mounds and small headstones of Hogarth children, Andrew and Isabella, John, Maria, Elizabeth, Jimmy, and Smithy, all chubby laughing little ones with the light auburn hair, pale skin and freckles, cousins and brothers and sisters, all dead of a fever before their sixth birthday. Kate leans back to rest against the stone of her mother, on which is also engraved her father's name, lost at sea like so many, and no remains to bury. Now, thinking of him, she looks out towards that unknowable expanse of water and its grey emptiness, matching her mood. How is it that the sea has nothing to say to her even though she has been its companion all her life? And when she has gone the sea will not grieve but remain what it is, the appalling, monstrous sea. As for Kate herself, she needs some time now to say goodbye to these old friends and to walk along the Spittal shore. She must leave Spittal soon. The earth she has trodden upon every day since she could walk must be left behind for Spittal is now an empty place. The families have left and only a few old folk remain to receive news when from time to time it arrives of their childrens' grand lives, if reports are to be believed, in America where there is undreamed of wealth and opportunity. Her own family have gone to follow the money that is to be made in the shipyards of the North East. Once sea-faring folk, used to the open air and the great forces of wind and water, they have now imprisoned themselves in dark streets where fog and bitter cold attack the men who cling to the scaffolding and must, with hammer and rivet build vessels on which they will never sail. The limits of each family's allotted fishing area, once so fiercely defended, are now unattended and no-one keeps watch to see that his space is not invaded. No longer does it matter if nets are spread to the very limits of a boundary threatening to encroach on a neighbour's tenancy and the flat bottomed boats of the salmon fishers lie beached like dying sea creatures on the sand. The great salmon trout has not deserted the waters but the money to be made from this harvest was always uncertain and money is the force that has driven the families, one after another to seek a more certain and prosperous life in the pits and shipyards of the Tyne, Wear, and Tees.

Kate Hogarth's daughters, Ann, now Levenson, and Margaret, now Laidlaw have gone with their children and are living in a dark brick house with three storeys and proper stairs in a street of dark brick houses, newly built by a group of speculator landlords. The Levensons, who moved there first occupy the two rooms downstairs, and the Laidlaws are above, with Robert and Catherine, named after her grandmother, and little Marjorie. The boys will work in the yards and bring home their regular wages, and there will be no more anxiety for the women, for the smuggling, that for centuries had been accepted as the way of life for every Spittal family, has become too risky and the penalties too great. Already several of the young men have been transported to Australia against their will and to the sorrow and suffering of their dependent families and these have been the lucky ones who have escaped the fate long ago of poor Richie Mendham, hung at Jedburgh for nothing more than arranging a few escape tunnels and secret hidey holes in the cottages and setting up a wee still in the cellar of his Inn and seeing that each man got his fair share of the gains. Richie murdered no-one, nor did anyone harm but he died for a few barrels of strong liquor and a few pipefuls of tobacco.

Now new people have arrived in Spittal, who will not be pursuing the salmon or risking their lives at sea, or waiting for a chance to unload a Dutch lugger in dead of night. These people come with the law and the authorities on their side. The cottages have been declared hovels which must be pulled down and the tenants that remain, evicted, because there is now a more abundant harvest to be reaped. These people are the entrepreneurs who have noticed that families who make money in the newly industrialised areas will want to take holidays and Spittal, easily reached, has a fine stretch of sand and sea. In place of the dwellings of poor people, of whom the new working class will certainly not wish to be reminded, solid boarding houses and hotels are to be built and there will be shops and Public Houses to supply their needs. Spittal sands, once so bare and seemingly stretching without limit into the Northumbrian sea and sky, will become a playground with sideshows, and trinket stalls that sell plates and cups with 'a present from Spittal' painted on them and the gulls that swept the sea for fish will now waddle in ungainly fashion to search the beach for the remains of food amongst the litter discarded by the trippers. Altogether there will be new life and with it, noise and commerce, gaiety and greed, and who is to say that all this will be worse than before. Only those who remember things as they were, unchanged for centuries, will mourn the past, but they are old and their time is over. There is no place now in Spittal for the likes of Kate Hogarth and she will move to the dark streets of Monkwearmouth Shore to live with her daughter, Margaret Laidlaw. Only Johnny, Margaret's husband, has remained true to his calling. Now a Master Mariner, nothing, not the promise of wealth, or the anxieties of his wife will ever part Johnny Laidlaw from the dangers and uncertainties of the sea. All around, in other dark brick houses in parallel rows of streets, the community of Spittal has resettled and is living a life that will bring them and their children things they have never had before, things that will be bought with the regular wages that each of the lads will bring in from the great shipyards. Catherine Hogarth, that was Kate Tatun born, ponders on what these wonders may be that can only be had through dirt and noise and the loss of all that has been familiar and pleasing. "There is but ain thing, lass," she says to her daughter. "The thing ah've nay had, nor ye, nor yeer ain lasses, an ah knaw not whether it be found on Monkwearmouth Shore."

"Why, Mam, arl them things can be here."

"Weel, if ye're bairns, the lasses as weel as the lads can get the education, tha' education tha' we ne'er ha,' then the life o' Spittal wull be well lost."

"The lasses will learn the readin' and the writin' noo, Mam."

"Tha's a guid thing, Margaret, but the education tha' ah niver ha', tha's aboot thinkin', thinkin' straight an true, an' learnin' ti think, which is nay easy, an' learnin' ti think fer yersel' fer nat arl that is telled by them tha' hae set theirsels up, is right, an tha' ah ken fer sure. If the new life we're gift in dirt an toil an foul air can gie us an our bairns the education, then it wull gie us arl', an we need nay mair."

§

Yet none of the promises of wealth and education can ease the ache of ending, which lies like a slow dying on those who feel it. With the departure of people from a place that was theirs for generations, a grieving settles that becomes part of them and is made more difficult to bear because the land is indifferent and detached. The whoring land will seem to share the sorrow of its loss but will soon go on to accommodate the lives of the newcomers in whatever way is necessary as if the old had never been.

MONKWEARMOUTH
1870

CHAPTER SIX

A History of The Sundered Land. Being also a Commentary on the Present State of those Lands Sundered by the River Wear.   1870

My name is Cardew Quinn and in the springtime of my life, as one might say, I admired greatly and continue to admire the works of Mr. Eneas Mackenzie sadly deceased many years ago, having fallen victim to the cholera epidemic of 1832. I therefore decided to follow his example and record the past and calamitous present state of the North shore of this, a Sundered Land.

I begin thus: "Permit me if you will, to describe to you that sweet shore which forms the North side of the fair river Wear, as it was before the present dual calamities of Industry and Greed came upon it. The river, descending from the Pennine Hills, causes a deep cleft to occur in the rock so that a gorge is formed which sunders the land as the water rushes onwards and outwards to the sea, but on the northern side the land makes a swift and sudden descent of more than sixty feet in two or three hundred yards and here, not more than a century ago, fresh meadows sloped gently towards the bank on which were the humble dwellings of fisher folk and farmers. Here surrounded by pleasantly cultivated pasture and orchards, amidst the fragrance of wild flowers stood the Monastery and Church of St. Peter founded by Benedict Biscop in the reign of Ecgfrith, King of Northumbria, where the young child Bede was born, lived and studied and was venerated amidst the sweetness of that sacred earth and where his eyes could contemplate the unimpeded sweep of empty skies interrupted only by the curving vast horizon of the sea. The land of Monkwearmouth was dedicated in those long ago times to meditation and the religious life.

It is this that we must bear in mind as we view the place today, for it was only when the shining black wealth under the Durham earth was discovered and mined that the changes gradually but inexorably took place and the land was scarred, the Holy earth desecrated, and the free fresh air so necessary to the growth of fair body and mind, was poisoned with black dust and grit and sulphurous fumes. The joyous song of birds was smothered by the clanging and hammering of iron on iron and the clattering of wheels on setts and cobbles, with now only the demented shrieking of gulls to remind us of Nature's enduring presence.

Until recently even the Church of St. Peter itself was almost obscured by the irresponsible tipping of sand ballast against its walls for the brigs emptied their ballast, sand from many a foreign shore into the keel boats, which then transported it and deposited it wherever, without too much trouble, they could, at first near to the water but then gradually further and further inland to the very walls of the church so that they could re-fill with coal to deliver to the empty holds of the waiting brigs. Over the decades the sweet land, once pleasant shore and pasture became covered with layer upon layer of sand, an area of miniature, man-made mountains. Sand of all colours was piled wherever the keel men discharged it without respect even for the ancient walls of a monastery that was once home to the Venerable Bede of whom all England has heard. Such is the power of Greed and the pursuit of money, that it cares for no-one and nothing except the blind acquisition of personal gain. Only now with the steam and iron of the new ships, when water ballast is preferred, can this appalling disfigurement of sand mountains be brought to a halt but the fair meadows are lost and upon these artificial hills within just one square mile are built the habitations for hundreds of human kind who live like rabbits in burrows, breathing foul air, and whose ears never receive the gracious blessing of silence. Even the relief of darkness as it descends on God's earth is no longer a blessing, for the fires to heat the rivets and the plates are not extinguished and the night is rent with the noise of men made bold and bellicose in the Public Houses of which there is one on every corner. The temptations that accompany men, liquor and easy wages are all too evident. So much for the Holy earth of Benedic and Bede. All this is brought about by Industry. The worship of iron, engines and steam has superseded the Saints.

With all this new wealth, this initiative and invention of Capitalism spreading itself from master to all ranks and levels of men, what would one expect to find? A happy and healthy community living in the warm but airy terraced cottages which private enterprise has provided for them in the last decade, each with its own tap to bring fresh water to the occupants so that the former plagues of cholera known in our Northern and Southern towns particularly ports, are a thing of the past? Far from it! As the families have migrated from their ancestral shores and fields they have piled themselves layer upon layer like the ballast sand, into each cottage, so that now it is people, not sand, that create the unwieldy heaps. One family and lodgers live in two rooms above, and another probably related occupies the ground floor of two rooms. In all, more than fourteen or fifteen human beings, men, women, children and howling babes, are crammed together into four meagre rooms. As one family moves to Monkwearmouth Shore lured by the promise of work and wages even for young boys, word is sent back home for brothers, sisters, mothers, nieces, nephews and all those connected with them to come and join and seemingly no matter how many, they are all accommodated within the cottage of the first family thus reducing the rent for all and entirely doing away with the necessity of furniture, since apart from mattresses for bedding there is no room for such luxuries. And does this thrift and economy of space produce, in time, a prosperous community who have benefited from regular wages and who can move on and up in the world? The answer is no, for the more wage earners there are working in the pit or the ship-yard, the more alcohol is needed to fuel their labour and dull the pain of the endless grind. Many a weekly wage never reaches the domestic hearth but is consumed in liquor long before. Now the long rows of houses, each row leading to a great berth where a giant ship over-towering all is being constructed, are blackened by the soot of fires, and the women, a hardy and courageous breed without whom this community would sink into a slough of iniquity and despair, strive to wash their children and dry the clothes of the family in air no longer fresh but laden with the grim and foggy miasma of Industry."

§

At number 24 Hardwick Street, Monkwearmouth, Margaret Laidlaw measures out four tablespoons of plain flour and puts it into a large mixing bowl.

"Is they good uns, Margaret?" her mother Kate Hogarth calls out from the chair permanently placed in the corner for her, and from which nowadays she rarely moves.

"Heaped, Mam."

"See tha' they is, mind, hinny. There's more than eight, maybe ten if arl the lads is in, today."

Margaret takes the big pitcher of water and carefully pours off half a pint into the smaller measuring jug. Then she adds a little milk, so that the clear water in the jug becomes lightly clouded.

"Dinna waste the milk, lass. Water'll do. A guid Yorkshire willna' suffer for a lack o' milk."

"It's only a wee drop, Mam."

"Water'll do, lass."

In a minor act of defiance, as daughters will, Margaret adds a little more milk.

Three boys are bringing in wages now, and Johnny Laidlaw himself is ashore having returned lately from ports in France, Spain and Portugal as Mate on the Clarissa. Money is coming into the household and Margaret can afford to use a little more milk. She takes an egg out of the bowl in the alcove cupboard beside the hearth in which is a black iron cooking range already heated by the coal fire in the grate. Then she cracks open the egg and breaks it into the mixing bowl with the flour. She adds a good pinch of salt.

"Missis Todd is mighty proud of her Yorkshire, Mam."

"Aye, tha' she is, but there's nay skill in it. There's nay skill in a Yorkshire tha's made wi' twa eggs."

"Does she tak twa eggs, Mam?"

"Aye tha' she does, though she willna' say so. But her batter is nay pale enough for one egg only."

"Tis a waste. Eggs is dear."

"Eggs is dear and nay guid Yorkshire needs twa eggs. The secret's in the beating an the standing an the heat. A Yorkshire canna stand a lazy slummock who willna' beat."

Margaret begins to add the milk and water to the flour and egg. She pours a little of the liquid to make a paste, then gradually adds more, beating vigorously with a wooden spoon.

"Gie it ti us, lass. Ah may as well be beating it as sitting here doing naught."

Margaret passes the mixing bowl to her mother and Kate places it between her knees to steady it while she beats. Margaret adds more of the liquid but leaves a quarter of a pint in the jug for the standing.

The smell of the joint, a shoulder of lamb, now spitting as it roasts in the oven fills the room and escapes out through the open front door into the street where it mingles with cooking smells from every house. The air is heavy, rejoicing and swelling in the jubilant fragrance of a hundred Sunday dinners from a hundred ranges and on the street corners men spill from the public houses, The William Pile, The Clipper Ship, The Aberdeen Arms, The Zetland, The Bull and Dog, and The Boilermakers, or the Duzzy House where men not duzzy when they went in, will be duzzy when they come out. The sweet sour smell of the beer now mingles with the odours from the roasts, crisping in their juices in the fierce heat of the ovens.

Now the bubbles rise to the top of the beaten mixture in the bowl. They begin to break as they reach the surface and Kate Hogarth stops beating. The batter must rest for an hour before the remainder of the liquid is carefully poured in so as not to disturb the beaten in air which will make the pudding rise. The extent to which it will rise will be the measure of its triumph.

The potatoes, parboiled, are placed in the tin around the joint, to roast. They are already fluffy so that they will emerge crisp and flaky, flavoured with the fat and meat juices. Unsuccessful roast potatoes are those that though roasted on the outside, remain smooth and are nothing more than boiled potatoes on the inside.

Near one o' clock, dinner time, the men return to the house and gather on the street outside the open front door to smoke and wait to be called in. Young Marjorie Laidlaw, sixteen years old pulls out the folding table and lays it. She is now of an age to be trusted to help with the Yorkshire and she removes the meat, the potatoes and most of the fat from the red hot roasting tin. Now Marjorie pours the batter carefully into the tin and the women listen for the satisfying spitting as the cool mixture full of air meets the sizzling fat. Holding it carefully and well away from her apron to avoid splashes, Marjorie puts it back into the oven. Her mother stirs a little flour into the remaining meat juices to make the gravy and Marjorie chops up the mint to add to vinegar for the sauce.

"Plenty o' gravy, mind," Kate Hogarth calls from her corner.

There must be enough gravy for the first course, which will be the Yorkshire Pudding, and then for the meat, potatoes and vegetables for the main course. A Yorkshire is not ready until it is ready, and to know when that is must be a matter of experience and intuition, for the oven door must not be opened before it is, to check. If it is, disaster will follow. The risen batter will collapse and calamity will stare all in the face over the dinner table. As soon as it is taken out and placed on the table it must be served and eaten, for a Yorkshire in all its glory will tarry for no-one. Late-comers to the Sunday dinner table cannot be tolerated and to miss the moment of the Yorkshire would be to violate the unity of the family and insult the authority within the house of the womenfolk.

At the shout of "Ready, lads" from the house everyone takes their places around the table. Five year old Thomas wriggles in between his mother and his sister Marjorie. Kate Hogarth, now over seventy years of age and partially crippled with rheumatism is helped to her place and the elder daughter, named Kate after her Ganny, struggles to hold her baby, Burlinson, on her knee while Johnny Laidlaw takes his Carvers seat at the head of the table. When everyone is seated, the oven door is opened, and Margaret Laidlaw carries the Yorkshire over to the table. Its outside edge forms a crust and is light brown and crisp, whilst the centre of the great pudding is cooked to perfection, golden and slightly moist to absorb the rich meat gravy that now appears in its tureen with ladle emerging through the hole in the lid.

The company around the table lets out a great groan of satisfaction and admiration and Johnny Laidlaw rubs his strong brown and weathered hands together in anticipation of the feast. Before the Yorkshire is cut and shared out however, there is one more thing to be done. Even a risen pudding in all its glory must wait on the Lord. Johnny Laidlaw, pushing himself up from his chair stands before them with clasped hands.

"Weel, here we are then, Lord, anither Sunday dinner, an we thank ye, arl on us, for these guid victuals set before us, an fer ye're many mercies. Aye, we do."

"Aye that we do" echoes the company.

"Aye and amen" pronounces Johnny, "an noo woman, let's get at tha' Yorkshire."

The plates, piping hot from the hearth are piled up before the pudding which is now sliced up and served with a ladle full of rich hot gravy on each slice. When everyone is satisfied an unusual silence falls over the company as they apply themselves to the full enjoyment of the Yorkshire.

Johnny Laidlaw's blue eyes, so astonishingly light, appearing almost pale against his dark brows and tanned skin, move hesitantly around the table as if in a patient endeavour to collect together in a lasting memory, his family, his flesh and blood, which remains in some way that he cannot understand, remote, as if they are no real part of him for they are now land creatures, whereas he is of the sea. It is never long these days before certain anxieties begin to creep like slender fingers, probing his mind. Sometimes they seem almost to threaten his sanity and he escapes them only at sea. There, on ships, he is at one with himself, emotions that confuse him are calmed and he is where he was born to be. He is Head of this family and yet he cannot tell them that it is becoming harder these days to get a ship. Only two or three years ago he was taken on as Master aboard the Lady Abadour and the Pallion, but now he must accept that with the Never Despair and the Clarissa he has been lucky to be signed on as Mate and taking orders from another. In truth, though he is not an introspective man, he knows that he has never loved anyone more than he has loved a good ship and has never given himself more completely to anything than to the sea whose savage ways he knows and understands and where shipmates, men of his own cast of mind, place him in company of an uncomplicated sort well suited to his temperament.

"Ye're quiet, Johnny lad," says his mother-in-law.

"Our Johnny is nay a mon o' words, Mam, ye should know tha'."

"Are ye no weel, then, Johnny?" Kate persists.

"Aye, aye, ah'm weel enough, mother. It's a fine Yorkshire, Margaret."

"The finest as ye'll get anywhere on Monkwearmouth Shore on a Sunday," says Kate.

"An how d'ye know tha', Ganny Hogarth?" asks young Robert Laidlaw.

"Wha'? Know wha'?"

"How d'ye know that this Yorkshire is the best in all Monkwearmouth Shore?"

"Ah know because ah know!"

"Ye canna know Ganny Hogarth, because ye'd have to gan aroun' an' tasted arl the Yorkshires in arl the houses this Sunday before ye could be judge."

"Gerraway ye young limmer," says Kate Hogarth, "do ye think ah've lived seventy years and ah dinna ken the best Yorkshire when ah see it?"

"Tha's no what I'm saying Ganny Hogarth. I'm no saying tha' ye dinna ken a good Yorkshire, I'm saying that since ye havna' tasted all them hundreds o' Yorkshires in Monkwearmouth this day ye canna say what ye sayed."

"Ah may be awld, lad, but ah'm no silly."

"Yes, ye are Ganny Hogarth, because ye canna understan' the what I'm saying."

"Robert!" says Margaret, "Hae respect for yer Ganny. Johnny, tell Robert to hae some respect for mi Mam."

"Aye" says Johnny.

"Aye wha'?" says his wife.

"Weel, aye, do wha' yer Mam tells ye, Rob."

Robert mutters to himself and quickly finishes the slice of the pudding on his plate.

"Dinna fash yersel,' Mam" says Margaret.

"Ah'll nay be fashed for tha' young limmer is right in what he says."

Now the knives and forks are laid aside, and the roast shoulder of lamb, with its crisp coating of fat on the outside, is taken reverently from the oven and placed on a meat dish to be laid before the Head of the household for the ceremony of carving. This is followed by the vegetables, cauliflower in a peppery white sauce and carrots, with the flaky roast potatoes arranged around the meat. The rich gravy in its tureen is topped up and passed around the table with the vegetables and Johnny Laidlaw stands to carve. Whatever is left over will be eaten cold on Monday and as Shepherds pie on Tuesday.

"Mam," says young Marjorie, "have ye seen the new lodger next door at number 23?"

"Yesterday I saw him, though no ti speak."

"He's a canny lad, Mam."

"Aye," Robert mimics his sister's voice, "he's a canny lad, Mam, but too canny for you, Marjorie Laidlaw."

Marjorie ignores her brother's jibes.

"Is he a mariner, Mam?"

"A mariner! Tha' white faced nacking gowk! He'd no last a day aboard ship wad he Da!" continues Robert.

"He's a shipwright an a guid journeyman a' tha," says Margaret, "Missis Todd sayed it, an I understand tha' he hae served his 'prenticeship in the South, one o' the southern yards, and is well thought on, an – " looking at her son, "is weel past rivet heater an sich."

Kate Hogarth raises her eyes from her plate for a moment to interrupt. "He's nay gowk. Tha's a bonny lad fer arl he nackers Englishman lich."

"Why aye, now we knows fer sure," says Robert, "fer Ganny Hogarth says tis so."

"He's nay great kevel, like yersel' Robert," says Marjorie.

There is once again silence whilst everyone applies themselves to the business of eating.

"Aye," Johnny Laidlaw rouses himself just as the discussion seems to be over. His intervention is all the more unexpected because he does not relish such family debates preferring to keep most of his thoughts on all subjects not directly relating to the sea, to himself. "Aye, he's nay a bad lad."

They all turn to him. This surprising comment commands immediate attention for Johnny Laidlaw rarely voices an opinion and when he does it would appear to be significant.

"Hae ye seen him, then Da?" asks Marjorie.

"Aye, an spake wi' him too."

"Is tha' right, Johnny?" says his wife.

"Aye." Having offered a crumb of information Johnny Laidlaw lapses into silence, then loads his fork with meat and potato which he puts into his mouth. The company waits.

"Wha' did he say, then, Da?" his wife asks when he has chewed and swallowed the forkful of food.

"Ah canna remember."

"Haway man! Ye can remember. Wha' di he say?"

"Ah telled ye ah spake wi' him. Ah didna say tha' he spake wi' me. Ye yammerin' wimmen is arl the same. Ye wants ti kna' every little thing. Wha' did he say, wha' did he do, how di he look when he sayed it. Ah dinna remember ah tell ye."

The company chastened, fall silent. Their disappointment palpable, descends gloomily over the dinner table. All that can now be heard is the clicking of knives and forks. Then suddenly, "He telled me his name, John Richard Balcombe, an his age, three an twenty. He telled me he come up to Monkwearmouth Shore fer the shipyard work at Thompsons Yard. He come up fer the iron ships from where his family is. Tha's Sussex way."

"He telled ye arl tha', Johnny?"

"Aye, an more, which ah canna remember, so hae done, wimmen."

"Will we ask him ti come roun fer supper, then Johnny, seein' tha ye've spake wi' him?"

"Wha' for, woman? Ah spake wi' him. Ah didna offer him ma victuals or the worriting an naggin' o' ma wimmen. Let the poor lad be."

"Aye, but Johnny he hae nay family."

"He hath a family. His family is in Sussex which is in England, or sich like place."

"He hae nay family here, Johnny."

"They dinna mind tha', they Southerner English. They dinna mak too much o' families. Wha' they like is freedom. Wha' they dinna want is mair families."

"Puir lad!" says Kate.

"Aye, poor body! Missis Todd is nay provider Mam. Best if the lad comes in wi' us fer his victuals" says Margaret.

Johnny Laidlaw sighs, "Weel now! Offer him ma roof, an the end o' me sons' bed to sleep on a' neet, an whilst ye're aboot it, offer the lad me daughters, in or oot of wedlock an arl."

"Johnny! Dinna say sich things in front of the bairns an me Mam."

Johnny Laidlaw applies himself to his dinner and the women are silent. Suddenly he puts down his knife and fork and raises his head. His wife, mother-in-law and his assembled family interrupt their eating to look at him. Such a deliberate placing of his cutlery can only mean that he is about to make a pronouncement.

"Arl tha' he told me ah kenned afore he telled it."

"Wha'?" says Margaret.

"Ah kenned afore he telled it, woman. How d'ye think he knowed to come to the Monkwearmouth Shore from tha' Sussex, where ah heerd he hath a whole town named for him. Monkwearmouth Shore is no the great port of Marseilles ye kna', wi' wealthy folks an rich pickins, an it's no gay Paree neither, nor no Genova nor sunny Napoli — "

"Dinna tak us fer fools, Johnny, jist tell us wha' ye knaw."

"Ah knawed his Da. Jacky Balcombe is his Da, a shipmate o' mine mony an mony a time o'er. He telled me his son was a canny lad, an a hard worker, nay a drinkin' mon, a good riveter, wantin' tae work on the new iron ships, nay wooden boats, an wantin' to earn guid money. Ah telled him tae send his lad up here. Tha's arl."

"Aye then Johnny lad," said Margaret, "then it'll be incumbent on arl o'us to mak' the lad at home."

"Where he'll no be at Mistress Todd's," adds Kate.

"Wull ye see the lad an bring him roon' here fer cold victuals tomorrow, then John?"

"Cold victuals. Is tha' arl ye can gie him, wife? They wadna be eatin' cold victuals down there in English Sussex."

"Gerraway wi' ye Da," says Marjorie.

"Cold meat and hot gravy wi' guid tatties, husband, an —"

"An a guid jam roly ti follow, mind," says Kate.

"Wi' plenty o' custard, Mam," adds Marjorie.

Johnny Laidlaw rises from the table. He straightens himself slowly and surveys his womenfolk.

"Ye'll sink the poor lad. He'll be guid fer nay mair hammerin."

"Nay, Johnny, he'll need the nourishment of victuals 'ginst the cold in the yard."

"Weel, ah'm brought ti wonder how the lad has carried on wi'out ye arl," says Johnny.

"An' so am I, Da,'" puts in young Robert.

"An' so ah be too, on wha' he gets at mistress Todd's," says Margaret.

"Very weel, ar'll ask the lad fer ye. But not fer tomorrow, tis too soon. Fer the day after."

"A bit shin o' beef then, an see if the butcher wull throw in a bit ox kidney fer the guid gravy, Margaret."

"Aye, an the jam roly poly, Mam."

"An the custard, Ganny Hogarth."

"Now, let a mon hae a bit o' peace, tae smoke his pipe. Tak yeer yammering wi' ye ti the dirty crocks. Man dinna live by bread alone as it says in the Bible."

"Nay, but he canna live wi'oot it, nay matter wha' it says in tha' buik. Tha' Jesus wa'a mon, an nay doot there was guid wimmin seein' tae his victuals, mony's the time," says Ganny Hogarth.

"Did ye hear wha' me Ganny sayed," shouts young Robert, "me Ganny sayed tha' tha' Jesus was a mon, an he wasna', he was God's son, tha's nay a mon, Ganny, an he didna need them victuals."

"Did he na'? Ah weel, that'd be a savin' if he comed here." Kate Hogarth heaves herself up from the table and reaches for her chair by the fire.

"An wull ye ask him, Johnny?" says Margaret.

"Ah hae said ah wull, woman."

Young Robert escapes outside, leaving the street door open as usual. Ganny Hogarth lowers herself carefully into her chair in the corner and the other women stack the plates and carry them over to the enamel bowl which is filled with hot water from the kettle always simmering by the fire.

"He's a canny lad, Marjorie," whispers her mother.

§

John Richard Balcombe makes an assessment of his current situation. This is not so much concerning his physical surroundings as his less tangible circumstances. The facts so widely believed about him and in all likelihood scattered as seeds in a light and apparently random fashion that inevitably impresses those on whom they chance to fall, soon swelling to form the full grown flowers of truth, were strewn before his arrival, by his father, also John Richard, a mariner, and a Sussex man indeed. But this is not our John Richard's first setting of foot on Monkwearmouth shore. Three and twenty years ago he catapulted into the world rather like Our Lord, onto straw at the back of Back Stables, near the North Shore and within sight of the sands and the great sundering river itself. There were other similarities to the Biblical account. His mother, Mary Ann bore the same names as Our Lord's mother and grandmother and happened to inhabit Back Stables because there was no other place for her to live. When he was still only a toddling child his father returned from sea, offered his name to Mary Ann and took young John Richard to stay with his parents in Sussex. Mary Ann, extreme poverty having taken its toll on her health and strength died soon after, but the opportunities for work and advancement in Monkwearmouth with the boom in ship building has brought him back to the place of his birth, where in fact he is not quite the stranger that it suits him to appear, since he has relatives on his mother's side with whom he lodges. Amongst the poor, as amongst other areas of society, there are levels of social respectability and though Mary Ann could no more help giving birth to her child in Back Stables than Queen Victoria could avoid the more opulent surroundings of her own confinements, it was somehow assumed to be Mary Ann's fault and she and her offspring provided a satisfactory cushion of blame above which others might rest in greater comfort secure in the knowledge that there was at least one layer below them. It was for this reason on discovering that little was known of him, and as his relatives have no wish to disclose facts which might link them once again to the unfortunate Mary Ann, that John Richard is happy to allow himself to be believed a stranger and a Southerner, since the South is unknown territory where it is generally assumed that folk are wealthier and more refined. John Richard has in any case proved his worth to himself by serving a seven year apprenticeship and is proud of his status now as an iron shipwright, master of his craft and trusted with the charge of apprentices himself. Conditions in shipyards are not for the weak and over-sensitive. The men who work there are hardened to a life that is toughened in the relentless cold. Their bodies and minds must be able to withstand the onslaught of every kind of harshness and indignity and this fortitude is usually nourished by access to plentiful supplies of beer and hard liquor available on every street corner. Rising at five thirty in the morning in the bitter cold of winter when there are still three hours of darkness ahead, these men in woollen longjohns and thick vests, pull on their jackets and trousers, over which they wear their two-piece overalls. Then grabbing mufflers and caps and unshaven they leave their houses, so that at three minutes to six every morning nothing can be heard but the gigantic clatter of hundreds of hobnail boots on cobbles. At six o' clock the public houses are legally entitled to open up to the men who find cups of strong tea and nips of rum and whiskey already ranged along the bar. There is time to gulp this down and make a run to the gates of the yard which close at five past six. Despite the apparent noise and chaos of this mad rush of men, grabbing their drinks and burning their throats with the hot liquid and the fire of the spirits, the landlords keep a precise tally of each man's consumption and the debt is paid when the wages come in. At five past six this seemingly unstoppable Gadarene surge has passed beyond the gates into an inferno of fire and thundering machinery. John Richard is not a hard drinking man, though he takes his measure of whiskey like the rest of them to ward off the cruelty of the cold, for by nature he is slight, though years of physical labour since he was no more than a boy have hardened and toughened his muscles and caused his face to take on a serious and somewhat challenging expression as if to convince those around him and more importantly, himself, that he is not a man to be toyed with. At three and twenty years he considers himself well used to harsh conditions and in accepting them as his unalterable lot in life he has little time for those men who sit in huddles and whisper of action against the employers and organisation of labour. He knows no other work and his pride is in thinking of himself as an iron shipwright, a builder of ships. Not of course as a shipbuilder, that is a term relating only to the bosses and those who put up the money to build, but John Richard's pride is greater than theirs for he uses his skill and strength to make a great ship, to see it rise from nothing to tower in its forest of stocks, throwing its vast shadow over everything with all the terrifying presence of a mighty, unimaginable mountain, and know that without him and those like him the visions of the owners and even the engineers would be only so much paper. It is this strong belief in the power and dignity of the shipwright that colours his opinion of many other things.

Even so John Richard has a sense, not entirely comprehensible to himself, of being a man out of his element. He drinks little, that is to say, he drinks enough to quench his thirst and an iron shipwright has a great thirst on him, but he never drinks to excess. Where the entertainment and relief of others is found in the oblivion of the senses brought by alcohol, until all the money so grindingly hard earned has gone with none left for wives and bairns, John Richard, although a single man, puts money by and dreams of days to come. What these days may be he does not care to think of too clearly in case his experience of reality and the impossibility of dreams will crush the all too delicate hopes he sometimes dares to cherish. Though he keeps himself a little apart from the other men he is respected as a hard worker and one who can be trusted.

His father, John Balcombe, is a mariner and old shipmate of Johnny Laidlaw and in truth John Richard would prefer to spend his leisure time with the two older men, listening to their tales of sea and storms. Never a great talker himself, he relishes their yarns and the way in which their eyes seem always fixed on a much further horizon than that before them, which inspires him to believe in a world beyond the hammering and the blackening of smoke and the yelling and swearing of men. He has considered a life at sea for himself, but no young man can afford to ignore the boom in shipbuilding and the money, sometimes as much as six shillings a day, to be made by a skilled journeyman. A seafarer's family is aboard ship and he finds himself ill at ease, even amongst his own on dry land and for himself, John Richard has hopes of settling down with a quiet and pleasing girl, who will not lash him with the sharp tongue that some women have, and who will bear children and enjoy the settled comforts of family life. It is March 1871 and his arrival in Monkwearmouth has happily coincided with the laying of the keel of The Pearl, J.L.Thompson's first iron ship, a steamer which it is hoped will raise the fortunes of the yard and revolutionise the future of ship building on the North Shore. John Richard is taken on without difficulty because he has had experience of iron ship building in the south, and is a qualified shipwright with all the old skills, and as able in the fairing of lines and the laying-off on screeve boards and on the mould loft floor as in riveting when the keel is laid and the ship rises in the stageing. The Thompson family know that the only yards to survive will be those that can move forward with iron and steel and the thrusts of progress in engineering. It is not for nothing that they have named this ship on which their future success and hopes are placed, after the very first ship that Robert Thompson and his three sons built on the North Sands in 1846 which started them in business with its profit of £300. The launching of the first Pearl, an eighty foot long brig on July the 8th 1846 had been a triumph for the brothers and their father who with four other hardworking men designed and built her themselves, and now with the building of the second Pearl it is intended that new wealth will be brought to the Yard. John Richard has few illusions about wealth. He knows that increased profits mean a leap up the ladder of opulent living for the owners of ships and yards that will not be accompanied by a similar rise for the men, but all he expects is the promise of secure and steady wages and a family that is properly and proudly his own with a roof over their heads and a good fire in the hearth. With this he will be satisfied and ask no more.

CHAPTER SEVEN

John Richard works a ten hour day with half an hour for breakfast at eight and an hour for dinner at noon. On a Saturday he works for five hours. These hours have been the focus of a long running dispute with the employers for the men under the leadership of Strike Committee President, Andy Gourlay, have been threatening to stop work until the Nine Hour Day has been agreed. In a working world where only those who are tough enough to withstand the harshness of the conditions and the hardness of men can survive, Gourlay is the undisputed leader. Rough, hard and fiery as he needs to be amongst men who are the toughest in the world, he has a skill which the others lack. Though he can take on any man in a fist fight and though he fears neither spilt blood nor the threat of it, it is his ability to use words, to frame and manipulate the language of persuasion and if necessary, confrontation, that gives him the magnetism of leadership and makes him into the most hated opponent of the employers. Where men's tongues are oiled and freed only by drink, when what they have to say is not worth listening to, Gourlay's biting intelligence never abandons him. It is the steel against which his wits and his words have been sharpened. His life is dominated by hatred of those he sees as exploiting the ignorance of the working man whose greatest fear is of poverty and starvation and he understands that the employers will never capitulate to moderation and reason until their own livelihoods are threatened by the solid withdrawal of labour, the ultimate weapon of the Strike. Neither the bosses nor their opponent Andrew Gourlay have the gift of negotiation. There can be no settlement except by head-on collision and Gourlay is prepared for it. He has already had the experience of his confrontation with Charles Mark Palmer in Jarrow in '66, and he will not let the men be pacified again by such tricks as dances for favoured employees and luncheons and picnics for the workers and soothing words about loyalty and 'family' and 'I'm one o' ye, lads' and all, such as Palmer looking down his long nose gave them. Then the men, like the peasant stock they came from, tugged their forelocks and doffed their caps in that long habit of obedience and agreed to drop their legitimate claim for shorter working hours and the Newcastle Chronicle compared the beneficent influence of Mr. Palmer, now Sir Charles, to that of The Venerable Bede! And whilst this veritable saint sat back in satisfaction to dine with his arrogant friend Lord Armstrong, the men slunk away to live on wages insufficient to save their families from malnutrition and worked until they dropped, health and will broken by fatigue. When he is sure that his influence over the men is strong enough, for that was his failure against Palmer, he will call for a Strike. The employers will respond with a lock-out and head-on the two sides will fight it out.

John Richard, returning to his lodgings at Missis Todd's on that March day in 1871, sees Mistress Laidlaw standing in the doorway of 24 Hardwick Street. She calls out to him but to tell the truth her thick speech in a manner all of its own seems to be neither true English nor true Scots making her difficult to understand, more so than her husband Johnny Laidlaw, whose way of speaking has doubtless been eased by contact with foreigners and native savages across the world. John Richard hopes to satisfy her with a nod of his head in greeting but Mistress Laidlaw is not to be deprived of her opportunity to introduce the young man into her family.

"Good evening to you, Missis," he calls, touching his cap. The gesture is not lost on Margaret Laidlaw, who perceives to her satisfaction that the new neighbour is civil and mannerly.

"Wull ye come indoors for a cup o' tea an a bite o' supper wi' us this night, young man?" she asks.

"That's kind of you, Missis Laidlaw, but Missis Todd will have my supper ready I'm thinking."

"Weel then, tak a cup o' tea wi' us fer now and come an share our victuals on Sunday."

"I'll be pleased to do that, Missis."

John Richard follows her into the house, having no wish to snub his neighbours, but after the long hours of hammering steel on steel, his limbs ache and he is in no mood for conversation, which at the best of times he avoids.

"Ah hae asked ma mon ti speak ti ye, but ah daresay he hasna for his mind is oot there somewhere." She gestures in the direction of the sea.

"Your husband is a fine man, Missis Laidlaw, and respected everywhere I hear."

"Aye, so they say."

Margaret Laidlaw ushers her guest into the room which is the main living space and kitchen for the whole family. Her mother, Kate Hogarth sits in the one armchair in the corner, and several young children sprawl over the floor. There is a good fire in the range but still the room is penetrated by sharp draughts that swirl around the feet because the front door to the street is never closed. The reason for this, as John Richard soon understands is because the older children run in and out all the time, to be followed by their crawling younger siblings, who being slower, run the risk of being trapped in a closing door. A constant draught is thought to be preferable to screaming infants and blasts of cold air as the door swings to and fro. Mistress Hogarth, the Ganny in the corner has her knees and legs well protected against the cold by a many coloured blanket made of knitted squares.

"Good evening to you, Missis," says John Richard, who has removed his cap, and now slightly inclines his head in Kate Hogarth's direction. She says nothing but nods to acknowledge the greeting. Still he is aware that her eyes are alert and watching him.

"Marjorie," Missis Laidlaw calls to her daughter. "Marjorie, leave them clothes be, noo, an come an greet the neighbour." The girl comes in from the yard with a basket of clothes which she has taken down from the line that is stretched across the back street with all the other lines from the other houses as if long-johns and night-shirts, petticoats, aprons and rags blowing crazily in the air thick with soot and smoke are there to create a wild festival of flags.

John Richard notes that she is a slight girl with pale skin lightly freckled and fair to auburn hair, yet she has her father's dark eyebrows and light eyes. She is not a pretty girl, but pleasant enough to look at though she wears an expression of anxiety that she would prefer to conceal.

"This is ma second daughter, Marjorie. She's a guid girl an all. An this is ma mither, Ganny Hogarth, an these bairns is me sister's an mi eldest daughter

Kate's who's at the rope works, an Marjorie an me looks after her bairn along wi' the others. An mi sons isna' here fer they's working fer JLs like yerself an willna' be in til they hae wasted their money in the Duzzy House."

"Mam, our neighbour doesna want to hear all that about our family an all" says Marjorie.

"I'm pleased to meet you, Marjorie," says John Richard.

"An wha' may we call ye, Mister?" says Ganny Hogarth from her corner.

"John Richard Balcombe is my name, Ganny."

"Weel we're neighbours noo, Mister Balcombe, an ah hope ye'll no be a stranger," says Margaret.

"Mam, our new neighbour here have more to do than ti be listening to our gabbing an noise."

"My name is John Richard, Marjorie, and I'd be pleased to talk with you and your family when I'm free from working."

"An are ye a drinkin' mon, John Richard?" asks Margaret.

"I like a nip when it's cold, and a pint to slake my thirst, but I'm not one to spend much time in the public houses, Missis Laidlaw."

"Then yeer a wise young lad," calls Ganny Hogarth, "fer there's nay future in it as an occupation."

"Weel then ye're welcome wi' us, an ye shall hae a guid Sunday dinner wi' us." says Margaret.

"As guid as the Queen hersel' in her palace in London eats o' a Sunday" calls out Ganny Hogarth, "aye an maybe better. Do ye like Queen o' Puddings, lad?"

"I daresay I do, though I can't say I know what it is."

"Dinna ye eat Queen o' Puddings in the English South?"

"I can't say, Ganny."

"Ah canna believe they dinna eat Queen o' Puddings doon there, Margaret."

"Nay matter, Mam. John Richard needs ti build up his strength against the cold here, fer ah hear tha' 'tis always balmy and soft weather in the South. Tha's why they dinna eat Queen o' Puddings doon there."

"I'm happy to eat any kind of pudding with you and your family, Missis Laidlaw,"

"Wha' aboot Spotty Dick?" calls Ganny Hogarth.

"He'll nay ken Spotty Dick, Mam, if he dinna ken Queen o' Puddings."

"Any kind of pudding will be all right," repeats John Richard.

"Spotty Dick isna' any kind o' pudding, young man," says Ganny Hogarth, "tis a pudding could be eaten by the Prince o' Wales, God bless him."

"I'll be glad to try it."

When the new neighbour has finished his tea and made his excuses to leave them, Margaret Laidlaw turns to her daughter, "A canny lad mind, Marjorie."

"He's a' right."

"A' right! A lad tha' doesna drink!"

"He never said he doesna tak a drink."

"In moderation, lass. Nay-one wants a body tha' doesna tak a wee dram noo an again, nay-one wants a swere poker faced fellow, fer there's many a mon who doesna drink who is nay mair than a cuddy-wafter in secret."

"Wha's tha', Mam?" little Thomas looks up from the floor where he has been trying to build a tower out of pieces of cold cinder from the fire.

"Wha's what?"

"Wha's a cuddy-wafter?"

"Mind yer own business."

"Wha's a cuddy-wafter, Ganny Hogarth?"

"Dinna bother yer Ganny, lad."

"Either tell the lad or dinna say things like tha,' Margaret," says Kate Hogarth.

"Forget it, noo!" Margaret is anxious to drop the subject and return to a discussion about the merits of John Richard, who though not particularly handsome is at least a bachelor earning six shillings a day, with a need for a home and a wife and more importantly without a mother to keep him tied to her side. Thomas, sensing that he has touched on forbidden and exciting things is not now going to give up so easily. "Wha's a cuddy-wafter, Ganny?"

"Tis a person who does every thing wi' the left hand, Thomas."

"Is that a'?" Thomas senses that in some way beyond his understanding, he has been cheated.

"Aye, tha's it."

Now it's Marjorie's turn to be surprised. She turns to her mother and whispers, "Is that right, Mam?"

"Aye, tha's as yer Ganny says."

" Why does the new neighbour do everything with his left hand, Mam?" asks Thomas.

"He doesna. Now let it be."

"Aye an let tha' learn ye no ti bring up things like tha' in front o' yer bairns, Margaret," says Kate, settling the blanket more firmly around her knees.

"He's a lad tha' knaws his manners too, mind," says Margaret.

"Southern manners," Kate Hogarth sniffs to signify that manners from the South leave an odour not entirely pleasing to the noses of Spittal folk.

"Southern manners is guid manners, an guid manners is the same everywhere. Here or in Eskimo land."

"The lad's nay strong. He looks like a weakling. He willna last."

"Stop tha', Mam. He's nay weakling. He canna be a weakling if he's working doon yonder lookya."

"Aye, an willna tak a drink wi' the lads after," counters Kate.

"An' willna waste his wages, Mam." The two women fall silent, each with their own thoughts about John Richard Balcombe.

"He's no like your Johnny, Margaret. He's no like your Da, Marjorie."

"Ye're right there, Mam, but wha's the guid of a man tha's never there?"

"How can a mariner be wi' his folks all the time. He's got a good bit o' crackle and spark to him, has Johnny. My! Ye never seed a mon like Johnny fer the twinkle toes. He could dance the awd Devil roun' the moon," says Ganny Hogarth.

"That were lang times ago, Mam."

"Aye, ye should a' seen them, yer Da an yer Mam, Marjorie, they was a couple."

"Tha' was in the awd days in Berwick," says Margaret quietly.

"When ah thinks o' Johnny Laidlaw and then ah thinks o' the new neighbour —" Kate Hogarth continues.

"Will ye hush," says Marjorie, "poor lad to be bantered around by the two of ye. What matter if he is no like me Da Twinky Toes? He's just the neighbour, that's all he is, mind."

"Did ye like him, Marjorie?" asks her mother.

"How do I know if I likes him or no, with the two o' ye never letting anyone get a word in, wi' ye talking of nought but puddins and such. A lad from the English South don't care nought fer puddins."

In truth Marjorie Laidlaw is not as indifferent to the young man as she pretends to be. She has been observing him somewhat stealthily, every day since he arrived for what young girl of sixteen who hopes to marry and have children can resist being curious about a lad who is new to the neighbourhood. Those already around, friends of her brothers, are too well known but someone new and moreover from the south can be dreamed of which is as good or better than anything else. Marjorie's dilemma is that she fears she has no way to make him notice her, why should he? She is no more than a plain lass with no gift of words and the skills that she has inherited from her mother and grandmother for needlework of every kind do not mark her out as different from scores of other young lasses of her age. Apart from that, the young man has only seen her with her hands and arms red and wet from the labour of the wash-house and the mangle and she has had to listen in silent embarrassment to the all too obvious efforts of the other women in the house to entice him in with their talk of dinners and dishes he has not heard of as if folks never ate in the South of England where, Marjorie is sure that they have puddings far more sophisticated than Spotty Dick. It is reported that the Queen herself has puddings made to look like swans and all of cream and ice. No Spotty Dick or Jam Roll could ever be made to look like a swan. In any case, as Marjorie knows all the other Mams and Gannies will have noticed the new young man and before long he will be fair stuffed with dinners and high teas whilst daughters far prettier than herself are sent for to catch his eye.

§

April 1871. It looks as if Andy Gourlay is succeeding this time. If he can persuade the men in the engine works to withdraw their labour until the nine hour day is agreed with the employers he has no need to go to the shipyard workers though most of them are with him and will strike particularly now that business is booming in the yards and the employers need all the men they can get. John Richard Balcombe, now a frequent visitor to the Laidlaw house, is not a Gourlay man.

"Ye'll no' be wi' us then, John Richard? Why's tha' then lad? You scared o' Mister Willie Armstrong and Charlie Palmer and yon Thompson boys? Eh?" Robert Laidlaw, Margaret's eldest son, rivet heater and now plate handler in the shipyard is never tired of taunting the young neighbour.

"I'm not scared of them or you or anyone, Robbie," says John Richard, "but I didna come all this way and spend seven years in learning my craft to be told I mayna' work, lad. You got four thousand Irish wi' you here, and not a man o' them has a skill to be proud of. They'll join you for sure, but I'm a proud man and I'll no be told when to give my skill and when to keep it at home."

"Scum Irish is they? They'll mak short work o' thee, boy. An what o' the Scottish lads? How does they figure in your book?"

" Most of them is skilled men."

"So ye're a bosses' man are ye, John Richard? Mak no mistake, lad, they'll hae nay particular respect fer thee, mon. Ye'll no be suppin' at their table or marryin' wi' their daughters fer all yer pride in yersel, an neither will them tha' comes after ye, yer bairns and yer bairns' bairns as far as ye can stretch. They'll keep ye and arl yours doon. An why? Because they's not fer sharin' wha' they've got wi' the likes o' ye, lad. An why? Because when they start sharin' oot the riches there's less fer them an theirs, an they might lose the perches tha's they's on, an you might start a-climbin' up there wi' em an —."

"An why is they on them perches then?" Suddenly the crackle of Kate Hogarth's voice comes across from her corner of the room, "an how did they gan up on them perches, eh, Robert?"

"Shut yer mouth, Ganny Hogarth. Ye're an awd woman. Ye kens nothin' aboot it!"

"Ah kens everything aboot it. Wha's the difference between Wullie Armstrong an Charlie Palmer an Robbie Laidlaw then?"

"Money. Tha's the difference, an it doesna tak a scholar ti see it."

"Nay lad, money is wha's come oot o' the difference."

"Gerraway wi' ye, ye knaws nothing."

"Ah knaws this, there's one thing that'll raise a man above anither an tha's education."

"Weel an ye're a guid one ti talk o' tha' Ganny Hogarth, fer ye canna read."

"Ah canna because ah had nay schooling, but education is no the same as learnin'. Ah've met mony a one wi' learnin' tha' could read an write a canny hand, but education tha's different. Tis like the dancing, learning is knowing wha' the steps is, but education is knowing wha' the steps is an how to mak something oot o' them. Education is wha' maks the mind grow, lad, an tha' fair fleet an agile mind, weel it can leap this way an tha', an it fears naught. An tha's wha' maks the difference." She pauses and looks around to make sure that she has the attention of audience, "an then, let me tell it ti ye arl, when ye're bairns an ye're bairn's bairns an' arl tha' comes after them, when they has the education, an their minds is agile an free an can jump ahead an arl aroon,' then them bosses an them wi' the gran' hooses an the gran' names, then they wull be lookin' aboot them fer fear an arl."

This unexpected delivery from the old woman takes Robert Laidlaw by surprise. He shrugs his shoulders not knowing how to counter the argument.

"Ah'm right, isn't I, John Richard?"

"Of course you are Ganny Hogarth, and that's why they's setting up Institutes and evening classes and such for the working man. Trouble is, what's they learning, eh? I'll tell you, they's learning Tom Paine and Karly Marx, and what they think is the power of the proletariat."

"The wha'?" Robert can see that the argument is slipping away from him.

"The proletariat, ye dolt," says Ganny, "'tis ye, the working man."

"And the trouble with that is," continues John Richard, " that the proletariat only have the power when the wealth of the bosses depends on them working. But when times gets harder and the orders ain't coming in for ships and engines, then it's out for the workers, and no Andy Gourlay or Tommy Paine can help them."

"The orders is coming in, ye knaw tha,' lad," says Robert.

"They is now, but there's been many a time when ships has been half built and then stopped for lack of a buyer."

"Ah'll tell ye when ships is needed most, lads," Ganny Hogarth calls from her corner, "when there's a guid war, tha's when. Ye'd best pray fer a war. It was fifty-six when tha' Crimean struggle ended, an after tha', fifty seven, wha' ye got, eh? Naught! Tha's wha' ye got fer yeer pains. Nay ships ti be built, nay food fer bairns an wimmin, an many a guid lad lost ti Mericky an gone ferever. Pray fer plenty o' wars, lads."

"Wha' nonsense is ye yammering, Mam?" Margaret Laidlaw comes in from the wash-house, "we wants nay wars. Nay sons nor grandsons o' mine is ti be lost in nay wars."

"It's not wars only, Ganny Hogarth, competing and price cutting between the yards, specially the London yards. It's good now, but there's no man can say for sure how it will be," says John Richard.

Kate Hogarth tucks the blanket firmly round her knees again. Her hands are long but the veins stand out covered only by a thin stretch of skin, once pale but now so freckled with age that the pigment meets and gives it the appearance of lightly scorched paper from which the joints of fingers and knuckles protrude angrily.

"Ah've one mair thing ti say," she says, "an. then ah'll say nay mair. Now mind ye listen, and ye too, Margaret. Ye'll work an ye'll toil an ye'll labour, but ye'll get nowhere. Long after ah'll be gone ye'll be here still, an ahl the others like ye. Ye'll be here because o' yer women-folk. Tis very well fer men ti get themselves a bit learning wi' their Institutes an like, but ye'll never raise yersels till yer women gets their chance at learnin' too. So mind ye see ti tha'. Ah had no chance an neither did my Margaret here, though ma lads did, but Marjorie has a bit learnin.' One day, mind, there'll be women like Marjorie, aye an her sister Catherine, an Ann mi girl that's noo Ann Levenson, an they'll have learnin' an education too. Then ye'll get up on yer feet the arl o' ye. Tis the women that'll pull ye ti yer feet."

Margaret Laidlaw picks up the baby as he tries to crawl towards the hearth. It is Burlinson, her grandson, her eldest daughter's son, born out of wedlock. Burlinson is looked after by his Ganny and whoever else is in the house.

"He stinks," says Margaret, "Marjorie, tak Burlinson and change him. Tak him oot the back, lass, he smells." Marjorie tucks the baby who is now screaming because his desire to approach the hearth has been frustrated, under her arm.

"Noo! Who wad be washin' babbies' dirty behinds, and cleanin' oot the grates, and seein' ti the victuals and manglin' them claes, eh, if arl the women was busy wi' the educatin'. 'Tis naught but clavers tha' ma Mam talks. Tak nay notice, lads. Ah've heered tha' there's women who wants this an wants tha' an wants ti vote an decide things in the parliament. Tis naught but clavers. Let the men do tha' kind o' thing an leave us be ti gerr on wi' matters o' mair note. Ah'm right, isn't ah, John Richard?"

"Well, there's a lot in what you say, Missis Laidlaw. If all the women was out all day learning and working and running the parliament, we'd be in a pretty mess."

Kate Hogarth draws her shawl closely round her shoulders, "Singin' to a different tune now then, is ye Mister Balcombe? Education fer some, eh? As long as they's men."

"Men and women is different, Ganny Hogarth."

"So ah've remarked o'er the years o' ma life, an' it's taen nay educatin' ti see it, but if ah'd had the blessin' o' a bit education ah'd have noticed tha' they is no as different as arl tha'." She leans back in her chair and closes her eyes. Since there is no privacy into which to retreat she has learnt long ago to withdraw herself from all that is going on around her so that the little space she occupies in her chair becomes an island, unreachable in its isolation.

§

Whit Monday 1871. Traditional day of celebration and demonstration for Shipwrights.

Closing time for the Public Houses where many of the men have been taking their leisure for most of the evening and a good part of the day too, and they are not ready or willing to return to their homes whilst the night still offers a good deal of sport. The piano has been pushed out into the street and the singing which had reached a crescendo inside the saloon bar continues outside. It is not a warm night but the revellers whose sensitivity to the cold has been blunted and burnt by the fire of alcohol surging through their veins are now well fortified and lean against each other, men and women mixed and linking arms.

Kate Hogarth's chair has been carried outside as well and she is helped to reach it and sit down by the open front door. She has wrapped a shawl around her head, and the blanket that usually covers her knees reaches the ground where her feet tap out the rhythms on the cobbles. At the open front door along the street sits Ganny Robson, her shawl tightly round her shoulders, and on her head a man's cap. Ganny Robson smokes a clay pipe of tobacco.

"Guid evenin' ti ye, Ganny Robson," calls Margaret.

"Aye". Ganny Robson nods and grunts a response, unwilling to remove the pipe from her mouth.

The children, mostly without shoes, chase each other, shrieking with excitement and the young men and girls stand around in groups, for this is an opportunity to flirt and preen and engage in all the subtle intricacies and interactions of courtship, love and longing, triumphant or unrequited. The setting for such a web of feeling can hardly be said to be romantic even though spirits and in some cases, hopes, are high. Apart from the general smoke blackened atmosphere caused by the soot of hundreds of chimneys from the lines of terraced houses there is the overlying tang of urine and the occasional splashed sprawl of vomit, which, if it does not rain, will by the morrow spike the air with its acrid smell. It is for this reason that Margaret Laidlaw has summoned most of her family to guard the doorway and the territory around it. Only by their determined presence can they ensure that those who have drunk too much do not empty their bodily contents on the step of number 24 Hardwick St. In the morning most of the women will be out early to clean their steps and the street around, for no matter what goes on inside the house there is a solid belief in keeping criticism and moral judgment at bay by maintaining an exterior appearance of good order and cleanliness. In any case the noise of music, singing and general mayhem makes it impossible to sleep and it is therefore better to watch and exchange a neighbourly word here and there, even if one does not join in. Those who create the most trouble are without doubt not the men of the shipyard or even of the pit, they are the scores of Irish labourers who have come over as single men, untroubled by family responsibilities, to pick up the unskilled work wherever they can find it, who lodge in a fifth or sixth share of a room and rather than sending their pay back to their dependents in the old country, which of course was, and is, their intention and purpose, find themselves unable to resist the lure of the horses and the hostelry.

Johnny Laidlaw, never one to place himself at the centre of any such gathering, watches from the doorway and Margaret fetches a cracket stool to sit beside her mother.

"Wastin' their money, look ye," says Kate Hogarth, "wastin' all they has on sich revelry, an on the morrow 'twill be gone an naught but sore heads an bruises inside an oot to show fer it."

"What other is there, Mam? Wha' else is fer folks like us?"

"Naught else fer certain if naught else is ti be thought of."

"Wha's tha' to be meanin', Mam?"

"There was plenty else when I was a bairn. There was haymakin' an Harvest, an dancin' an God's guid fresh air. Aye, an there was cobles tui row across ti the Holy Island itself, an watch ti see the great tide cover the causeway, an yersel' an the Isle cut off an lonely from the land. An then there was time an space ti think. Ye canna think in this place. Ye canna even breathe."

"Mam, that was Spittal. These days noo is different."

"Different, as ye say. These days is progress so they say. These days ain't

Spittal tha's fer sure, but ah rue the day tha' put the leavin' in ahl the folks heads. Johnny Laidlaw kens ma meanin', dinna ye Johnny?"

"Aye, Ganny."

"Aye weel Mam, ye're safe there. Johnny Laidlaw'll agree wi' ye jes so he can be left in peace."

"Hey man!" It is Jimmy Bell, the big Pitman who calls out. "Ye're no away at sea, then Johnny, lad?"

"Waitin'. Waitin' fer a ship, Jimmy. Ah'll be gone any day noo."

" Give us a horn-pipe, then Johnny. Come on lad."

"Nay, Jimmy, look ye, there's yon Irish lads ti gie ye a reel."

"Ye gan ti let them Irish boyos show ye how ti do it, Johnny?" It's Will Levenson who calls out to him now.

"Ye've nay fiddler, an nay piper, an ah canna perform fer ye wi'out a guid musician ti aid me"

"Fetch Swanny. Fetch Swanny Mills over," shouts Jimmy Bell.

James Watt Mills, known as Swanny, just fifteen years old and a fine musician is pulled out of the group of young people. "Get your smallpipes, Swanny, lad, and Johnny Laidlaw here'll show us a rare dance."

"Is me Da going to dance, Mam?" asks Marjorie, "tell him no, Mam, it's no right for a man of his age. He'll mak a fool o' himself."

"Wull he indeed ! Johnny Laidlaw was never nay fool." Says Margaret.

"But Mam, he's too old now."

"Auld nothin'! Ye knaws nothin' aboot auld."

Swanny takes up the smallpipes and one of the Irish boys takes the fiddle. They discuss the reel, their heads together, with Johnny, and then the two musicians try out a few notes, tapping their feet to catch each other's rhythm.

"Off ye go, Johnny, lad, Gie us yer best," Will Levenson urges him.

"Are ye fit like, Captain Laidlaw?" asks Swanny.

"Fit an ready" replies Johnny, as he draws himself up straight to his full height, and his strange blue eyes take on a look of rare intensity, then in an instant focus again on that thing that is inside him and yet somewhere else a long way off, maybe in time or on the distant horizon. Arms by his sides his feet begin to tap out the rhythm of the reel and the remembrance of their old dexterity and the patterns of movement come back and they move as easily as when he was a young man in Berwick at the May Flittings.

"Come an join me, Margaret, ma wife," he calls, as the crowd clap in time to the clicking of his feet on the cobbles. Then Margaret who thought she had forgotten how to be young, leaps forward to her husband's side and together, their feet matching in movement and beat, they perform the reel as if it were only yesterday that they left the Hirings. The crowd now shrieks with delight and another fiddler joins Swanny, catching the rhythm as it speeds up, the crowd beating it out with the clapping of their hands and the stamping of their feet, until breathless, the couple signal to the musicians to stop, and acknowledge the applause with waves and smiles. Marjorie has never seen her father smile and respond with such enthusiasm before. Six year old Thomas stops running around and holds onto his sister. "Is tha' me Mam?" he asks.

"Ah thank ye, Johnny" whispers Margaret to her husband.

"Thank me, wha' fer?"

"Weel, fer askin' mi."

"Fer the dancin'? Why not? Twas ye an me tha' was used ti doin' it tigether in the auld days."

"Nay, no fer the dancin', fer somethin' – ah canna say. Jes' fer rememberin' mi again. Ah canna say."

"Ah always remembers ye, lass. Ah remembers tha' ye wanted a great clock one day, an ah remembers tha' ye ain't got tha' clock yet. But ye shall hae it, Margaret, ye shall."

"Hey, Johnny Laidlaw, is that the great Captain Johnny Laidlaw?" A rough looking seaman breaks through the crowd and tries to grab Johnny's arm.

"Ye knaws me weel enough, Tim Leary. Ye're drunk, man. Gerraway hame."

"Aye. I knows ye. We been shipmates many a time. Tell the people wha' happened in sixty seven, then Johnny, tell them, tell yer wee wifey here wha' happened aboard The Abadour eh!"

"Get ye hame, Tim, ye're drunk."

"A rare fine dancer is yer man, Missis, he can do a fine side step o' the law when he wants."

"Shut yer mouth, Tim." Johnny Laidlaw wrenches the seaman's grasped hand from his arm.

"I shut my mouth fer ye, Captain, an I've had nay a ship since."

"Ah'm sorry fer tha."

"Sorry ain't no good to me, Captain Laidlaw, but then you ain't no Captain now I hears. I hears that sudden The Clarissa has a Mate named Johnny Laidlaw, an then I hears that Never Despair has a mate called Johnny Laidlaw an I thinks, well now, is that the same Johnny Laidlaw as was Captain of The Lady Abadour in sixty seven when —"

"If ye've got any complaint wi' me, Tim Leary, ye'll gie it me when ye're sober. Now gerraway."

Johnny Laidlaw pushes the drunken seaman with an unexpected force so that he falls and sprawls full length on the cobbles. Then he turns to his family and ushers them back into the house.

"Marjorie," he says, "Help yeer Ganny back inside. It's late. Time fer nay mair o' this nonsensical merrymakin' an fal-de-lal."

"Wha' were he gabbin' aboot, Johnny?" asks Margaret.

"Wha' do drunks gab aboot, eh? He's nay but a limmer rogue, Timothy Leary."

Kate Hogarth hangs on to her granddaughter's arm as she hobbles back into the house followed by Thomas who tries to carry her chair with the cracket stool balanced on top.

"There's mony a limmer so ca'ed tha' is nay limmer," she murmurs, "Ah heerd the Wallace ca'ed a limmer once an he were nay one, tha's fer sure. Thomas, lad, dinna try ti carry ma chair, tis ti big for yi. Marjorie, ah'll steady mesel' on the door here, an' ye'll fetch ma chair in."

"Wha' were it Ganny?" whispers Marjorie, as she bends to lift the stool. "Wha' were that Timothy Irish sayin' ti me Da?"

"Yeer Da's a guid mon, an a guid mariner, lass. But he's a Spittal mon fer sure, an he wadna be a Spittal mon if he didna carry a bit mair than's set doon on paper in a ship where he is Captain, an nay one is the worse fer tha.'"

"But Ganny, what of the ship owner? Do he know about me Da?"

"Wha' is nay care ti the ship owner is nay anxiety fer he. Yeer Da wull save the owner frae anxiety, let's say, but I do hear tha' they Excise did find a wee bit something on The Abadour which yeer Da was Captain of. The Excise, weel, there's mony an Excise tha' wadna put the hand on Johnny Laidlaw, tha' kenned him from a boy, but since tha' it's nay been sae easy fer him tae find an Owner tae gie him Captain. Tha's arl. Dinna be tellin' wha' ah've telled ye ti nay one. Ye're a Spittal lass.

"Does me Mam know?"

"Ye're Mam is daft fer yeer Da. She'll hear nay thing against him. She'll hear nay word. Tak me chair indoors lass, an be sharp. Am ah ti stand holdin' ti this post forever. Tak me chair in an come an gie us yer arm. Be sharp, Marjorie."

§

"Most seamen lead, if one may so express it, a sedentary life. Their minds are of the stay-at-home order, and their home is always with them – the ship; and so is their country – the sea. One ship is very much like another, and the sea is always the same. In the immutability of their surroundings, the foreign shores, the foreign faces, the changing immensity of life, glide past, veiled not by a sense of mystery but by a slightly disdainful ignorance; for there is nothing mysterious to a seaman unless it be the sea itself, which is the mistress of his existence and as inscrutable as Destiny. For the rest, after his hours of work, a casual stroll or a casual spree on shore suffices to unfold for him the secret of a whole continent, and generally he finds the secret not worth knowing."

Joseph Conrad   Heart of Darkness

Jo Korzeniowski's last ship excluding a brief term as second mate on the Adowa, was his two year service as second mate on the Torrens. She was the last full-rigged composite passenger clipper ever built, tall and slender with bows graced by the figurehead of a woman and she had the ability to run before the wind in the roaring forties at 300 to 350 miles a day without shipping a sea. She was built by Laings on the Wear, the oldest and proudest of the shipbuilders. Korzeniowski never forgot the exhilaration of his experience aboard the Torrens. He tried unsuccessfully to get another ship like her, but his career as a seaman more or less ground to a halt. For a mariner to find himself beached, stranded on shore without a ship is to be homeless and purposeless, especially for those like Jo Korzeniowski and Johnny Laidlaw whose whole life and ambition it has been. Fortunately for Jo Korzeniowski he emerged as a genius when he set his hand and mind to writing and only had to change his name to Conrad, which in any case it had always been (for Konrad was his real name, though his ship-mates called him Jo). There is no such luck for Johnny Laidlaw. Lacking Conrad's ability to speak three languages perfectly, indeed, battling against the tide on occasions to speak the one to the satisfaction of the true English, he finds it increasingly difficult to get a ship. Family life on dry land, though within sight of the sea has become strangely meaningless to him. As meaningless as what might be thought of as strange in foreign lands but which he has taken so much for granted all his life. His curiosity has blunted. He has dismissed the variety and exoticism as being too frequent, too incomprehensible and too irrelevant to interfere with his remit as a seaman. His place is aboard ship, his concentration and energy directed solely to the movement of that ship safely from one location to another. His allies and his adversaries are the weather, wind and the water. He knows the characteristics of the sun, moon and stars better than those of his children and a life deprived of the necessity to struggle and challenge those cosmic forces that for so long have provided both mystery and familiarity perplex and distress him in ways that even he cannot identify. His eyes with their long habit of staring into a vast space seem to have lost the ability to concentrate on a smaller or narrower focus and so it is with his mind too. He smiles at his wife and children but his smile slides over them to reflect the distances and expanses contained within the unknowability of his thought-hoard. He is one with that ancient Anglo-Saxon Sea-Wanderer whose wailing reaches out over a thousand years, 'where has it gone, where has it all gone?'

It is certainly true that Johnny Laidlaw has been less than circumspect in some of his adventures. When men of a sea-faring temperament are confined together without hope of escape in a ship, far from land and over many weeks, with nothing around them but the heaving forces of the sea, tensions are aroused and for the Master, inevitably there are those who oppose his judgment, yet must conform and therefore enemies are made. If Johnny Laidlaw had not taken a risk or two with the contraband, a risk after all that was shared with his crew, whether they liked it or not and mostly they accepted the risk willingly because of the profits in which they would also share and if in '67 when he was Master of the Lady Abadour he had not had to be towed into Ramsgate Harbour from Cronstadt with both fore and main topmasts gone, provoking unusual interest in his crew and cargo he might well have remained a Master Mariner and retired from the sea honourably in old age. It is useless for the likes of Tim Leary to blame him now for their predicament. They knew when they signed on with him that he was a Spittal seaman and that certain risks were in his blood and they would have been happy enough to share in the spoils. If his narrow escape from the clutches of the law have made the finding of another ship more difficult, he will take more risks. He knows that in old age he may hope to sit with the other ancient Captains on a seat by the shore, his spyglass to his eye, searching the vast expanse of water, spending his last days quietly re-living past voyages and dying in his bed at home, but Johnny Laidlaw is too much of the sea and without it he is lost. Even though space for living is limited aboard ship there is the freedom of wind and salty air and he cannot settle to a life of confinement in the over-crowded house, surrounded by women and their domestic concerns. When his end comes he earnestly prays that it will be at sea, dying in whatever circumstances, as a man, a true and strong seaman to the finish.

CHAPTER EIGHT

Marjorie Laidlaw helps her grandmother to steady herself against the kitchen doorway and goes back outside to fetch the old lady's chair. As she bends to pick it up she feels the strong grasp of a man's hand on her shoulder.

"Are you going indoors now, Marjorie?" asks John Richard Balcombe.

"Aye, it's late and me Mam and Da wants us in now."

"Your Da is canny on his feet then."

"Aye, he's a twinkly toes an all."

"Did you know he could dance a reel?"

"I heard tha' he could do it, but I never seen it. My Da is no a man o' many words. He would never say."

"Will you take a little walk with me, Marjorie?"

"Wha' now?"

"Aye now."

"I canna. Wha' would me Mam say!"

"I don't know what your Mam would say, lass, I ain't asking your Mam. It's you I'm asking."

From the kitchen doorway comes the voice of Kate Hogarth, "Are ye leavin' me here ahl night, Marjorie? Where's ma chair, ah canna stand here much longer, girl, ma strength wull fail mi."

"Tha's ma Ganny," says Marjorie, "I have to go indoors now."

"Will you come for a walk with me tomorrow then, tomorrow after tea?"

"Walk? Where to?"

"Up Cage Hill maybe. Up on the headland. Take a look at the sea."

"Wha' for, look at the sea? I can see the sea, every day of me life."

"Look at the fields then?"

"Wha's to look at in a field?"

"I'm asking you to take a walk with me, lass, I canna tell you what to look at. I canna go on asking. Will you take a walk with me or will you not?"

"Maybe."

"I'm not going to call at the house and ask. If you want to take a walk with me tomorrow after you've had your tea, you come outside here and I'll be waiting for you."

"Wull ye come an help me, Marjorie, ah wants ma chair," calls Kate Hogarth.

"I've got to go," says Marjorie.

"I'll wait for you tomorrow, but if you don't come I won't be asking again." John Richard turns away, and Marjorie picks up the chair and takes it into the house.

Lying in her narrow bed she can hear Burlinson's snuffles as he sleeps in the bed alongside, with his mother, her older sister, Catherine, called after their Ganny, but known as Kitty. Marjorie cannot sleep. She wishes that somehow she had accepted the invitation to take a short walk with John Richard for then it would have seemed natural, indeed nothing to remark on, but merely the end of the evening when everyone was out in the street and by now anyway, it would be over. It would not have been noticed. Now she must lie thinking and worrying and she must make a decision, not just to go walking with a neighbour but whether to meet him and walk out with him, with others looking perhaps from their open doorways. Everyone knows what walking out means and although she has long had girlish dreams about the neighbour, dreaming and facing the reality of a formal understanding with him, are two different things. On the other hand she asks herself what her life is to be if she does not find a man who will marry her and John Richard is pleasing enough, though she has noticed that he appears to know his own mind and there is a stubborn twist to his mouth when he doesn't get his way.

Throughout the next day Marjorie hugs her secret and tells no-one but she is aware that she cannot go out after tea without saying where she is going. The Hogarth women are people who understand the values of propriety. They are not feckless, unheeding folk like so many around them for they take a pride in their good but modest clothes which are always clean and mended, and just as in Spittal in the time before their arrival in Monkwearmouth they are regular church-goers with a proper sense of right and wrong as it is put before them by the clergy of St. Peters. 'The rich man in his castle, the poor man at his gate' seems to them to reflect the natural and undisputed order of things, best accepted and not easily changed. Marjorie is aware that to announce that she is going out to meet the neighbour, though he is often made welcome in the house, will give rise to much comment and questioning about intentions when in fact she herself has very little idea of what may follow an innocent walk up Cage Hill with a young man who has a reputation for hard work and apparently correct behaviour. For the first time she feels the strangeness of John Richard Balcombe. He is a man and one she does not know except within the security of the family. To face being alone with him is something that she has not thought about before and she finds herself lacking in confidence. A man has the smell of a man about him which is absorbed in the company of other men or within the family, but on his own the smell of a man may be unwelcome, threatening, and it must be reckoned with. At last she decides to say something. She hopes that the words she has formed in her mind will sound easy and inconsequential.

"Mam, will it be- I mean will it — " The words will not form themselves properly. "I was thinking I'd go outside for a bit walk after tea, Mam. Maybe call on Bella Shaw. She's had a bad cough I hear."

"Aye, ah'll come wi' ye. Ah've a bit cake ti tak fer Bella," says Margaret.

"Well, I was thinking that maybe the neighbour would be walking up there with me, Mam."

"The neighbour! What neighbour's this, then?"

"Well, you know Mam, him next door, Mister Balcombe."

"John Richard! Has he asked to tak a walk wi ye?"

"It's no important, Mam. Just if I was goin' up to see Bella, look ye, he might walk me up there."

"Did he say tha'?"

"Aye."

Margaret turns to the chair in the corner where her mother sits with the rug over her knees. "Did ye hear tha' Mam? Marjorie is oot walkin' wi' John Richard."

"It's no like that, Mam." Marjorie feels herself blushing and wishes that she had said nothing. By now any interest that she had in John Richard Balcombe is appearing as no more than the day dreaming of a silly girl and deeply to be regretted.

"If the lad asked ye ti walk, ye'd better gan, but nay mair than a half hour, mind."

John Richard waits in the street outside Missis Todd's house. He hopes that the cigarette he is smoking and the way in which he leans against the wall gives him a casual air. Here is a man, who after a hard day at the yard is easy with himself, in no way made nervous or apprehensive by a plain girl of seventeen or thereabouts, at least five years younger, whose experience of the world has extended no farther than the street in which she lives. In truth it is these very factors that are of the greatest importance to John Richard for he is no sophisticate and cannot hope to attract the interest of a different sort of girl. To be noticed he realises that he must seek someone likely to be impressed by what he perceives to be his own limited charms and he has little idea of how to fascinate a girl by means of conversation or flattery. His tactics in previous experiments with women have centred on few words and unmistakeably plain physical explorations that make up with enthusiastic activity what they lack in finesse. If she does not come out, he tells himself, he will certainly not pursue her. There are other girls like her, plenty of them, who will need little encouragement.

When the front door of number 24 opens and Marjorie Laidlaw steps outside, John Richard affects an attitude of indifference.

"Are you coming then?" he asks.

"I'm taking a walk to Bella Shaw's. Me Mam has some cakes for her since her cough is bad. If you want you can walk wi' me."

John Richard removes the remains of his cigarette from his mouth with his finger and thumb and drops the stub on the setts. Then he grinds it with the heel of his boot. "As you wish," he says, "I don't mind going with you that far."

They walk, side by side in silence, having very little in common to talk about, but the silence is uneasy as both of them wonder whether this venture has anything at all to recommend it apart from a vague tingling of the nerves. Now alone with him without the familiar and comfortable interruptions from her mother and Ganny Hogarth, the young man seems to be much more the stranger than he was when he first arrived in Hardwick Street. She longs for their voices and the normality of talk about puddings and such like which have embarrassed her so much before. Finally the silence is broken.

"How old are ye then, Marjorie?"

" You knows how old I am."

"Why don't you just answer my question. How old are ye?"

"It's a daft question when ye knows the answer."

"Right, then, I'll not speak." They walk in silence again.

"Seventeen last birthday," says Marjorie at last.

"You got a sweetheart then?"

"I dunna bother myself wi' things like that."

"You must know many a young lad."

"Aye, I do."

"No-one in particular then?"

"I telled you."

"So what if I was to say that I like you?" John Richard is not entirely sure that what he has just said is true but it is the only way forward that he can think of and girls seem to require some such declaration before allowing any further moves to be made.

"I wouldna believe you."

"It's true, mind." It seems to him that the saying of it makes it more true than he had previously suspected and that if he goes on saying it he might eventually convince himself that he means it. Marjorie does not answer. Response is not possible. No-one else has ever said such a thing to her before and though the truth of it seems unlikely, she cannot help but be pleased. It is as if someone has put a gift of unwieldy size into her hands and left her with the problem of opening it. "D'you like me then?" asks John Richard.

"Ye're well enough, but I don't know you hardly."

"You've seen me plenty."

"Aye, but ye dinna talk to me. To me Da an me brothers, an then about mens' stuff at the yard an all that."

"Well, you willna get to know me at all, lass, if we walk only as far as Bella's and then mostly saying naught."

"Maybe we could gan a little further, but not far, mind, I mustna be long."

"Well thankyou, Marjorie. The cobbles are not so easy to walk on. Take my arm, ma'am." Marjorie takes his arm and giggles for she is no ma-am, nor ever will be. They walk as far as the Thompson gates and though it is getting dark now they stop and stand beneath the huge presence of the rearing hulk and the forest of stocks that surround it. His talk is of the yard, the business of a riveter and a plater, of problems with the apprentices who have no proper indentures and can be used to put skilled men out of work and Marjorie listens as if she has never heard such fascinating stuff before. When they return and he leaves her, she goes back into the house with an unusual pink colour in her cheeks.

"Ye're back then," says her mother, "an how was Bella?"

"A good bit better."

"Ah'm glad ti hear it, fer ah was telled she was nay so good today."

"Well, she hasna been so good."

"As she's a bit improved ah'll relieve ye of them cakes ye's still got in yeer bag an tak them ti her. It's no Bella ye've been passing the time wi'. Now mak some tea fer yer Ganny. Ye'll soon come doon ti earth,my lass."

§

John Richard Balcombe and Marjorie Laidlaw have been walking out together on a Sunday for two months. In this time Marjorie has learnt one of life's paradoxes, for the very strangeness that frightened her so much in the first place is in fact the essence of the attraction and the part of the other that cannot be fathomed is the most significant part which fades more or less inevitably when the other becomes predictable and known.

"So," says her mother, "is there an understandin' between you an him?"

"He hasna said so."

"Weel! Has he no? Then yer Da will be obliged to speak wi' him."

"Nay, Mam, let him be."

"He canna set the tongues o' all the neighbourhood waggin' an all the hearts o' the young lasses breakin' an no say a word ti ye aboot weddin.'"

"Who says that I want to be weddin' him anyway?"

"Ah do, lass. Ye ain't livin' in fairy land here, ye ken. Nay Prince o' the fairies is comin' fer ye o'er the hills back yonder. Ye ain't nay Queen o' the fairies neither. Ye'd best lap up warm in wha' ye has. He's as guid as ye'll get an better than most o' the others. He'll provide fer ye as best he can."

"Is that what weddin' is then, Mam? Is that all it is?"

"Wha' did ye think? Tak wha' ye can an put up wi' the rest."

"Aye an there's a deal ti put up wi' in marriage," calls Ganny Hogarth, "pray ti become a rich widow, they's the ones wi' the canniest o' wedded bliss."

"Rest ye're tongue, Mam," says Margaret, "tha' lad is nay limmer. A Southerner, but nay rogue."

"He ain't nay Southerner, an he ain't si guid as arl tha.'"

"Gerraway, Mam!"

"He's nay Southern gentleman, though he may hae lived a wee while doon there in England. His mother was Mary Norman who was livin' in Back Stables. Livin' wi' the horses wi' oot a penny ti her name. An if ye ask me how ah come to know, ah'll tell ye. Ganny Trott telled me aboot it. Jacky Balcombe come up from the South an gift her that bairn, an he took it after she died, poor body. She wasna nay better than she ought, but she went, an may the Lord rest her soul."

"It doesna matter, any road, Mam" says Marjorie, "tell Ganny Hogarth to be quiet."

"An may the Lord look after arl them lasses tha' has bairns ootside o' wedlock, an in particular them lasses in this family, tha' their Mams and Gannies can rest wi'oot ha'eing mair bairns an babbies ti disturb the hoose an the peace o' their las' days." She glares at Burlinson, who has learned that sticking out his tongue will usually provoke a reaction.

"Ah want ti hear nay mair, Mam," says Margaret.

"Ah'll say nay mair." Kate Hogarth pulls her shawl about her and tucks the rug more tightly around her knees.

It is a disappointment to learn that the neighbour is not as much a stranger as he has appeared. Indeed the family of John Richard's unfortunate mother had been known in Monkwearmouth long before the relatively new arrivals from the North. They had been living in the Sundered Land since the days of the Monastery and may have known and served the Venerable Bede himself, even their name of Norman originated from the days of the Norse invasion and now it appears that the lineage of John Richard Balcombe, despite the rude intervention of his father from the unknown South of England, is impeccable and unchallengeable. As for John Richard himself, by June 1872 he has allowed himself to slip with relative ease into a relationship with Marjorie Laidlaw and though nothing is said between them, there is neverthless a growing assumption about which he is becoming not altogether comfortable, that they will marry and that sooner rather than later. The business in the yards is booming and being paid by the half, quarter, and whole day, he can earn a minimum of six shillings a day and sometimes as much as seventeen shillings. Out of this he must pay his rivet heater and his helper who are sub-contracted to him and not employed directly by the Thompsons, but neverthless he has money in his pocket and money enough to support an undemanding wife and a family. He is not a religious man, nor has he been brought up to attend any Church or Chapel, but Marjorie's family have inherited a largely theoretical Presbyterian outlook on life which has lately been modified a little by their attendance at the Anglican Church of St. Peter, and they seem to take it for granted that he will become a church-goer and respectable member of that congregation.

Gradually John Richard finds himself drawn into the Laidlaw family expectations, though in truth he hardly knows why except that to disentangle himself at this stage would require an effort of decision and strategy that after a day's labour at the Yard is beyond his limits of energy. Each day he lets go by without any positive decision one way or another diminishes his chance of escaping the situation. He supposes that he has become comfortable with the arrangement; undeniably he enjoys the cooking of Marjorie's Mam, and largely because of that he can tolerate the astringent tongue of the old Ganny who never moves from her chair in the corner. There is no need to be too much concerned about an old woman who can neither read or write and whose allotted span of life must be nearing its end. As for Marjorie herself, though she is very plain with her light auburn hair and pale freckled skin, and though she lacks the fiery temperament that makes some girls so attractive to men, she is homely and kind with a gentle disposition. She is skilled at the sewing, and even more temptingly she is fast learning how to cook like her Mam and put a tasty bite on the table when it is needed. Simple pleasures and a kind word delight her as much as more expensive demonstrations of affection, which is just as well, since John Richard would not be happy to see the money earned by the sweat and pain of muscle being spent on such fripperies as some females require. Marjorie makes her own clothes or alters those of others handed down to her and does not complain. She is not coarse in speech or manners and for all these reasons John Richard considers himself to be at least fond of her. She is not a girl who would inspire a more unsettling passion in a man and she certainly regards him favourably, he is sure.

It is true to say that marriages are not infrequently made between people who choose each other for no reason except that they see themselves reflected satisfactorily even flatteringly in someone else's eye and few can resist this magic since almost everyone is born with a vague but worrying feeling of being less in all sorts of ways, than others, even indeed that whilst others were meant to be born one's own humanity is somehow a mistake. Certainly it is this that helps to convince John Richard that he is on the right track with the unremarkable Marjorie Laidlaw since through her he is enabled to see himself in a more admirable, even desirable, light. There are those who would go so far as to describe this process of self appreciation through the perceptions of another as that of falling in love, though in love with who or what would be in doubt, but the realist in John Richard has never expected to fall in love and is therefore never at risk of disappointment.

On their walks he has found her to be not unresponsive to his physical advances, at first an arm around her waist, then a kiss followed by a more exploratory kiss and then, rather more. Marjorie, on the other hand, cherishes a more romantic notion about the relationship. For her the strong arm that hammers the iron rivets into submission all day and that now creeps around her waist or shoulders, so unlike a woman's arm, gives her a new thrill of excitement and the first kiss which is the first kiss of that kind that she has ever received is almost terrifying in its intimacy. It may well be asked how a young girl brought up without benefit of privacy, in the closest proximity possible with four brothers, a sister and her parents in what has never been more than three rooms, with the hurly burly of a street full of uncles, cousins and neighbours of every kind pressing in on her, fails to understand even the basic principles of the sexual act. Babies arrive by the score, and Marjorie has seen many a woman in labour and helped her Mam when necessary, to deliver babies which always emerge from beneath a sheet covering the lower regions of a woman's body, but still she knows very little about conception except that it is a secret thing and a dark secret at that, not talked about. Girls who Marjorie knows, willing or unwilling virgins, whisper amongst themselves but after marriage Marjorie has noticed that those with whom she has shared whispers and giggles join the ranks of the enemy who know things that cannot be told except to those who have experienced the same and this is true even of her own sister, Kit, Burlinson's mother, with whom one night she was giggling under the bedclothes and the next night sharing a puzzled silence and a bewildering withdrawal.

There are few places where a young couple can be alone in the streets or the houses, but after dark there are the back streets deserted by the fishwives with baskets on their heads, and the washer women, and the children who run bare foot to chase each other and these alleys afford a little privacy apart from the occasional drunk who staggers and props himself up as best he can against the smoke blackened walls of the backyards and then slides to the ground where he lies insensible against the wall. Nowadays their evening walks usually end in the back street where Marjorie finds herself not altogether displeased with the sensations which are new to her of his increasingly urgent kissing and the activities of his hands.

"Ye shouldna be doin' that, John," she says half- heartedly pushing him away.

"An why not?"

"It ain't right. We're no wed."

"Aye, but we will be soon, we're as good as wed."

"Is that so! Nay-one spoke ti me about tha."

"No, but you knew."

"So when will this weddin' be then?"

"Soon." His hands begin a more forceful search and his breathing, audibly urgent, leaves him no resources for further speech.

"Nay, John, don't."

"Too late for don't now, lass," he struggles to hold her against the wall with one arm whilst his other hand burrows its way up through the folds of her skirt. His urgent excitement and arousal will not be restrained now. She turns her face to one side and feels the roughness of the brick against her cheek protecting her from the violent thrusting of his mouth on hers. Though she dare not move her head to look down, she is aware that he is fumbling with his own clothes and then she knows nothing except for the rhythm of pushing and the ache that enters her body between her legs. Suddenly it is over. He releases her and her crumpled skirt falls back around her legs. Silently he buttons his trousers and adjusts his belt. They have nothing to say to each other. At last he takes her by the arm, "You'd best be getting home now," he says as if to a stranger.

"Ye shouldna ha' done that, John," she says.

"Dunna be daft, girl, everyone does it."

"What'll me Mam say?"

"You won't be tellin' your Mam will ye!"

"Don't do it again, John."

"We'll be wed soon anyway, so it don't matter."

When they reach the door of number 24 he does not pause to take her hand, but seems to be in a hurry to leave her.

"In you go, now" he says, "You're alright, don't worry."

Confused and anxious she looks at him. He has spoken of marriage and yet he now seems more distant when surely he should be closer to an intended wife. For her part she feels no elation or joy at the prospect of becoming a bride and yearns only for an explanation of what has happened between them that has changed every thing.

"John?" she says

"Goodnight now," he says, moving away from her briskly. There is nothing for her to do except enter the house. She knows that she must find a place away from her Mam and Ganny to examine the area of the throbbing ache and dry the wetness that runs down her legs but which is concealed by her skirts.

John Richard Balcombe stops on the step of number 23 when he hears the door of Marjorie's house close. He steps back onto the cobbles and lights a cigarette. The familiar movements of his hands as he takes the packet from his jacket pocket, picks out the cigarette and puts it in his mouth, brings the box of matches from his right trouser pocket, strikes the match twice, and cupping the flame in his hand to light the cigarette, brings back a comforting feeling of normality. He inhales and the rich warming savour of the smoke fills his lungs. He feels better. Instead of entering the house he walks off down the street towards the gates of Thompsons Yard. There are men coming out of the pubs, standing around in groups talking, but John Richard merely nods and moves on. The tobacco is soothing to his head and his mind. Two things are waiting to be cleared away in there and a drink will help. He enters The Grapes, the next pub that he comes to, and orders a whisky which he drinks down quickly and without enjoyment. Then he moves on. The walking, the tobacco as he lights another cigarette, and the powerfully warming sensation of the liquor perform their miracles of easement so that perhaps after all there is nothing much to be considered, or at least, not to be considered now. Some later time will do. After all he only did what all other men do and what women must expect particularly if they have permitted a few liberties already. Lasses like Marjorie Laidlaw should not go walking with men who spend their days in hard physical struggle and trials of strength if they want to be treated like angels. It alarms him if he spends a few minutes thinking about it, that he has been obliged to mention marriage, so he dismisses the memory. In his situation which had not been entirely premeditated what else could he have done? With luck he need not mention it again. If the subject is brought up it can be dealt with as pending, in the future, when things are better. He turns back and reaches his lodgings. Sitting on the side of his bed, having removed his shirt, vest and trousers, he reaches for his matches which he had taken out of the pocket and put on the stool beside the frame of the bed and feels for another cigarette. He inhales, exhales, and slumps on the sagging springs of the mattress as he holds the cigarette loosely between his fingers. All is not as well as he has told himself. On the contrary everything is a mess and he is lost. He stubs out the cigarette and rolls his body heavily under the sheet. Pulling the ragged eiderdown over his head he is smothered in despair.

§

"Kitty!" Marjorie reaches out to nudge her sleeping sister.

"Whisht, Marj!" Ye'll waken the bairn. Ah canna be doin' wi' it. Ah have to gerrup early."

"Kitty can ye just tell me, when ye knew – when ye knew about Burlinson, how did ye know?"

Kitty sits up in bed, alert, and turns to her sister. Even in the darkness she can see Marjorie's round eyes full of anxiety.

"Wha's happened, Marj?" she says, "is you expecting?"

"Ah doesn' know."

"Have ye had yer bleeding?"

"No."

"How long?"

"Only a few days, but I feels so sick."

"Marj, I think ye're havin' a bairn."

"Oh no, Kitty - whar'am ah to do?"

"Tell me Mam."

"Ah canna. She'll kill us."

"Ye must." Both girls sit up in bed looking at one another in silence.

"Who was it, Marj?"

"Ye knows."

"Him next door? John Richard? Wha' me Mam likes so much?"

"Aye."

"Ye mus' tell me Mam, Marj."

"Maybe it'll come to naught, Kit, maybe it'll gan away."

"It willna. "

"Ah canna tell me Mam, an what will me Ganny say?"

"Will he marry you, d'you think, lass?"

"He dinna come near us now. Dinna say naught to me Mam, Kit. Ah dinna ken how it happened."

"Aye that ye do, ye dimmock. It aint no different from no-one else. It aint no 'maculate conception."

"Maculate conception? What's tha'?"

"Like Our Lady wha' never had it done to her."

The sisters fall quiet again. Overcome with tiredness, Kitty lies back and turns over onto her side to sleep.

"Tell me Mam," she says before closing her eyes.

Marjorie lies on her back, staring up at the ceiling, and she does not sleep until the light begins to show at the window and the clatter of boots on cobbles and doors opening and shutting announce the morning. Kitty gets up silently and pulls on her clothes in order to get to the rope works. She glances first at Burlinson still asleep in the bed she shares with him and then at the pale sleeping face and dark shadowed eyes of her sister.

"Poor bairn," she says.

Margaret Laidlaw is aware that her younger daughter's face is drained of colour but the girl was always pale like most children who breathe the foul and sooty air all day and never have the freshness of the fields or the shore without the pall of industry overhanging. Now, in the mornings Marjorie is sick, though she tries to hide it, and wretches into the slop bucket which she hurries to empty into the communal earth closet before anyone notices. Her determination to keep her secret and deal with it in her own way, futile as it must certainly be in the end, gives her the new manner of determined courage over weakness. She welcomes the awful morning sickness and thinks of it as an attempt by her body to rid itself of the intrusion and the more sick she can be the more chance she feels that she has of expelling the thing within her.

Her mother instinctively senses the toughness of her daughter's frailty but has no time to be concerned, for suddenly Ganny Hogarth who has never been slow to add her opinion to any discussion or argument, appears to have lost the ability to speak. She tries to utter a few words but the sounds fail to come together in any way that makes sense and she shakes her head as tears that never fell for the death of children, or when she left her own beloved home in the Border Country, begin to escape her eyes.

"Wha's the matter, Mam? Wha's up wi' ye?" asks Margaret kneeling beside her mother's chair. Kate Hogarth shakes her head. She tries to lift her hand to brush away the shameful tears but the hand with its familiar pattern of freckles remains on her lap refusing to obey the instruction of her brain.

"Ah'll fetch Dr.Blumer, Mam," says Margaret.

Inside her head Kate Hogarth is saying, " no doctor, it's too late. Just stay wi' me here,lass," but words so clear in her head will not transform themselves into speech except for a jumble of low moaning sounds. She tries to put out her arm to stop Margaret from leaving but the arm lying on her lap is no longer hers. Margaret, crouching beside her mother's chair, looks up into Kate's face and sees the anxiety. She knows that this is no time to be running for the doctor.

"Marj" she shouts, "gan round to Dr. Blumer's an tell him ti come quick to yer Ganny. Tell him ti come right away. Be sharp now."

Then she puts her arms around her mother cradling her and stroking her head.

"It's all right, Mam," she whispers.

Kate Hogarth can neither speak nor move except for her head, but her thoughts are as clear and quick as they have ever been. She wants to say that this is a very important time, the time of her dying, or rather of her life ending and that she has no sense of finality. The words of some of the strict Presbyterians in the Spittal of her childhood swim to the surface of her consciousness, words that are as black as hell, red as fire and bloody as sin, but she is aware that they have no power to disturb. She has lived long enough to see that learned men are often fools and hypocrites and understand nothing of real things. On the brink of death Kate Hogarth smiles to herself. She was right all along in what she knew, and life and death are one, inseparable but not enemies.

There is no finality. She feels the gentle caress of her daughter's hands on her hair and observes the round and frightened eyes of her sickly grand-daughter, shocked at being in the presence of a dying old woman, the Ganny she has known all her life transformed from the reassuring ordinariness of a familiar presence in the corner of the room to the widening space of an awesome mystery. Kate blesses the girl and the unborn child who she knows is waiting to take her place in the long chain that stretches in front of her and behind. She relinquishes the struggle to make her thoughts known and looks down on her silly freckled hands, so disobediently helpless. Useful, friendly hands, she sees them now with affection. Saying goodbye to the body she has known intimately for so many years is not easy, as parting from faithful friends never is but it is she herself saying goodbye, still herself. The room is silent, lips move, entreat, instruct, she is aware of that, but there is no sound. Dr. Blumer rushes in with his large medical bag crammed with the equipment of his calling. Poor man, what desperation to save lives as if lives were all.

She sighs, her eyes close.

"It's over Mistress Laidlaw," says Dr. Blumer kneeling to take Kate Hogarth's wrist between his thumb and finger, "there's nothing I can do, she's gone."

"Oh me Mam! Oh me poor Mam!" wails Margaret.

"I'll send my wife round to you directly, Margaret," he says, and turns to Marjorie standing terrified, her fists tight and pressed against her mouth. Go and fetch Ganny Mills, lass. The Gannies will know what to do. Off you go lass."

He turns to leave, pushing Marjorie out ahead of him. "I'll send my wife round, Margaret," he says.

Margaret Laidlaw is left alone in the room, still crouching on the floor, her arms around her mother.

Upstairs, Burlinson wakes and cries.

CHAPTER NINE

John Richard Balcombe smells the warm richness of the hot-made lardy crust pastry and the savoury meat fillings, pork for the pork pies and lamb for the Scotch pies. He waits his turn in the line of customers that snakes around the white tiled walls of the pie shop and ponders on life's satisfactions which after all outweigh its sorrows when it is possible to buy and eat such tasty fare. It is Saturday, a half working day, and the cold of this November has made the labour high up on the gantry platforms against the side of the ship a trial of endurance. Muscles have been pushed and strained beyond pain but the promise of a hot pie, rich with oozing pork jelly together with the meltingly moist crunch of pastry has cheered him and raised his spirits. As he slowly shuffles forward with the queue of patient customers, he lights a cigarette and blows the smoke out lazily through his nostrils until the comfort of the tobacco and the promise of tasty food with half a day of freedom ahead seems to be all a young man could wish for. He turns round to see how many are in the queue behind him, and finds himself looking into the eyes of Kitty Laidlaw.

"I'm sorry to hear about your Ganny, Kitty," he says, "she'll be missed will Ganny Hogarth."

"We dinna want yer sorry, John Richard Balcombe," she says, "we can do wi'out yer sorry."

The customers sense that the tedium of waiting in a long queue is about to be relieved by an interesting argument, fodder for gossip. The chatter ceases as everyone waits for John Richard's response.

"Why's that then?" he says.

"Ye should know. How long is it since ye seed our Marjorie?"

"What d'you mean by that, then, Kitty?"

"What d'ye think I mean?"

John Richard discovers that his appetite for a Kennedy's meat pie is diminishing. The girl is being deliberately insinuating but it cannot be anything more serious than his apparent neglect of her sister. Everyone knows that a girl does not fall into the family way on the first time.

"I really don't know, Kitty. I'm very fond of Marjorie as you know."

"Then I'll speak plain to ye. Our family has enough to take care on without your bairn."

The line of people now wait in anticipation. There is nothing better than a good tale as it unfolds before the eyes and ears.

"Aye, well you should know, Kitty lass. The only bairn I knows of that burdens your Mam is yours."

Kitty Laidlaw's face flushes red with anger. "Burlinson's Da was lost at sea before we could wed," she says.

"So you say!"

"It's true. He didna walk out wi' me and then walk away when it suited."

"Nay, he just got lost."

"He got lost at sea, man. I'm tellin' ye." The tears that fill her eyes start to trickle down her cheeks.

John Richard has reached the counter and he smacks his money down on the glass. Mrs. Kennedy wraps the pie smartly with the air of one who is much too busy to listen to tittle-tattle, takes the money and then turns briskly to the next customer. The pie is hot and steaming from the oven. Its juices are oozing into the paper in which it is wrapped. John Richard turns briskly and without a word to Kitty strides out of the shop. A dozen faces turn to watch him go. Tongues click and someone remarks that she has heard that the man is from the South. "Aye, an ye never know with them folk." says another.

John Richard continues to stride away from the streets towards the open sea front. When he reaches it he sits down on the sand and looks out over the grey sea across which is Germany, Scandinavia and the Baltic Ports, places to which at the moment he wishes he could escape. If it is true and Marjorie Laidlaw is having his child he will have to leave the area and the security of work and not come back, or he will have to marry her. He unwraps the pie carefully and bites into it, wiping the fragrant juices that spread around his mouth with his hand. For a moment the dilemma does not seem to be so pressing, the pie is good. As he eats and ponders his options it seems to him that the second has a good deal to recommend it. After all he is fond of the girl and it would be more comfortable to live at number 24 where meals are regular and tasty, than in lodgings, and certainly it would have advantages over leaving for an unknown place with all the attendant insecurities. Moreover, as he considers it, number 24 has just lost its Ganny. The old woman will no longer be sitting in the corner smothered in shawls, seeing all and keeping up an uncomfortable and unwanted commentary on every situation. He takes another bite of the delicious pie.

§

Marjorie Laidlaw picks up the washing basket and carries it out into the back street to hang out on the line that stretches across to the opposite yard. John Richard Balcombe has been loitering in the narrow street even though it has meant losing a Monday morning's pay. It seemed as if it would be the only sure opportunity of coming upon Marjorie alone. As he approaches her he notices how pale she looks.

"How are you, Marj?" he asks.

"Me Ganny's died."

"Aye, I heard. I'm sorry."

"Where've you been? I ain't seen you for near a month."

"Working, Marj. It's hard work and always plenty trouble down there, what with riveters laid off and doing holders-up work, and holders-up making no end of trouble and noise, along with Gourlay and them others."

Marjorie begins to peg out the clothes.

"You all right, Marj?"

"Why're you asking?"

"I heard something."

"From who? What's to hear?"

"I heard from your sister. You're in the family way she said."

"She had no business to say such thing."

"Is it true?"

Marjorie does not reply. She continues to take the wet garments out of the basket and peg them up.

"Is it true, Marj?" John Richard grasps her wrist as she squeezes the wooden peg against the line.

"Marj, is it true?"

"So it seems."

"I told you we'd wed, and so we will."

"Who said I'd wed wi' you, John Richard Balcombe?"

"Marj, if you will marry with me, we'll wed."

Marjorie shakes her wrist free and continues to peg out the clothes.

"How did your Ganny die, then Marj?"

"Her heart gived up, Dr. Blumer said."

"Everyone's heart gives up."

"Aye. It weren't her heart. She was seized. She couldna speak or move her hands. It was sudden. Sudden like, she couldna say nothing, only moaning. It was terrible. I see'd it. It was the worst thing I ever seed. It was terrible, John." Now the tears flood from Marjorie's eyes and John Richard holds her against himself in his arms as she shakes and sobs. "It was really terrible, mind. She was me Ganny."

John Richard takes a clean handkerchief from his pocket and wipes the tears as they roll down her cheeks.

"An that was not the worst of it for me Mam said tha' Ganny Hogarth was a Spittal lass an must be laid out Spittal way."

"Aye well never mind, Marj."

"Aye but I do mind, John, I canna get it from my mind."

"Aye well —"

"Me Ganny Hogarth was laid on the bed, covered wi' a best sheet, an a plate wi' salt on was put on her chest, an then the little mirror was covered, an a candle lit an put by tha' plate, an me Mam said tha' if a dog or a cat should come in an walk over tha' plate we must kill tha' animal, but we has nay dog nor cat," she pauses, "aye but I could not sleep for thinking tha' a dog or a cat might creep in an want to know what was on tha' plate on me Ganny's chest because they is always looking for scraps, an then who would do the killing?"

"Aye well —"

"An me Mam said tha' that plate should ha' been of pewter which is a metal plate, but we have none, only a plate with cherubs on that says 'a present from Spittal' which me Mam said would be the same as pewter." She moves away from John Richard's arms and looks up at him, "She was me Ganny," she says.

"So, we'll wed, shall we, Marj?" he says, "it'll be all right. We'll wed." Marjorie looks at him. Her eyes are red and the skin around is puffy with tears. Her nose is running. She nods her head in assent.

§

The morning of the 18th November 1872. Outside, the fog which had descended on the previous evening has grown thicker and out at sea ships moan like bewildered souls in grief. There are no wedding bells to mark the ceremony that unites Marjorie Laidlaw and John Richard Balcombe only the mournful sounding of foghorns from the looming shapes of those sad sea monsters signal their near invisible presence. Marjorie Laidlaw wears a high necked jacket in dark blue sateen with long sleeves that widen into a fall at the wrist. It is drawn in to the waist and fits over a full skirt of the same material. At the neck it is adorned with a posy of artificial flowers and her light auburn hair is drawn back into a thin chignon, whilst over her forehead a few strands of hair have been pressed overnight into two stiff curls on either side of a middle parting. Marjorie and her mother made the outfit which has three pintucks and a frill around the edge of the skirt for decoration and will serve well in the future on most foreseeable occasions, since neither anticipate any possibility of a need for ball gowns or more frivolous attire. Marjorie also wears her mother's drop ear-rings.

John Richard already possesses a best suit and waistcoat into which he uncomfortably squeezes himself from time to time, mainly on Sundays at church, since his potential acceptance into the Laidlaw household has made church-going an obligation. The suit consists of a short length cut away coat with wide lapels reminiscent of a style popular in the previous century, a high cut straight waistcoat also with lapels and trousers somewhat in need of a crease. He wears a stiff collar and a white neck scarf which is tied in the manner of a cravat. His shoes are old but well polished. On this day, however, his new status as respectable and serious married man is marked by the looped gold watch chain that stretches across his waistcoat. Neither the bride nor the groom offer any facial expression indicative of joy for both are deeply apprehensive and unsure of the day itself and of a future that now seems to stretch out before them with a grey predictability in which the principal requirement will be endurance. Of their shared uncertainties they have said nothing to each other lest the disturbance of talk upsets the balance of the situation to which they have submitted themselves.

After the ceremony, the couple along with the bride's father and mother and her youngest brother, Thomas, take a walk across the Wearmouth bridge to the new photographic studios of Mr. Clem Humphries to have the day recorded for posterity. There against a painted backdrop of stone pedestals, urns of flowers and majestic steps which hint at the presence just out of view, no matter how unlikely, of a stately mansion, they are posed, and by the time that Mr. Humphries has placed them in the favoured positions and retired to view the effect from behind his curtained box on its stand, the faces of his subjects have become rigid with apprehension. At first Margaret Laidlaw is seated with six year old Thomas standing to her right side against her knee. Behind them stands Johnny Laidlaw, his fringe of beard around his chin neatly trimmed in the mariner style, his hand resting on his wife's shoulder. Mr. Humphries views the composition and discovers the result to be unfavourable. Desirable though it is to have the Head of the family standing to denote his upright status, Margaret Laidlaw is five feet and a bit tall whilst her husband is six feet, and therefore either his head or her legs from the knees must be lost, together with the whole of young Thomas if this option is applied. The parties are re-arranged; Johnny Laidlaw now sits and his diminutive wife stands by his side with her left hand on his shoulder and her right hand tense with readiness to restrain Thomas, whose hair has just been slicked down with spit and who has suffered more than enough already on this day, what with being crammed into a hand-me-down suit with trousers that are a little too short, a silly waistcoat and cut-away jacket and worst of all by far, a frilly white collar which has just been adjusted to lie neatly and conspicuously over the jacket. Thomas makes a mental note to avoid marriage at all costs. The composition is now decided upon, but the awkwardness of the unfamiliar setting of the family amongst urns, pillars, looped velvet and gold tassels, albeit only as a painted screen precariously placed behind them, has set their faces into expressions of grim concentration covering deep unease. Only Thomas's face portrays his true feeling which is a mixture of extreme boredom rapidly turning to bursting fury at having been held in one place for so long.

The bride and groom are not photographed together. For some reason which appears to them to be perfectly justifiable, each is posed not with the other but with an elaborately covered chair, its legs, seat and back ledge smothered in fringed velvet. A chair, indeed that is the very symbol of modesty, even chastity, a chair that lends the weight and dignity of its appearance to the notion of the newly weds as properly respectable. The chair is placed against its own painted background which suggests the interior of the stately mansion just out of view in the previous photograph. Marjorie is posed with her hands leaning against the back of the formidable chair as if in need of a little graceful support and her face has the look of blankness and uncertainty that she feels. John Richard stands with one hand carelessly placed against the chair ledge to indicate that in his case he is in no way dependent on it. His moustache reinforces the line of his mouth which hints at an almost pugnacious severity such as should be worn by any man about to become the head of his household even if at the moment the household is no more than his seventeen year old wife. As the resulting photograph will not be detailed enough to display Marjorie's wedding ring, Mr. Clem Humphries has assured the family that he will paint it in afterwards in strong gold paint. On the certificate of marriage John Richard gives his occupation proudly as Iron Shipwright.

The young couple then resume their lives as before, except that Marjorie Laidlaw is now Marjorie Balcombe and they live at number 24 as a married couple requiring a separate room which causes some problems of overcrowding in the six roomed house where there are now some fifteen inhabitants including babies and children. On June 9th 1873, their first child, called Margaret Ann is born.

MEGGIE BALCOMBE

1883

CHAPTER TEN

"Many are the homes and families in abject wretchedness and poverty today, that but for the foolish extravagance, over-indulgence and wild speculations of their principal might be in a comparative state of comfort and independence. His investments have been foolish and badly made – in the public house instead of the Post Office. Capitalists, monopolists and millionaires have each in their turn been denounced and held up to obloquy as the greatest enemies to social progress and social reform but are we not safe in saying that Intemperance and gambling are vices that present far greater dangers than either of them? We have more to fear from the Brewer and the Bookmaker than from any combination of Capitalists of whom we have ever heard. Let us appeal to you to combine with Temperance and Thrift and to replace 'The Sporting Life' and the 'The Racing Calendar with 'The Wealth of Nations' and 'Progress and Poverty'."

Robert Knight. General Secretary of the United Society of Boilermakers and Ironshipbuilders. 1870.

'My name is Margaret Ann Balcombe. I live at number 24 Hardwick St. I am near ten years of age.' This is what Miss Dale, our teacher made me to write in me new writing book in me best hand, wi' thicks and thins of pen. The thins is easy, but for the thicks ye must press so hard on the nib that the ink may spread and spoil the letter and that is where the cleverness comes in, which I have mastered well, so says me teacher. I am named Margaret after me Ganny, who is Margaret, but we all calls her Ganny Laidlaw, and she lives in the upstairs of our house. Before we was born she lived in the downstairs wi' me uncles, that is her boys, an me Anty an her bairn, Burlinson, but me Anty is gone now to live wi' Burlinson's Ganny, an she don't live here no more because she don't like me Dad. When I was little me Granda lived upstairs wi me Ganny Laidlaw, but he was a mariner and not often in the house and then he wasn't seen no more. He was gone, an that was the end o' him. I dinna know why I am called Ann. I thought it was because me Dad's

Mam was called Ann, but me Dad didn't have no Mam. Some folks dunna have Mams nor Dads. Me Mam an me Dad an me Ganny an me brothers calls us Meggie. I am a scholar and at school me teacher calls us Margaret, but me little companions calls us Meggie. I can read and write a canny hand, but best of all I likes to sew. When it was the first sewing lesson I liked it straightaway. It made me more happy than all the other things to learn in the school. When we is sewing, lookya, we is quiet in ourselves and content, but still we can have a bit talk with our companions, mind.

I have three brothers, and I wishes often that I didna. I wishes that I didna have nay brothers at all because brothers is great trouble and naught but noise. They is younger than me an causes annoyance, standing on me scholar's writing book or pulling at me sewing, or taking the stitches off me needle in the knitting. I can knit on four needles and do socks and gloves, which me and me Mam and me Ganny does for all them lads in our house. Them boys is hard on socks and soon as the sock is done they makes big holes and then we three must sit in the evening and do naught but darn. I wishes them lads would darn for themselves, for it is my belief that there would ne'er be so many holes, which they makes on purpose to vex us.
Of me brothers, who is John, Jimmy and Tom, I likes best little Tom. I likes his little pointy face like an elf's face I do believe. He is more quiet like me and he would be more quiet than that even, except he is led on by our John and Jimmy, who teases him which is a shame. John is the eldest one of me brothers an he is really John Richard after me Dad, who is John Richard. Me Mam is Marjorie, an one of her Gannies was Marjorie, but that was up near Scotland, long way from here, where we have been once to stay by the sea. Them Gannies and Anties talked like me Ganny Laidlaw, an it was hard to understand. They did neither read nor write an thought it a marvel when me Mam showed them my fair hand though tis nothing like the fair hand wrote by me Granda Johnny Laidlaw for that was masterly, said they, but he ain't with us no more.
Those that live up the stairs wi' me Ganny are me uncles, Robert and Thomas. They say that our little Tom looks just like me Uncle Thomas when he was small, wi' pointy face an all, and fair, and them large eyes which are a blue an

full o' wonder, but if that be so I canna hardly believe it for me Uncle Thomas doesna have a canny look now. I canna see it. Both them lads, me uncles, works in Thompsons yard. Sometimes they dunna work,which is a great trouble to me Ganny Laidlaw. Sometimes me Ganny says to one o' them, "where was ye today, ye wasna at the yard" an me uncle says "I was." An me Ganny says "Ye wasna because I knows where ye was. Ye was in the Duzzy House." Then me uncle says "if ye knows that, what for are ye asking me. Since ye knows all dinna ask silly questions, woman." Then there is a lot o' noise an me uncles bangs about a lot which can be heard from down below where we is, an me Ganny cries, an me Mam says to me Dad to gan up there an mak them men stop blathering, which me Dad does do, but sometimes it don't stop, but gets worse. It was not so bad when me Granda was living. He was married to Ganny Laidlaw, an his name was Johnny Laidlaw like I said. He was a tall man wi' blue eyes like pools of clear water that sometimes is seen down on the Roker shore when the blue sky passes over them. Ye'll nay see much clear water here on Monkwearmouth Shore. He was a mariner, was me Granda, an some say he was a smuggler. Me brother John says for sure he was a smuggler, me Granda Johnny Laidlaw, an everyone knew him for it. Then one day when he was expected he didna come back an me Ganny was told that he was lost at sea an wouldna come back no more, an he didna. Ganny Laidlaw cried and cried, an me Mam said it was because she really loved that Johnny Granda an she could never think tha' she'd see him no more. I knows tha' she will see him more, mind, because he will be in heaven waiting for her to die, but if he was truly a smuggler he might not be allowed in that place an Ganny would have to gan where he is if it was allowed. I asked me Dad about it an he said that Granda Laidlaw was a sort of smuggler because one time he got caught, but he didna go to prison because he was clever, an what he done was good.

Best of all in this house I likes me Mam and me little brother Tom. Then I likes me Dad an me Ganny, but now she is always sad on account o' that Johnny Laidlaw. I dunna like them two uncles upstairs because they says bad words and frightens us at night, so when I hears them going on I pulls the covers over me head so's they won't see us if they comes in to us downstairs.

So in this house which is 24 Hardwick Street there is mostly men, me Dad, me three brothers, me uncles, and me Granda Johnny who isna here nay more an never will be for he is lost. On the top floor is an old woman an her man. I dunna ken who they is but they is always living here an they has no children which is a blessing for we dunna want more rowdy boys who comes home an throws up on the stairs for me Mam an me Ganny to clear up.

An now I tells a secret, which is my secret an all. That is that I have had enough of lads an men an boys an uncles an brothers, except for Tom an me Dad, an I intends never to marry, never at all. I'll have nay men in a house wi' us. An that's me secret which I intends and will not change.

§

John Richard Balcombe, now a proud member of the Church Institute and head of his household, stands in front of the fire warming his hands which are white and mottled with the cold. Reviewing his situation after ten years of marriage to his wife Marjorie, he finds himself not at all displeased. Though the marriage itself had not been entirely what he had wanted at the time he has as one might say, grown into it. No longer is he the visitor, the outsider, the apparently motherless and fatherless stranger from nowhere. He is Head of Household and if he has had to jettison his image as the man from the enticing mystery of the South there have been notable gains. Things have changed a lot since the days when Mistress Laidlaw and her sons, Robert and Thomas and her daughter, Kitty, with the troublesome child, Burlinson lived downstairs, and Johnny Laidlaw was Head of Household, even though he was seldom at home. Moreover John Richard's essential honesty compels him to admit that he is thankful for the demise of Ganny Hogarth, that lurking presence in the corner of the room who would not be ignored. It was not right, in his opinion, for a woman, and an old one at that, one with no learning or schooling who could neither read nor write and whose husband when he was alive had been no more than a farm servant or fisherman, to insist on expressing her mind so irritatingly amongst her menfolk. She was forever disturbing folk whose views and opinions were long formed, with a single word and no-one could say how she had done it. That old woman's release from the chair in the corner was a blessing and a mercy even if poor Marjorie still mourned her and now the chair itself, the only tangible reminder of Kate Hogarth who was without any possessions of her own, had gone upstairs to the new Ganny, Ganny Laidlaw, her own authority in the household much diminished too, since the loss of her husband. With a wife, a daughter and three sons and with his mother-in-law a widow, removed to the upstairs he is able to take proper care of his family and has zealously avoided many of the pitfalls that await a working man, even a journeyman riveter at JL's if he is not rooted and grounded in the teachings of the Church and his own sense of responsibility.

As for Marjorie, his wife, his feeling for her has never been one of passion. It has never been as it was with his mother-in-law whose eyes softened and followed every movement of her husband around the room and whose misery at his loss was like a weight suspended in the air above them, threatening to descend and smother them all. There was a time when if he could have extracted himself decently from his relationship with the girl, he would have done so but he has come to realise that affection and respect have much to commend them. He is fond of Marjorie as an honest and loving companion, wife and mother to their four children. John Richard has already learned one of life's most valuable lessons, that if you come from nothing and are nothing you appreciate what you gain by your own achievement and do not undermine your sense of yourself in the restless pursuit of ever more and more.

He leaves the shipyard at four o' clock in the afternoon in winter when the failing light makes work impossible. Unlike the other men, unable to bear the weight of a day's pay in their pocket and who must quench their thirst and numb their minds and aching limbs in one of the scores of Public Houses,

John Richard goes home without delay to 24 Hardwick St. As a skilled worker and a member of the Church Institute he is not prepared to waste his time and wages. There will never be any need for Marjorie to stand in shame outside the yard gates with the other wives who must catch their men and empty their pockets before all the money is gone nor will she make the trip to the pawnbrokers as the other women do or beg a few bones from the butcher with promises of paying later. Marjorie is the one they turn to when they need help and because of her thrift and his hard work there are always a few pence or shillings to lend, sometimes in the knowledge that it can never be repaid. As he enters through the open door, John Richard smells his tea, a piece of boiled bacon with onions and carrots and with peas that have been soaking all night ready for the pot. Other men's wives will have spent money on buying in the victuals, pie and pease pudding from the shop, but Marjorie has learned her mother's skills at cooking and there is always something freshly cooked and tasty for the family. To tell the truth, John Richard is not entirely happy about the food which he labours to provide having to be shared more often than not with Ganny Laidlaw upstairs. It is not that he objects to the sharing but he resents the fact that his brothers-in-law do not feel it necessary to participate in any household responsibility.

"Tak some tea, John. The kettle's boiled and it just needs to mash. Just give it four minutes," says Marjorie. He hangs up his jacket and cap, loosens his necktie and seats himself before the good fire. Slowly and with pleasure he lights a cigarette and draws in the smoke which he exhales through his nostrils.

"Isn't there smoke and soot enough round here for ye, John?"

"Aye lass, but the lungs gets used with it and must have it for their health."

They smile at each other, content in the easy comfort of home.

"What d'ye think they've come forward with now, then?" he asks.

Marjorie pours the strong tea into a mug, adds two spoonfuls of sugar and a dash of milk. She stirs it vigorously and hands it to her husband.

"New sign boards on the gantries. Big boards wi' bold writing, and what do they say? Is it a matter of great importance to the building of the ship? Can it be to do wi' the better working o' the men? Nay!"

"What are they then, John?"

"Will you believe it! 'Do not urinate against the side of the ship.' "

"What's that, Dad?" asks Meggie.

"What d'ye think of that, then, Marj?"

"I dunna know what to think. I never thought about it before."

"What did ye imagine, then, lass. That we held on all day up there?" He bends over and crosses his legs in mock agony. "Oo! Ouch!" he says.

Meggie and the two older boys begin to giggle. Little Tom looks up at his Dad in alarm.

"I never thought of it," says Marjorie.

"'Do not urinate against the side of the ship,' " he repeats.

"What does it mean, Dad?" asks Meggie again.

"It means do not piss."

The older children giggle behind their hands and little Tom who has no idea of what the merriment is about, joins in. "Ha! Ha! Ha!" he chuckles, getting louder and louder to outdo the others in his appreciation of the joke he does not understand.

"What do they want us to do, then?" John Richard continues, "piss over our work fellows down below? Take our dainty china pos up the stocks wi' us and tippy-toe down again to empty them? 'Do not urinate against the side of the ship' I ask you!"

The children rock about on the floor enjoying the shared merriment that draws families together.

"Ye could tak Ganny Laidlaw's po, Dad," says John, "it has roses painted on the outside."

"He! He!He!" Little Tom shrieks with enjoyment. The joke is about chamber pots so it must be funny.

"Well, I don't know," says Marjorie. "Anyway John, what does it do to the side of the ship? I mean pissing."

"Spoils it, so they say. Ammonia into the new steel plates, but its nonsense, that's all it is. Bosses got naught else to think about. Ship gets launched, goes to sea, washed clean.   'Course if you're talking about the stink, that's another matter. Piss water ain't so bad when it's fresh an warm, but when it's old and dried on - the stink would knock you over til you're used with it. Can't do nothing about it though. Labouring men wi' a big thirst on them – they can put up as many placards as they like, can't do nothing about it."

"Oooh!" says young Jimmy in a mock high voice such as he imagines is used by the gentry, "I wants my po!" Little Tom rolls around the floor with merriment.

"Will ye gan to Gourlay then, John?"

"Gerraway! Gourlay's yesterday's man. He knows naught but fight. Mr. Knight's our man now. He's clever wi' the bosses an all, but I doubt he'll have time to talk o' pissing."

The door to their warm room, where the kettle simmers gently on the fire in the range and the table is neatly laid for supper, suddenly bursts open and the lumbering body of Rob Laidlaw heaves itself into the room and collapses on to the chair that has been drawn up to the table. The children stop laughing and crouch in the corner of the room, watching from a safe distance. Rob Laidlaw is never actually drunk these days, his body is so soaked and marinaded in alcohol that he remains permanently under its influence. Those who have seen him sober say that his manner is so dour and uncommunicative that they long for him to take a drink and will lend him money or encourage him to go to The Clipper Ship or The Duzzy House to restore his spirits back to what for him, is normality. His relatives who knew him where he was born in Spittal and speak the Spittal way say 'Robbie Laidlaw is dron,' for that is the word they use for the man who lives inside his own head and cannot be persuaded out by any but the Demon Drink.

"So, sister," he says, calling to Marjorie. "ye're mon here wi' ne'er back us in our fight against the forces o' – forces o' – capitalisism."

"What forces are these, then, Rob?" asks John Richard drawing on his cigarette and blowing the smoke out in a great swirling cloud.

"Forces, lad, forces of Capitalisism and Monopolitisism. Forces o' bosses against the workin' man."

"Aye, well, ye'll have nay need to worry then, Robbie lad, if tis against the workin' man then that's no ye, is it, man!"

"The workin' man, lookye. The honest workin' man." Robert tries to get to his feet as if to impress with his full height as he beats on his chest to indicate honesty and pride but he falls back helplessly on to the chair.

"Marjorie, can ye see an honest workin' man in this room? Can ye see a skilled worker that knows his trade," asks John Richard.

"Yourself John Richard Balcombe," she replies.

"And any other may I ask?"

"None other that us can see."

"There now! Ye're sister canna see any in this room excepting her husband that would fit yon description."

"Forces of monopolitism will get ye, lookya, if ye dunna mind out," says Robert, seemingly impervious to the insult which has come sliding towards him, "an if we dunna stand together, man to man, shoulder to shoulder, face to face – nay, no face to face – against the forces which – which is against us – we'll – we'll – "

"What, Rob? What will be happening to us then, man?"

"Sink! We'll sink. He don't stand wi' us, Marj, your man. He's no wi' us in the Union."

"Howay man! Unions is about confrontation. Gourlay is for that. I go wi' Knight. He's for negotiation. There's nay such thing as power for workers. There's economics, that's all. When there's plenty work at the yards, aye, then the lads has a bit power, but when the orders dunna come and the books is bare like it has been and will be again, and ships is standin' in the stocks half made and the ways stands idle and goin' nowhere, then where is ye're workin' man and his power? And let me tell ye that the day is comin' when machines not bosses will put the workers, skilled or no out o' work, and when them days arrive, be sure there will still be capitalism to draw the prizes, but men, no matter how they protests in their Unions will be without work, and come that day most on us will be ruined. I hope I dunna live to see that day. There'll be no more proud working class o' men, only the likes o' ye, Rob, the likes o' ye, sinking in ye're own sloth!"

"Tha's enough!" Robert tries to rise to his feet again, but fails. "Ye comes in this house, marryin' wi me sister tha's in the family way as we all knows, an ye taks o'er the house, wi' me Mam pushed upstairs. Ye thinks ye're better than all on us, but ye ain't nothin' but a bosses man."

"I ain't no bosses man. I ain't no-one's man but me own. Now gerrup from tha' chair and see to ye're Mam. Be sharp!"

Robert swings his arm loosely in a half circle as if to strike someone, anyone, but his clenched fist falls and hits the table with a crash that sends a tremor through the laid out crockery and utensils. The children huddle together tightly and Marjorie stands in front of them.

"Best get upstairs, Robbie, lad," she says, "Me Mam will have ye're tea ready fer ye. Young Thomas is home a while back, they'll be waitin' on ye." Robert heaves himself up and staggers towards the door. Marjorie puts a hand on his shoulder to steady him but he pushes her away with the force of an arm that cuts a wild swathe through the air. "Gerraway from me, ye slatterly jade," he says, "ti let ye're ain brother be treated so." He clutches at the doorway and lurches towards the newell post against which he falls into an ungainly sitting position, both arms embracing the post. After a few moments of silence when he appears to consider his position with surprise, he shouts at the door which has now closed behind him, "I'll have ye, ye limmer, if ye move tha' post again."

"Dunna be too hard on him, John," says Marjorie.

"I'll be as I likes wi' him. He's nay better than Smithy Mills and all the rest on 'em. They'll ne'er raise themselves when as fast as they gets it they spends it. They has nay purpose, nay goal. They lives from day to day and canna see the slump coming before it's on 'em and they has naught, and their women must beg for bones and tak everything they has to the pawn shop. Then the likes o' you, Marj, ye'll be letting then have a little bit here and a little bit there of what we've saved wi' thrift, because I dunna spend me time in the Duzzy House, and ye're a good woman that knows how to cook and mend and keep the bairns clean and fed wi' good beef dumplings an all. I tell ye this, Marjorie, there's no a day goes by when I dunna thank the Lord for bringing me to wed wi' you, lass. Remember that Meggie. Ye're Mam's a canny woman, an a good mother an wife, cunning in her ways wi' money."

"Me Ganny Hogarth used to say, I heard her many a time to say it 'when poverty comes in through the door, love flies out o' the window.' "

"Aye, that old woman was all there in the head," says John Richard, privately thankful for his release from the sharp interventions of her tongue.

Margaret Laidlaw, her door open, hears the dull thud that signifies the

heaped body of her son, Robert, as he slumps to the floor and embraces the
newell post. She leaves her chair, the chair that was her mother's and goes
out on to the landing.

"Get up here, ye drunken slummock," she shouts. Below the door opens
and John Richard stands in the hall-way, his arms folded as he surveys the
collapsed figure of his brother-in-law.

"Gie us a hand there, John Richard, man, ti lift this lout, this twanking
slummock up the stairs."

She comes down and though she is small and seemingly slight she surprises
with the strength of her shoulders and arms as she heaves her son up against
the post.

"Tak the ither side, man," she says.

Between them they pull Robert, his feet dragging lifelessly behind and
clumping on each stair. Then they drop him on the floor of the upstairs
room which he shares with his mother and Thomas, who at fifteen is quickly
learning how to live like a man in the manner of his older brother. Margaret
closes the door as her son-in-law retreats down stairs. She wishes that the
young man from the South, which is how she still thinks of him, though he
has mostly lost his old way of speaking, did not have to witness the shame
that Marjorie's brothers are bringing to the house. The rising anger in her
voice cannot be mistaken nor can it be confined within the room.

"Wha're ye doin,' Robbie? Ha'e ye nay pride? Ah'll nay hae ye here oot
o' yer wits wi' the drink – nay dinna answer wi' me – ye'll nay come here
wi' yer daft talk, an ye're jades neither. Wha're ye thinkin' of ? Can ye no
remember ye're guid Da, tha' Johnny Laidlaw? Wha' wad he be thinkin' o'
ye noo?"

A low mumbling from the floor indicates that Robert is endeavouring to rise
to the challenge of what his mother has said to him. Margaret's voice rises
to a shriek.

"He were a guid mon, a mon o' pride an virtue like nay ither." The
mumbling from the floor gets louder and more assertive as Robert tries to
raise his head.

"Virtue, lad, a word ye dinna ken, an a brave seaman too. Ah'll no hae ye
say nay ither, Robbie."

Now Robert tries to articulate more effectively the thoughts that are so clear in his head, but the sound emerging is still apparently confused. This is the undoubted fault of others who willfully fail to understand in order to cause him additional irritation.

"He weren't nay limmer rogue, yeer Da. He did wha' ony mon o' spirit wad de to mind after his kin. He weren't nay drunken, twanking slummock. He cad read an write a lovely hand, no like ye, Robert tha' can barely hold a pen wi'oot droppin' it."

The door opens and John Richard stands half outside. "Is he givin' ye trouble, Ganny Laidlaw?" he asks.

"When does he no give us trouble, an look ye at Thomas there, nay better, wi' nought but what his brother leads him tae, doon the paths o' the wicked."

Now Robert heaves himself to his feet. The righteous presence and re-appearance of his sister's husband appears to invigorate him and the pupils of his eyes which had seemed to drop like stones below his lower lids rise as if by some superlative effort and blaze.

"An who is he?" he roars, pointing unsteadily at John Richard. "Who is he to be sae welcome, sae up-nosed in this house. Ah'll tell ye, Mam. He's Mary Norman's bastard. Bastard! Born of a slut an reared like an animal!"

"Say tha' again, man," John Richard squares up to him.

"Dinna harm him, John. Dinna fash yersel' o'er him," cries Margaret running between them with surprisingly nimble feet, "he doesna' mean wha' he says."

Now Thomas who has been watching from the back of the room comes forward. "He means it Mam. Everyone knows tha' he's a bastard. His Da went off to Southern parts where he come from an wanted nay more to do wi' his slutty Mam, or the filthy back stable where he was reared."

John Richard, white with fury, clenches his fists and turns on the two brothers. "And where was ye then? What was ye, all on ye? Spittal folk, and there is no person who doesna' know o' them, Spittal trash, that ne'er did any good for anyone. My Mam, God rest her soul, and me good grandda and his wife were born and bred on this land, and all their folks before them, long before the likes o' ye ever set your god-forsaken, idle feet on holy soil and fouled it. If I hear ye say another word about my folks, I swear before God, and before

Ganny Laidlaw who ye dishonours wi' your words, and before my wife and bairns who is listening downstairs, I swear by my own pride in who I am, bastard or no, that I will kill ye, and I'll no pay the price neither, because you and your kind have made Monkwearmouth Shore into a place where the law dreads to walk and has no sway, when once it was a sweet place of honest folk and never will be again."

Downstairs, Meggie and little Tom crouch behind the door, whilst Jimmy and John stand clutching their mother's hand on either side.

"Is me Dad goin' to kill me Uncles, Meggie?" whispers Tom.

"Whisht! It's naught," she whispers back, her face white with terror.

"Nay, me Dad is goin' to kill me Uncle Rob," hisses Tom.

"He'll not," says their mother, "yer Dad canna kill no-one, it's just a way to talk."

The door slams upstairs and John Richard comes down, his face full of anger and determination.

"I'll do it, Marj," he says, "I'll do it if he crosses me again, no matter if he is your brother."

Marjorie's eyes fill with tears and Meggie rushes to her and puts her arms around her mother's waist, her face buried in the apron that gives off the good mother smell.

"This is no place to bring up bairns," says Marjorie, "this is no place for a body to live wi' all this struggling an fighting every day. There's other places, quiet, where a body can live wi'out all this."

"Aye" says John Richard, calmed by the sight of his wife's tears, "there is, an there's better ways o' life too, but I canna say if we'll gan there in our lives."

Marjorie dries her eyes, "We'll do the best we can, then, John. I must gan up to me Mam now, see that she's got a good fire and such, an that them boys havena' vexed her. Will ye get some coals in, please, John, an bring them up for me Mam's fire?"

§

Ganny Laidlaw don't come downstairs much now. Mam says that's because she's a widow. Me an Tom, we canna understand why widows stays indoors all the time. Some widows dunna. Ant Levenson, she's me Ganny's sister, she's a widow, but she gans about everywhere. Me Ganny don't, she is always resting, Mam says, though it ain't easy to rest when them lads comes in. They don't know nothing much about rest or peoples feelings. I thought I would go up an see me Ganny, but I had to wait until me uncles was out. Then up us went, and she was sitting in that old chair by the fire which was nearly out because them uncles hadna fetched in the coals. So I fetched them in, a bucketful, an made up the fire til it was blazing, an her waggety clock that Johnny Granda gived her, tick-tocking away in the corner. It seemed nice an homely an all.

"Are ye sad, Ganny?"

"Aye, lass, I am," she says, an went on looking in the fire as if she would see the Holy Ghost himself in there, for there's some that has seen that Ghost in the flames, though not meself, yet I has tried that hard.

"Did ye love me Granda?"

"Arl wives must love their husbands, lass," she says.

"So did ye love me Granda?"

"I just telled ye ah did. Ma Johnny, he was everything on this earth ti' me. He was just the same to me now as when he was a young lad in Berwick." Me Ganny smiles. "We danced ye know, hinny, we danced so tha' every body in tha' place was lookin' at us. Johnny Laidlaw, he was the finest dancer in the Border country, aye an beyond. There was nay comparing him, he was sae nimble an fleet o' foot."

"Mam says that he was mostly away from here. Mostly at sea, on ships."

"Aye, his bra' heart was always awa' wi' the tide. Tha's why ah loved him sae much."

"How could ye, Ganny, if he wasna there?"

"Tha's a strange wee thing aboot love, lassy, Johnny Laidlaw he wad ne'er let any person claim him, no even his ain wife. He was always his ain man, an the more he was his ain man the more ah loved him for being it. Ah knowed tha' he wad ne'er end his days in bed. The sea was his haim and his bed, an it wad claim him when nae living body could. The sea took him at the end. Tha's what was meant tae be for Johnny Laidlaw, an me left to keen fer him. Ye're a bra' guid girl, Meggy. See tha' ye wed wi' a bra' guid mon."

"I'll not wed Ganny Laidlaw. I have nay liking them for sorts of human persons what is men. Always drinkin' an makin' noise an trouble."

"Then ye'll hae nay bairns, lass."

"Can ye no have bairns without a husband, then? Well if that be so I'll be well pleased an all, because bairns is trouble an crying an sickness an bairns does die too, which brings grief. When I grows up I'll be a lady, that's what I'll be, Ganny Laidlaw, an us'll bring ye to live wi' us in a grand house of me own, no a house filled wi' men an boys an them kind o' human persons."

"An wull ah be able tae sit in this awld chair in sich a fine hoose?"

"Us'll buy ye a better chair, such as a lady can sit in," I says with grand pride.

"Nay, it's nae mair than this chair ah'l want" she said. "It was me Mam's chair, Ganny Hogarth. She sat in this chair fer mony an mony a year."

"Then ye shall have it, Ganny, but maybe I'll sew ye a nice cover fer it, so that it will look proper in me house."

Ganny Laidlaw leans forward and touches us on the cheek, "ye're a canny lass," she says.

It seems there's nought but trouble in our house with me uncles upstairs and me Ganny so sad all the time. Sometimes I think that if me Ganny was not so sad, me Uncles would cheer up too, but me Dad says nay, they's lost. Sometimes when the rowing gets bad me and our little Tom goes down the street together to look at the big shapes of ships that's being built. Them big shapes that are so dark and still come on you sudden and you can feel the fright, but tis not them that interests us as much as the props that's used to hold up the platforms where the men like me Dad is working. Them tall wooden props was once trees. Every one of them was a tree an our little Tom he says to me, "Meggy, they's a forest." Then we half closes our eyes an we may see the green leaves an all, an little Tom he says that when he grows up he doesna want to work in the yard, but be a forest man, or a man that grows living things in a garden. So we looks up and up and we sees those wooden poles all sprouting up wi' leaves and maybe blossoms too like you see in the fields far yonder from where we lives. Then we pretends to hear the birds that flutter about between the leaves, singing with glad trills and warblings, not like them gulls which do but screech to make us think of screeching in our house an all. In the Autumn we sees the leaves all turning gold, but we never say that we can see them fall for then our trees would be but stocks again. Poor little Tom, I canna think that he will ever have a meadow or a wood or a grand garden of his own, for no-one here does work in any place except the Yard or the Pit.

But we have fun that is to come! Me companion, Annie Pringle who is not called Annie, but is called Issy by me, telled me of a grand Concert that's to be for children, across the water in the Victoria Hall. There's to be clowns and jugglers and them with dolls that do speak, only tis the men with the dolls that do speak really though their mouths do not move, and there's to be singing and dancing people too, and magicians to amaze us, an moving waxworks whatever they may be, but best of all, what d'ye think? It's said that there's to be presents. Presents for every child that has a ticket to be there. I asked Issy if she was sure about the presents and she said she'd heard tell that there was toys. And Issy's Mam has said that she and her little sister and her cousins may go though Micky is but five years old, and I am to ask me Mam if I can go with Issy, an she will say yes.

§

Now comes a big disappointment! The biggest disappointment and sorrow in me life so far. I canna think that there will ever be a sorrow great as this. Me Mam says she canna give us the money for the children's concert, though it is only one penny for a child. Why can she not when Issy's Mam can? She says that she must always be careful and strict with money, and I canna gan without me brothers, and there's three of them. Why can us ne'er gan anywhere without them brothers? Them brothers is a botheration.

Issy did cry and put her arms around me when I telled her I couldna come. We know that brothers is a bad thing, and when we are grown up Issy and me will live together in a house and not have brothers or uncles to torment us. Then Issy said no matter, Meggy, for she will get a present for us, an this is how. When the children gans up for their presents, Issy will rush to be the first, then when no-one is looking she will gan round again and get one for me, an if they say where is your ticket, she will say please sir, I lost it. But not to tell me brothers, for she canna gan round again four times for them an all.

The day of the concert is come, and I canna speak for sorrow. All over the town there is big signs pasted up that says 'Mr. Alexander Fay, Travelling Entertainer, presents the greatest treat for children ever given on Saturday June 16th 1883.' It will be the greatest treat for children ever given in the whole world, and there never will be another treat for children like it, ever, ever, ever, an me Mam will not let us go! Issy says that the Victoria Hall where it is to be, is like a fairy palace, with towers and spires and arches an all. When the time comes, I watches out for Issy to see her gan with her sister an her cousins. They can go by theirselves because Issy is the eldest and she has the little one by the hand for he is but five years old. The others is following close behind. Though she is sad for me, Issy is skipping with little Micky and he is doing his best to skip alongside and they is all laughing with happiness. Then Issy thinks on and turns and looks at me with me long face. Her eyes are shining and she says nought, but gives me the secret sign which means that she will bring me the present and it will be a good 'un. She will tell me of the tricks and dances and talking dolls an them waxworks an all an it will be just as good as if me Mam had let us come says she, but them words is just to glad me heart, for well she knows that nought could be as good as seeing them things for meself. Goodbye Issy, and now I must go indoors and bear with the cackle of me brothers.

§

An Untimely Harvest
From the Sunderland Daily Echo   Monday June 18th   1883

The dead reaper has, with amazing suddenness, put in his sickle, and with one fell stroke has gathered in a great but untimely harvest.... A multitude of happy children, conscious only of the innocent pleasures of early life, trooped merrily on a bright summer's afternoon to a special enjoyment. Parents sent out their little ones with the pleasing thought that they were going to an entertainment which would delight their young hearts and that they would shortly return brimming with the simple chatter which only fond parents know how to appreciate. Little did some of them think that within a few hours they would be mourning the loss of almost an entire flock. How this fearful change was wrought may be briefly told. The performance which consisted of feats of conjuring, the exhibition of talking waxworks, ghost illusions, and other trifles well suited to the juvenile taste, was attended with a special attraction. Each child had received a ticket, some of which entitled the holders to prizes. Naturally enough the element of chance thus introduced into the entertainment excited the little ones to a degree beyond what would usually have been the case. When therefore the time came to claim the presents falling to their lot, there was witnessed precisely the kind of joyous commotion which might have been anticipated. The occupants of the gallery rushed down the stairs to the area pressing upon each other with impatience. Such a stampede unless effectually checked, must under any circumstances have been attended with risk, but something now happened that transformed the scene of childish mirth and excitement into one of blank horror. A door on the staircase had unfortunately become partly closed. This obstruction arrested the progress of the children in front, and those behind came on with great impetuosity, crushing and crowding upon those against the door until a vast heap of struggling and gasping little ones was formed. Everything that was possible at that moment was done to mitigate the disaster, but how little the most desperate efforts could avail was shown in the awful rows of dead and mutilated children. In the area of the building, on the flags outside, and in other places near the hall, 170 little corpses awaited the arrival of horror stricken parents. No pen can fully describe the scenes witnessed. Shrieks and wails filled the air, mingling with the cries of an excited and surging multitude which had quickly gathered to the fatal spot Here was to be seen a distracted mother showering kisses and caresses on the lifeless forms of her children, while the father stood by with blanched cheeks and compressed lips – the silent eloquence of bitter woe……. Kindly and strong hands were not wanting, and the members of the medical profession hurried to the scene and did whatever human skill could do to save life. With regard to the culpableness or otherwise of those responsible for the arrangements, we shall at present say nothing. That matter will doubtless be fully investigated at the proper time. Meanwhile we can but express our profound sympathy with those whose homes have been darkened by this dire calamity, and who will long "treasure the looks they cannot find, the words that are not heard again."

Message From The Queen

"The Queen is terribly shocked at this awful calamity, and her heart bleeds for the many poor bereaved parents. She prays that God may support them. Her Majesty is most anxious to hear how the injured children are."

CHARLES GIRDLESTONE HOPKINSON
MONKWEARMOUTH 1883

CHAPTER ELEVEN

Charles Girdlestone Hopkinson, son of Benjamin Hopkinson, Gentleman, of Ambleside, Cumbria; Scholar of Pembroke College Cambridge; BA 1873, MA 1876; Ordained 1874; Priested 1875; unacceptable suitor for the hand in marriage of Miss Amy Lawrence of Liverpool; rejected by her family as inappropriate, unworthy and above all, poor. Though poverty in a young man is not in itself an impenetrable barrier if it is accompanied by high aspiration and single minded ambition, it is dreadful to contemplate in one whose vocation appears to disdain the acquisition of worldly goods and is content to consider the world and more importantly Society, from the lowliest point of vision and who (despite her infatuation, attributable to youth and immaturity) will never be able to provide a wife with the standards upheld and approved by her wealthy shipowner family. Moreover, quite apart from these legitimate concerns, as if not enough in themselves, Miss Lawrence's family must take into account that there are rumours. Those who have made the most diligent effort to crush unpleasantnesses in their own background, can surely not be expected to welcome and admit the peccadilloes of more careless families into theirs, threatening hard won respectability and the fruits of tireless social exertion with breaths of scandal and the whisper of irregularities. Enquiries having been made; it appears that the young man's father, Benjamin, so-called 'gentleman', was a man of uncertain means without profession or visible financial support and it was rumoured, though reliably so, that the grandfather or great grandfather of the young man, without shame or concern for the opinions of others, took as his companion (shall we say), his housekeeper, who bore him many children out in one of the Colonies. Now with no proper resolve to retrieve any family pedigree or fortune, this grandson, this Charles Girdlestone, decides that he has a calling within the Anglican Church, and not under the protection and patronage of some person of nobility in one of the English rural Counties where he and his proposed bride might at least occupy a modest yet gracious Rectory set in its own grounds thus acquiring for themselves some standing amongst the gentry of that locality (though never of course, the elevation afforded by wealth, so jealously guarded by the Lawrences), but of his own choice the young man has settled as Curate in the Toxteth vicinity of Liverpool with no idea to raise himself even within the limitations of the Anglican hierarchy, when, married to a Lawrence, an Episcopal aspiration might not have been misplaced. The young couple insisting that they were 'in love', seemed to hold to the quaint notion that such a declaration is a sufficient basis on which to balance a marriage. It cut no ice with her family. Where would the Lawrences have been if the various family members had been permitted to chase after butterflies of this nature? The transient flutterings on the wings of passion, not grounded in the solid earth of common sense which recognises the advantage of unions based on equality of wealth and status, must always soar in ecstacy, dwindle and finally fade altogether, whilst mature judgment will over the years, yield much more in terms of security and financial benefit. Love is all very well, but allow love to grow out of material well-being. Young men may fall in love as often and as deeply as they like but when they have learned the skills necessary to gain the centrality of their desires with the object of their fascination, they will find easy satisfaction followed all too often by boredom and release from the enslavement of passion. It is therefore a duty not to encumber themselves in this with the calamity of marriage, unless such a marriage can bestow significant economic benefits on both parties. Miss Amy, however, with all the stubborn stupidity of the very young, defies the wishes of her parents and in 1877 marries the Revd Charles Girdlestone Hopkinson very quietly and privately near his father's Estate in Cumbria.

Minor compromises are then agreed on both sides. The Lawrences, not wishing the world to witness their daughter's reduced situation, make some silver ware and furnishings available to the couple and the young man accepts a Curacy away from Liverpool, not, as might have been hoped in a country Parish or Cathedral city, but in the Northern town of Wigan an area devoid of charm or distinction. It seems that his head is in the clouds and he is incapable of appreciating the degradation of the surroundings into which he has chosen to place himself, indeed it is more than likely that he does not even see it.

In 1878 Charles Hopkinson moves from the Curacy to become Vicar of All Saints, Wigan, though there is little sign that either he or his wife are resolved on the pursuit of any path towards Social Elevation. Indeed they seem to rejoice in the company of the working class, amongst individuals whose lives and standards are so inherently abhorrent to the refined sensibility. The Lawrences then, feel this to be a marriage without proper foundation doomed to failure and in one sense they are right, for after the birth of a child, also called Amy, their daughter Amy dies. It is the belief of the family that she has been driven to her death by the exigencies of an almost servantless life (a cook and one housemaid), the dreariness of her surroundings, and the pre-occupation of her husband with the miseries of his flock which as everyone knows are largely self-inflicted. At this point, the Lawrences, who see no reason why good silver, cut glass and furnishings should be wasted on a young man who has brought nothing but disappointment to them and whose connection with them can now be severed without regret on either side, remove the items given from his Vicarage, and inform him that they have no further interest, either in him or in the child. Mrs Charles Girdlestone Hopkinson can now be fully resurrected and restored to happy memory as the Miss Amy Lawrence that she was and the unsatisfactory details of her marriage put aside forever without visible traces that they ever occurred. Charles Girdlestone sinks slowly down into the very depths of despair. He sits for hours in his Study with his head in his hands. He cannot work or think except of his poor lost darling. At first he had thought that piety and prayer would be his comfort but they have done nothing to quell the surging waves of grief that overcome him. Was he indeed to blame for Amy's death? Was her end brought on by his selfish absorption in the demands of his Calling, so that he failed to notice the delicacy of her health, failed to appreciate that she was bound to suffer in the humble conditions in which he had placed her. Failed to understand that though he himself was impervious to heat or cold and that any vessel could hold his morning tea as well as a china cup, all this was very different from the conditions from which he had plucked his darling flower. He takes comfort from no-one, and the needs of his

Parishioners go unheeded. Hour after hour goes by in which his misery and guilt flood his being and though he prays and endeavours to place himself in the hands of the Lord there is no solace in that source. Though he repeats the words 'come unto me all that travail and are heavy laden and I will give thee rest' there is no rest. The 'comfortable words' fail to comfort. How often then have they failed to comfort his humble Parishioners? It now seems to him that the means by which they subdue their pain and sorrow might have more to recommend it in practical terms and he turns as they do to the easements of alcohol. There is no need for him to find company and oblivion in the coarseness of the Public House when in the privacy of his Study he can take a glass of wine whenever he wants and indeed he gradually dispenses even with that little formality and takes a drink from bottle or flask as often as he wishes. As he sinks into this dependency he realises that the closeness he has always felt with the poor and the labouring classes is now no longer brought about by a sympathetic imagination, but by a bonding in misery and misery's palliative. And his condition is worsened by an even deeper sense of loss and rejection. The Faith which he took for granted has failed. The God who he has served with such certainty of belief has made no answer, yet the Demon in the bottle has come readily to his call and eased his burden of inner torment. Not only has he lost his beloved wife, but with her has gone what he now recognises to be his idea of God, and if in truth God is but an idea, then his life has become meaningless.

Out of this morass of doubt and despair, a friend emerges. Joseph Barber Lightfoot, Bishop of Durham, is an old friend from Cambridge days where he was Hulsean Professor of Divinity, a man who is prepared to examine St. Paul's Epistles critically and bring a clear, refreshing insight to bear upon the Biblical texts and their practical implications. He is one who has always believed in the young man's vocation and on hearing that Faith and Hope have deserted him decides on Charity as the way forward. He suggests that Charles Girdlestone accepts a living in the ship-building community on the North Bank of the Wear in the County of Durham. Monkwearmouth, he explains, is reputed to be the roughest working class area in England. There are of course, families who are hard working and honest but all are ground down by labour, harsh conditions, lack of education and drink. Many are suffering from disorders brought about by overcrowding and their practical and spiritual needs are urgent and daunting. What is required, says Bishop Lightfoot, is a clergyman whose own life has not been easy and who can inspire the people and lead them towards a sureness of comfort and purpose in the Lord.

Charles Girdlesone Hopkinson is now faced with an impossible dilemma. Though he longs to escape from a place filled every hour by memories and visions of Amy, his own Faith is like a guttering candle flame that one watches anxiously in the hope that it will not die, and he wonders whether his belief in his departed Lord is greater than that of his proposed flock. Moreover how can he talk to them about the corruptions of alcohol when he himself has become reliant on it? All of this he has the courage to put before the good Bishop, who remains unperturbed by the startling admissions.

"You have need of healing, Charles," he says, "go to Monkwearmouth and heal the people there, and they will surely heal you."

In Faith then, which he did not have, Charles Girdlestone Hopkinson becomes the Vicar of St. Peters, Monkwearmouth, and makes an oblation to his predecessor, The Venerable Bede, to be helped with the task before him. Arrangements are made for his child, Amy to be cared for by a good woman who has long had connections with his father's family. He is thirty three years old, and the year is 1883.

CHAPTER TWELVE

We has a new vicar at our church, that is the church of St. Peter. He is a tall man and he wears little spectacles in wire frames but behind them you can see his eyes that have lines curving upwards from the outside part of his upper eye-lid. He has a long face, yet not thin, and his cheeks are sunken inwards without much colour in them, but then who has colour in their cheeks living here where nought is breathed but soot. He has soft brown hair cut short and no beard. His nose is quite a big 'un but it fits well with his face and what is best about that face is the mouth which spreads out on both sides like his eyes, and is quite large. He does not smile with his mouth and yet the mouth seems always as if it was just about to smile. The same with his eyes, they do not smile but seem ready to smile all the time. One time I saw him smile though and it was as if a laughing sun did shine right through to crack his face in two. Me Dad says that he don't have much to smile about. He is a widower and his beautiful wife has died so he is always sad, and me Ganny says that if he was not sad enough before 'twill make him sad to be on Monkwearmouth Shore. When he is with us children at the Sunday School I know that he is not sad, though some of the lads is mischievous enough. His name is Mr. Hopkinson and he made us write that name in a fair hand on our slates. Me brothers and me calls him Hoppy for short and he hears us, but he doesna mind it. We ne'er had a clergyman before that didna mind if we called him by a nick name, which we sometimes did, but in secret, mind.

I does believe in God, as is right, but not all that much, though I wadna tell that to Hoppy. If God is good as they say, he would ne'er have let happen what happened that I canna even bring my self to talk about for the tears that fill my eyes and my heart so heavy with sorrow. I will ne'er see Issy more, no nor her little sister, nor her cousin little Mick an I knows that Issy was trying to get us a present an I canna think on it. How can I no see Issy more when we did see each other every day an I can still feel her arms around me an feel her breath on my face as she was telling me her secrets? I dunna know why God would do a thing like that, so many canny bairns lying on the ground and covered with a sheet, their grieving parents coming all day in carriages to turn back the sheets and look at the faces hidden there to find their own. Mam says that Jesus has taken them all to Heaven, but I knows that Issy would rather be down here wi' me for we did have fun, lookya. Issy's Mam canna speak for grief, though all the Mams and Gannies do go by to comfort her, but there's no comfort in it. Some now don't believe in God no more, like me Uncles, but me Ganny says that they better or they'll go to Hell. I dunna want to go to Hell meself, but I don't know where Jesus was when all them bairns was killed. It's a big question, mind.

I would like to talk to Hoppy, not with all them other children there, like at Sunday School, but by meself. If I talked to him I'd ask him for the answer to that big question, which surely he would know, for he is our Vicar. Every day that passes the question gets bigger an bigger in me mind, an though I goes to Church an Sunday School an say all them things in the Prayer Book, yet still there is nay answer to me question.

§

Ever since he took over the Sunday School, Charles Hopkinson has noticed John Balcombe's girl. She is not prettier or more lively than the other children, being pale skinned with a few freckles on her face and with fair coloured hair that some might call golden and others a light auburn. He has noticed that many of the working class children lack colour in their cheeks and yet this is not the whiteness of complexion so coveted by ladies, but a pallor induced by the constant inhalation of polluted industrialised air. It is the serious expression in her eyes as if she were always seeking to understand something just beyond her grasp that intrigues him. Perhaps she is like her father. John Richard Balcombe, a regular attender at the Church Institute, is a man whose eagerness for knowledge and whose respect for learning brings him almost every evening no matter how fatigued from manual labour, to listen to speakers on every subject. Like a mongrel hungry for scraps he avails himself of each opportunity to learn and through this learning he hopes to catch, in the end, an enlightenment he yearns with all his being to possess. Charles Hopkinson cannot help but compare this working man with some of his fellow students at Cambridge whose curiosity, whose hunger for enlightenment barely existed, so sure were they that they were born understanding quite enough and had no need of more. That strained, eager, searching expression that betrays its vulnerability is seen on the faces of both father and daughter and that same vulnerability which they are aware of in themselves and think of as inadequacy, gives them a strength that they do not know they have. He notices that the girl always stays behind to clear away the chalks and slates when the Sunday School class ends.

"Thankyou, Meggie," he says, "you're a helpful lass. Do you enjoy the Sunday School then?"

"Aye, I do, Mr. Hopkinson, for I loves my church. I loves the stories about Jesus, an all, but I canna see that all of them is right, mind."

"Why's that then, Meggie?"

"Well, them ladies, Mary and Martha. In our house there's plenty lads, and me an me Mam, we must be always at the cooking an cleaning an washing an mending – well, there's me Ganny upstairs, but she's too sad to do much now though we takes some of the darning up to her so she can do it where she sits, but if me an me Mam didna set to there would be nay fires an nay food an clothes an no-one to go for the messages. So if Our Lord Jesus Christ come visiting with us, Mr Hopkinson, we would nay have time to be sitting an listening, not if He was wanting to sup with us and I knows he would be offering his Holy words to our lads only. For meself, I would like to be sitting there all comfortable like that Mary, but me Mam an me would be cumbered about with much serving like it says, an I couldna leave me Mam to do all the work by herself. So I think that Our Lord Jesus Christ was not fair to

Martha because he was a man, an a man canna understand what a woman's life is when there is all men expecting their victuals an all. A woman's way is different from a man's an not of her choosing, me Ganny says."

"So is that what you think, then, Meggie?"

"Aye, an I canna help it, though I know it's wrong to say it, but that's what I'm thinking when I hears that story. My heart is with Martha, sir, for if she don't attend to the victuals an all there'll be nought for them to eat an no-one to clear it up after. Words is fine stuff but people needs food to fill their stomachs as well. You are a clergyman and knows more than me, an I should never speak this way I know, an never have before to any person."

"Meggie, you should say what you think, and I am glad to hear it."

"I have no book learning, Mr. Hopkinson, so I canna say what's right, only what it seems to me without book learning, an what they tells me that has the learning. Sometimes my thoughts is very wicked an I canna help it, for I knows that everything Our Lord Jesus Christ said is Holy, and is printed in red letters in me Bible, an is right."

"All of us have questions in our minds, Meggie, that's no bad thing at all."

"My questions is worse. I do not know where Our Lord Jesus was when all them bairns was killed, for I shall ne'er see my companion, Issy, more, and Lord Jesus did not save her even though she ne'er missed one Sunday at church." She turns away from Charles Hopkinson and wipes her eyes with the back of her hand, but the tears fall too fast and she pulls down her sleeve and tries to dry her face. Charles Hopkinson sits down on the bench and motions her to sit beside him. He takes a clean handkerchief from his pocket and gently mops up the tears, then hands it to her to blow her nose. She wipes her face and hands it back to him.

"You keep it, Meggie," he says

"Aye, for now 'tis dirty, an I will wash it an iron it properly for you, Mr. Hopkinson."

"You need not, for I have plenty of handkerchiefs."

"But I will, sir."

"Well, if you will I shall be happy to have it back."

"I'm sorry about them tears and I know that I shouldna say such things of Our Lord."

"And I have not answered any of your questions, have I?"

"Nay, but I was wrong to say them things."

"No, you were not wrong. You said some very important things, and you deserve to have an answer because when people do not ask questions out loud they often ask them inside their heads, and when they do not have an answer they lose their Faith. I don't know whether I have the answers to your questions, Meggie, but I shall think about them and I shan't forget, and when I have thought about them enough I shall come to you and tell you what I've thought."

"An will you be asking the Lord Jesus then?"

"Yes."

"There will be an answer for sure, because you are our vicar and can pray better."

"That I cannot, Meggie."

She looks up at him, not understanding, "Cannot?"

"No matter. Let us just remind ourselves that we believe in the resurrection, and we believe that Issy and all the children have eternal life with Jesus in heaven."

"That I know, Mr. Hopkinson, but I canna feel it. I canna feel eternal life and I canna feel what heaven is like, an I knows that Issy would best like to be here wi' me. And now I know that I am full of wickedness because I canna feel them things and you will be ashamed of me, Mr. Hopkinson."

"That I would never be, Meggie. You are right to say what is in your heart because that is the way to learn and then to be more sure. For the moment it is enough to say your prayers and try to believe even if you cannot feel it. That is what Faith is. Faith is always a leap out into the dark where you can't quite see where you are going, or for what purpose."

The child's eyes are filling with tears again and she turns away to hide them. Gathering up a pile of slates she takes them to the cupboard.

"I havena collected up the chalks yet," she says, "but I will do it, and put in order the benches and the tables so that all is left proper."

Charles Hopkinson looks at her and cannot speak. How can he tell her to believe what she does not feel. How can he tell her with all the assurance of his years of scholarship to believe what he himself cannot feel. He is lost in the child's presence. How can the hideous deaths of so many children be explained in the doctrinal formulae that glide so easily and steadily through his brain and move his tongue to form the words that can't be felt? Surely he has failed her and in doing so has failed himself. She has placed trust in what he has said and he is shaken further.

"Thankyou, Meggie, you are a good helper," he says, unable to think of anything else.

"Aye, well, and that Martha was a good helper an all."

"So she was, Meggie, but people who sit and listen and maybe ask questions and try to work things out, they are good too. So maybe you are a bit like Martha and a bit like Mary."

" I like to listen to you, sir, because I can tell you my wickedness and you will not say hush, and you will learn us something to make us understand better."

"But what you say lass, will help me to understand more."

"Oh, I have no learning, Mr. Hopkinson," she says "all learning is in books and we have none, but now I can learn to pray and to be better and to know that Issy is happy in heaven, because you have come to us, and you have books and can learn us everything."

"I can try and teach you a little, Meggie, but I cannot teach you everything."

"Oh sir, I shouldna have said 'learn us everything' for I know that is not correct. It should be 'teach us' not 'learn us'. There now you have learned us something straightaway." Her eyes sparkle with merriment and he catches the sparkle so that they laugh together. "Meggie Balcombe, you're a canny lass," he says.

§

Charles Girdlestone Hopkinson dips his pen nib carefully into the ink, pauses to consider his heading, and writes CONFIRMATION. He regards it thoughtfully for a while, and then underlines it, CONFIRMATION.
Looking up to the window as if the view of the darkening afternoon sky will somehow assist the process of thought towards purpose and clarity he begins to prepare his notes for the class, but looking down again, he crosses out the word he has written, pauses again, and writes BELIEF.
He notices the black outlines of the branches of one or two trees in the bare garden, as they appear against the sky. The leaves have fallen early and winter is well on its way but his eyes remain on the branches and the grey sky without really seeing anything. His mind rests. Then with a sharp movement he pulls it back to the task and stares at his new heading: BELIEF.
Underneath he writes a sentence to remind himself of his over-all theme, 'the attitude of the Baptised approaching Confirmation should be:

1) His back to Sin i.e Renunciation of World, Flesh and Devil.

2) His face to God. i.e Belief.

He pauses, lifts his head to look again at the branches slightly moving, or is it the sky that moves?
He thinks: Belief, defined as turning the face to God? Is that the definition of Belief? Never mind. He lowers his eyes to the page again and writes, 'We believe all the articles of the Christian Faith with its three-fold Revelation of Father, Son and Holy Spirit. With this in mind we see that each clause of the Creed grows out of the preceding.'
He pauses again, his concentration not holding to the work, then he writes: Sin.

Alpha: World = temptations from outside.

He glances up to check the positions of the moving branches against the moving sky.

Beta: Flesh = temptations from the body.

Gamma: Devil = temptations directly from Satan.

We renounce Alpha and Beta only in so far as they are sinful i.e not inevitably sinful; may be all right in proper place.

Gamma, always sinful. We can relate this to Genesis, Adam and Eve i.e World — tree pleasant to look upon, nothing wrong with trees. Flesh – good to eat for food. Devil — ' He pauses. 'Devil associated with both tree and flesh, the serpent of pride and deceit' once again he looks up and then adds 'etcetera'.

No longer quite sure of his direction he ponders on 'all right in their proper place' then brings his thoughts back to focus on his main heading : Belief. 'The Church requires nothing more than Belief from its Lay members. This means belief in the Creed. For the ordained there is another requirement, the assent to the formula that defines the doctrinal postulate of the Church of England as drawn up in the 39 Articles (16th C). NB. The ordained may not merely consent to let the Articles pass, they must align themselves in agreement, 'become' agreement. That is what 'assent' means.'

For the laity then, simple belief is enough, (but belief in the Creed is not simple!) The Creed requires exposition. How does the Creed relate to the laity? How do the laity relate to the Creed? How should they should perceive its three branches, its Trinity?

His mind drifts again to the young girl in the Sunday class. Can she understand the Mystery of the Tripartite God? How does she make sense of the things visible and invisible? For her it is enough to believe.

No. He looks up suddenly. No. It is not enough to believe. Belief is not enough. He is weary now of clinging to the thread of thought that must be followed. The fact is, that Belief and Faith are very different things. Faith is the same for laity and ordained alike, it is that mighty leap into the mysterious unbelievable that both must make. The rest, so called 'belief', can only be assumption, assumption learned by rote and thus ingrained by repetition, re-examined with difficulty. How then, to give his flock their daily bread, soul's food? Is it by insistence on the proclamation of Belief? Charles Hopkinson lowers his head into his hands, as the door to his Study is opened a little and his housekeeper, Clancey Jackson, looks in.

"I'm sorry to disturb you, Reverend, but Miss Blumer is here. I have told her that you've had your dinner put before you this day, but you've left it uneaten. I do not wish Miss Blumer to think that I doesn't feed you proper, Mr. Hopkinson."

"Why should she think such a thing, Clancey? I was not hungry that's all. It's not your fault. Everyone knows that you always do your best."

"It's just that Miss Blumer has brought a dozen eggs and some fruit, and a very big steak pie. I have told her that there is plenty in the larder, but your appetite is small, sir, and you neglect to eat. I have told her that there is no need of eggs and such here, and that you certainly won't be fancying a steak pie, for you are not a big meat eater."

"Well, we must not be ungracious, Clancey, though of course you are quite right and we have a well stocked larder, thanks to your own good management. Show Miss Blumer in, will you."

Laura Blumer is 30 years old and a spinster, the daughter of Dr. Luke Blumer. At such an age it is not expected that she will marry, and in any case she works all day with her father, tending the needs of the sick and even assisting him with surgical procedures when necessary. If Dr.Luke is called away, folk regularly ask for Miss Laura, who though she is not a qualified physician has been at her father's side since she was a child and knows nearly as much as him when it comes to medical matters. Many of the women patients who have 'women's problems' prefer to confide in Miss Blumer rather than her father. She is tall, straight backed and some would say handsome rather than pretty with good strong features.

"Miss Blumer, sir," says Clancey as the younger woman pushes open the door and enters the Study.

"Thankyou Clancey, I have left the things I brought on the kitchen table. I hear your mother is not too well today. I'll be over to see her directly."

"Thankyou, Miss."

"Please come in, Miss Blumer," Charles Hopkinson rises to his feet clumsily, scattering his notes and papers from the desk onto the floor around him. He looks down at them wearily. They reflect something of the confusion of his thoughts. "Never mind," he says.

"Good afternoon, Charles, or rather perhaps it is evening. The days draw in now and the darkness seems to come earlier. How are you?"

"Well enough, thankyou. Will you be seated?"

She looks around the room; books and papers cover every possible surface and all the chairs.

"Oh, forgive me, of course, wait, let me —" he shuffles around in embarrassment, lifting piles of documents and placing them at random on top of other piles so as to release a chair. She smiles and sits down carefully manoeuvring her feet into a tiny space so as not to disturb the things on the floor.

"Have you eaten today, Charles? Clancey tells me that you have not."

"I've been very busy, Miss Blumer, and to tell the truth I have rather forgotten about my meals. My concerns at the moment are related to the provision of spiritual bread for my flock."

"Of course, that has to be your concern, but let me venture to say to you Charles, that spiritual food is very well, but without actual bread to eat, both you and your flock will perish. I have brought you a large and tasty pie made this morning by our cook, Clara, and if you would be so kind as to ring for Clancey and ask her to bring it here, with a large knife and two plates, we will each enjoy a slice now. Please ask her to bring some bread and butter as well and some of the fruit I have brought for you. Oh and a nice pot of tea."

Clancey is summoned and receives the not entirely welcome news that she is to bring the food as requested by Miss Blumer.

"Will I lay it in the dining room, Mr. Hopkinson?" she asks.

"No indeed," says Laura Blumer. "We can eat here in front of the fire well enough without fuss."

Charles Hopkinson discovers that he is surprisingly hungry and that there is considerable pleasure to be had in balancing a plate, picnic style on his knees. Besides, the shortcrust pastry crumbles just as shortcrust ought to do particularly when the delicious meat juices have been allowed to soak into it and the meat itself has a wonderfully delicate flavour lightly garnished with herbs. The hot tea is also welcome and he realises that not having had the urge to eat all day, he has become debilitated and weary of trying to force his brain to focus on the nature of his task.

"So, may I ask what has been occupying you today?" says Miss Blumer, as she balances a piece of pie on her fork and raises it halfway to her lips. Charles Hopkinson's mouth is full and he chews enthusiastically whilst trying to respond.

"Confirmation" he says none too coherently before he swallows.

"What?"

"Forgive me, I had a mouthful of food. I have been preparing my thoughts for the Confirmation class."

"And how has that gone?"

"Well enough. The task of providing spiritual sustenance to those about to confirm their commitment to the Christian Faith is always demanding, but ultimately satisfying of course."

"Spiritual sustenance," she repeats.

"The bread of life. Our daily bread."

"Yes. It's a very bad time for the folk here. Many of them are reduced to searching for their actual daily bread from the pig troughs."

"From pig troughs! Surely not."

"Indeed." She stretches to reach her bag on the floor, " if I can find it, I know I cut it out of the report – yes here it is, an extract from the chief Medical Officer of Health sent to my father. Shall I read it to you?"

"Please do."

"'Homes are bare of furniture, their clothes are scanty' – this is referring to the Monkwearmouth folk –'the season promises cold, and fires are luxuries which they cannot afford. Food is now being taken from pig troughs.' That's what the Medical Officer himself says, and he doesn't see it as we do, my father and I. Many if not most of the bairns have no shoes and if they have no shoes they can't go to school. You hardly ever see a bairn around here that hasn't a running nose and we're not properly into winter yet."

"But, forgive me, I am relatively new here," He pauses to take a rather noisy slurp of tea. " Why is it so bad now, why is it worse?"

"The downturn in the Yards, Charles. The orders aren't coming in, and constant disputes between men and Managers means withdrawal of labour."

"Strikes?"

"Exactly so. The men have a grievance over the apprentice business and they're right but they can never win."

"The apprentices?"

"Yes, in previous times apprentices to shipwrights were taken on to learn their trade over a period of seven years, during which time of course they were not paid skilled workers' wages. Now the employers are taking on more and more apprentices and laying off the skilled men, because they say that the boys don't need seven years to learn how to rivet and the like. They can do it straightaway with fewer men to oversee them, and they can do it cheaper."

"So the men strike?"

"Of course they do. But as I said, they can't win, there are too many factors against them."

"Such as?"

"The slump in orders, which has been happening since '80, and the transition to steel."

"From iron?"

"That's right. It was the same when they began to make ships from iron in the '60's and '70's, obviously a lot of resistance which was futile and now it's the same thing, a steel plate is much bigger than an iron one and easier to handle. It needs fewer rivets, ergo, fewer riveters, caulkers, rivet heaters and so on. Everyone suffers. For example, a riveter pays his rivet heater out of his own wages, so if he's earning less he's not going to want as many boys to heat the rivets and he's not going to pay them as much. I can tell you, Charles, it's the women and bairns that suffer. The women never know where the next mouthful is coming from, they're worried out of their minds. There hasn't been much loss of trade in the Public Houses though!"

"But is it the same for all the families? The Balcombes for example, John Richard is a conscientious family man, and the daughter, Meggie, she's the one I know best, she seems always to be neat and well clad. I don't know the boys as well, but I imagine a well run household. I call in on Missis Laidlaw, the grandmother, from time to time."

"It's the same for all of them, Charles. Marjorie and John are thrifty and John doesn't waste money on drink, but when they've got a bit put by Marjorie is never slow to help her neighbours. They struggle like everyone else. Perhaps they're a bit more resourceful, that's all. It's certainly true that in the boom years a skilled journeyman like John Richard Balcombe could earn near enough to a pound a day, but now it's more like five or six shillings and the same number of mouths to feed and bodies to clothe. Those who understand thrift and prudence put away some money when they had it, and it serves them now, but the curse of the working man is his chronic inability to think beyond the moment and in truth who can blame him. I am sure that as a Reverend gentleman you have much to offer in terms of deferred reward, but it's of little comfort after a long day of manual labour with nothing to go back to except overwhelming responsibility. People need to laugh and enjoy themselves and get relief from labour and drudgery." She breaks off and looks at him noticing what she sees as signs of distress on his face, " I'm truly sorry, Charles, I should not have said all that."

"On the contrary, you should say what you think, and I should pay attention to it."

"I didn't mean to suggest that your mission to them is unimportant. Everyone values the work you do and the support and friendship you offer."

"I have to confess though, Miss Blumer, that I frequently doubt the value of my message. I sometimes wonder even if – " he breaks off in confusion. He had not meant to reveal so much about himself or his fears. She looks at him, waiting for him to continue, but then perceiving that he regrets having said so much, she continues in a matter of fact tone that she hopes will cover the momentary awkwardness that has arisen between them.

"This community relies on women like Marjorie Balcombe. If she's got a shilling put by there's fourpence for someone else who's in need, and she's always there for the laying out when folks die, and for the lying in as well, though God knows how she manages with those brothers of hers in the house."

"Meggie's a canny lass."

"She is that. She's but ten years old or thereabouts and yet she helps her mother and me with the laying out many a time. The Ganny, that is the old Ganny, Ganny Hogarth, she was a character, I can tell you. Broad Scots accent though she insisted that it wasn't Scots at all – very insistent that it wasn't that, she was, I've heard her take on the men and win the argument every time, though sometimes they didn't want to know it, mind. My father was very fond of Ganny Hogarth. He used to say 'if women were let into Universities, which let's pray they never are,' he used to say, 'Ganny Hogarth would soon have all the proud professor's brains spinning like tops, though she could neither read nor write. Never went to school, but she could think. How that woman could work things out!"

"She's dead then now?"

"Oh yes, more than ten years ago."

"You know a lot about these people, Miss Blumer."

"I've been living amongst them all my life, Charles. You learn a lot if you spend time and listen to them. The thing that most bothers my father is the working conditions of the men. Not many of the iron shipwrights can expect to live beyond forty five or so, the work is too hard physically, and that and the cold, well, the heart gives up."

"But don't the employers care?"

"Some of them do, but they don't do much about it. They've got their own concerns. Our family had a Yard some years ago. My grandfather was a ships' carpenter, only he pretty well owned the Yard, but it was the changeover from wood to iron that closed most of it down. The owners have to be ready for change and know how to adapt to it, otherwise they go down and that often means confrontation with the work force who inevitably oppose it."

"These people mean a lot to you, Miss Blumer,"

"They're my family. Well you know, not literally, but that's the way I feel about them."

"And you've never married."

"Marry! I've no time to marry. How would I have time to be a married lady, and help my father tend the sick and the dying all at the same time? I'm thirty years old and I've no desire to give up the life I know, and there's never been a man who would want to marry a woman like me who has no parlour talk and who embarrasses the men with her interest in industrial disputes and working conditions and who knows more about getting babies out when they're upside down and washing the soiled bodies of the dead than how to dilly-dally around with romantic fal-di-lals and the like."

Charles Hopkinson finishes the slice of pie in front of him, and she takes the plate and adds it to hers, placing the forks on top and balancing the dirty teacups on top of the pile.

"A very good pie. Thankyou."

"Don't thank me, I didn't make it. Our cook is excellent, she's been with us a long time now. It would be tactless to make too much of it in front of Clancey."

"I'll ring for her to take the plates."

"No, don't bother her Charles. I'll take them down to her now on my way out."

Miss Blumer stands up and sweeps a few stray crumbs from her coat.

"Oh my goodness, I am so sorry, I didn't even offer to take your coat when you came. I'm afraid I am a woeful host. Forgive me," he says.

"If I had thought to take my coat off, I would have done so, Charles. I never thought of it."

"But it's cold outside and now you won't feel the benefit of your coat."

"So, there is nothing to be done, is there. I have not far to go, and shall be perfectly fine. I'm in robust health, Charles. Now I'll gather up these plates, and if you could just open the door for me — "

"But your bag as well."

"Yes, I can manage it very well over my arm. Thankyou, Charles, for receiving me when you are so busy. I'll bid you good evening." She leaves the room and he watches her as she walks briskly down the corridor towards the kitchen.

"Good evening," he says to her retreating figure, "and many thanks for the pie and the—"

Too late, she does not hear him. He closes the door regretfully and goes back to his desk. He dips his pen into the inkwell, and then puts it down onto the blotting paper in front of him. He looks up and out of the window. It is dark now and he can hardly make out the lines of the trees, but he sits looking for a long time.

It occurs to Miss Laura Blumer that if she ever were to consider marrying, the widower vicar, Charles Hopkinson might make quite a suitable husband.

He is certainly in need of the attention of a woman, since it is reported that he frequently forgets to eat and is variously absent minded. Moreover there is a certain lack of pomposity perhaps better described as humility about him that she admires. Miss Blumer knows nothing of romance but she fancies that she could become very fond of the clergyman. The fact that they share many opinions in common and look at the world in much the same way, though she perhaps from a more secular perspective, would augur well for a long-term arrangement between them. However she has heard that he mourns the loss of a very beloved and beautiful young wife who was of a delicate disposition and Miss Blumer is all too conscious of her own rude health and not inconsiderable strength both of mind and body. Men are drawn to small women of slight frame who are subject to many sensitivities. Those of Charles Hopkinson's age do not marry a woman to gain a housekeeper or a nurse, she tells herself, and certainly not to acquire an intellectual companion. Marriage involves much more than that as she has heard from the many women who have whispered to her in her capacity as the doctor's daughter, in shame at the profound shock they have suffered on their wedding night. As she strides off down the passage she resolves to put thoughts of such a union with the clergyman, out of her mind and yet it is with unfeigned interest that she listens to her father talking about him that evening at dinner.

"Old man Armstrong was telling me a very droll tale about our new Reverend," says Dr. Blumer. He pauses waiting to be urged on with his story. His wife at the other end of the table simply nods and mumbles 'uhm?' He takes this as a sign to continue.

"A couple of nights ago he invited Hopkinson round for dinner over at Whitburn. Well, apparently Hoppy went there on foot, what, well, a mile or two I should think it must be, wouldn't you say so, and during the course of the evening it began to rain. If you remember it was the night of the terrific storm – one or two of the vessels out there at sea in a bit of trouble, you'll recall. Anyhow, old Armstrong says to Hoppy, 'look man ye'd better stay the night here at the Manse, the weather'll not let up 'til morning.' So Hoppy agrees. Then during the evening's entertainment when old Armstrong's daughters are offering a twiddle-de-dee or two on the pianoforte, Hoppy disappears. At first no-one is much concerned because, you know, it's the Armstrong girls on the pianoforte and er –"

"Luke, don't be unkind about those girls," she interrupts. He looks at her and then continues. "Anyway, time goes by, and no-one can find him. Nearly midnight and there's this frantic ringing on the doorbell. Servants gone to bed, of course, so old Armstrong answers the door himself. Hoppy standing there on the doorstep, shivering and wringing wet. 'Where've ye been, man?' asks old Armstrong. 'Well,' says he, 'if I'm staying the night I thought I'd better go back and fetch my pyjamas.' At this Dr. Blumer falls about in his chair with violent laughter. "I'd better go back and fetch my pyjamas!" he repeats.

"Nay, I don't believe it," says Mrs Blumer, 'ye're making it up, Luke.'

"It's true. As true as I'm sitting here, woman."

"Well, I'll not laugh at him, though you may split your sides," she says to her husband whose wholehearted merriment has ended in a fit of coughing. "Poor body, he needs someone to look after him. Invite him round for supper, Luke."

"Aye, I will, for at least he'll not have to go back so far to get his pyjamas if he stays the night here," and the doctor shakes with breathless laughter again. His wife and daughter sit looking at him without smiling as he endeavours to control his mirth, "Aagh ye women, with your po faces. Ye've no sense of humour in ye at all," he gasps.

"Don't make fun of the poor body. We'll have him round here more often, so that he won't be so much on his own, that we will."

Charles Girdlestone now becomes a more frequent and certainly not unwelcome visitor at the house of Dr. Luke Blumer.

§

At the end of the Sunday Class Charles Girdlestone Hopkinson finds himself anticipating with some pleasure the half hour or so that he will have to talk to eleven year old Meggie Balcombe who always stays behind to clear the slates and chalks. When all is neat again and in its proper place, they sit together in the porch, out of the wind, without any embarrassment.

"Here Meggie, I've an apple – in fact I've got two apples, one for you and one for me. A lady kindly brought them round to the Rectory the other evening. I'll not eat all the fruit she brought – there was enough to fill the trees in the Garden of Eden. I'll eat one now if you will have the other."

They sit together companionably crunching into the apples, and Meggie notices that Mr. Hopkinson frequently starts to talk with his mouth full, which she wonders at, because she has been told many times that proper folk chew their food and then swallow it before they speak, which her brothers never do. In fact they often begin to laugh with their mouths full of bread and though they endeavour to hide it behind their hands, they choke and splutter and it sprays all over the table. Hoppy does not choke and splutter she observes. With his mouth full of apple he turns to her and says, "I've been thinking about the things that trouble us, Meggie."

"What things?" she asks. Surely there are no troubling matters of hers that are shared with Hoppy.

"Sadness, lass," he says, "you know, when people die and bad things happen like you were telling me of your friend Issy, and all the other children."

"That is a big sadness, mind," she says.

" I know. Did you know, Meggie, that I have just such a sadness laying on me, because my wife, who was called Amy also died, and not very long after we were married. That made me so sad that for a long time I could do nothing but sit and feel distressed, and very angry."

"Angry?"

"Yes, angry with God who let that awful thing happen even though I thought I was his special steward, and serving as best I could."

"Well, I am not special like you, Hoppy, but that is how I am feeling too."

"I know it."

They crunch on the apples and sit in companionable silence together.

"But then," he continues, "I had this thought. When Issy died, Meggie, did you stop loving her because she wasn't there?"

"No, but that is the sadness. The love got more and more."

"Neither did I stop loving my Amy. Every day I was thinking of her and loving her more."

"But that is what brings all the pain and hurting."

"Yes, but the love doesn't go away does it? It doesn't ever die."

"No, but sometimes I wish it would stop."

"Well, but it will not leave you, Meggie, that is what God is. Not how he is, but what he is. It's hard to imagine what God is like, but we have to get to know him. I don't think it would be easy to get to know a bearded old man in the sky, do you?"

"The ones in our street like that was me Granda Johnny's friends, but I dinna know what God is even though I've come to the Sunday class and the church all me life so far."

"Well, let's make a start like this. We know how to love, and we know that love is sometimes wonderful and joyful. Sometimes it is, but sometimes it's painful too. Love is the most wonderful thing, but also the most mysterious, and the most unending. The thing is, Meggie, Love is God, and God is Love. Maybe that's all we really need to know about God.

"But what about Jesus, and all of that?"

"Well, once we understand that Love is God, the rest can, in time, follow and we'll understand more, but we must hold fast to what we know and feel, that even when love is sadness and pain and tears it is still God. I think there are lots of folk who've got it upside down. They look at it from the wrong side first, and they don't know that none of it makes much sense until you feel what God is, that is, Love, which is not always easy. Love has to include sadness and longing for lost things and puzzlement and joy and excitement, and all that is God."

She stops eating and sits silently for a few minutes.

"So is what I feel about Issy and them, is all that, that I feel, is it God?"

"It is. That's how you get to know God, but you know Meggie, I think that it's taken me a long time to understand that. Maybe you already know him better than me."

"Oh no, Hoppy. That can't be. You've been a scholar at a place of learning and read many books an all."

"That's been important in its own way, but you don't always find what God is inside a book. Some people have it in their hearts, and some have it but never find it, and some don't want to find it."

"But what about heaven, where Issy is gone. Does the love reach to her there?"

"Not very far from here there's an Island. Some people call it Holy Island and others know it by the old name of Lindisfarne."

"Me Ganny telled us of it, for that is near where she was born."

"There is a long and narrow path called a Causeway that goes out to the island, and folks can reach it by that path, but twice a day the sea comes up and right over it so that you cannot even see it, and you can't reach the island, nor leave it neither until the sea goes back again. Sometimes the sun shines on that path so that it glistens like a ribbon and the sea lies calm and silver around it, and sometimes the sea looks grey and troubled and covers it, but the path is still there. That's what the love is like. A glistening ribbon pathway that reaches right out to a Holy place, and comes back to us again from that place, shimmering and shining all the way back to us. Even when we don't see it or feel it, there it is, and it will never go away. It's always there to reach us."

"And is heaven like that island, then?"

"I haven't been to heaven, Meggie. I think it is a Holy place like Lindisfarne, but not a strange place for all its Holiness just as the Island is not. Folks may be quite at home there, so that they feel warm and easy and know that they are themselves not fearsome shining angels with harps and feathers for how would that be?"

"Very strange, I think."

They sit together without talking and the silence is easy for them. Then looking at the core of the apple in his hand he says smiling, "I'll bet, Meggie that I can throw this further than you." He hurls the core out into the Churchyard. She gets up laughing, "Why aye, Hoppy," she says, "that ye can, but I can near match it, lookye." Her arm moves backward to get a good momentum and the apple core in her hand spins forward in a wide arc, to land beside his.

CHAPTER THIRTEEN

It occurs to Charles Girdlestone Hopkinson that a well run household such as is kept by Dr. Blumer and his wife Elizabeth is a much jollier place to be than his dark vicarage, where the shadows of the past have unfettered freedom to invade and even though his thoughts no longer dwell on his lost Amy all the time, yet the emptiness of the house does little to interrupt a stream of melancholy to which he is prone. He is inevitably struck by the contrast between the vicarage and the doctor's house where there is always the buzz of industry and conversation and where over the supper table all manner of subjects are discussed openly and with authority, even by the women. That Laura Blumer has some regard for him he cannot help but notice and certainly he respects her vigorously expressed opinions and her energetic enthusiasm for getting things done, and he asks himself, having known a passion and exhilaration of a different kind, whether this regard can be enough. Laura is no Amy, but a match between them might have the comfortable approval of her parents and he suspects, the whole community who have long valued the young lady. If Laura's practical mind lacks the complexities with which he feels his own mind to wrestle, and which he senses somewhat disconcertingly in a child like John Richard Balcombe's daughter, does it matter? In effect, is it not better that the limitless questioning of faith, the doubt and analysis to which he gives so much time should not be present in a prospective wife where mutual descent into introspection might be damaging to both. He perceives that a union might be acceptable, even advantageous, and resolves to ask Miss Blumer if she would consider marriage. Having been single for so long and having a firm place in the community, he doubts whether his proposal will succeed. He therefore decides to broach the matter, as is proper, with her father. As they sit together by the fire in the library after supper one evening he embarks on some tentative enquiries.

"I marvell, Dr. Blumer, that Miss Blumer has never been tempted to marry."

"Miss Blumer? Oh aye you mean my daughter, Laura. Marry! Good God man! She is far too busy, and in any case she would never modify her vociferous opinions or forthright manner in order to subject herself to some man. Why should she?"

"Why indeed!" Charles nods agreement and stares gloomily into the glowing coals.

"No, I've never heard her express the least preference for any man," Dr. Blumer taps his pipe against the fender and takes out his tobacco pouch to refill it. He lights it and leans back in his armchair, drawing on it with contentment.

"Couldn't manage here without her help. Not that I've ever stood in her way as far as marriage is concerned, oh no. Never heard her mention it though."

"No, no, indeed." Charles feels himself to have reached a dead end as far as his own suit is concerned.

"Oh no, no, no," continues Dr. Blumer, "marriage is a wonderful state, a blessed state, as we all know, but not for everyone I'm sure you'll agree."

"Well—"

"Oh my deepest apologies, Reverend, of course, as a widower — yes— as a widower—the sorrow, yes, must be very great —yes, the loss — yes, really very tactless of me. Forgive me."

"Really, Dr. Blumer, there is nothing to forgive. Your comment was a general observation—"

"Oh entirely thoughtless of me, Reverend. And do you ever consider re-marriage— or perhaps the wounds of your bereavement are still too raw, unhealed, one can well understand that, my goodness."

"I have thought of it, I confess."

"You should, you should. It's not good for a man of your age, in his prime, shall we say, to live alone in such a large and in my opinion comfortless house. You have a housekeeper of course, but my dear man, a housekeeper is no solace, no soul mate. You are undoubtedly the shepherd of your flock, and a vast and disorderly flock it is, as I know, with many a lost and straying sheep to keep you busy." Dr. Blumer laughs as he re-lights his pipe and begins to puff at which point the chuckles become little breathless coughs.

Recovering his breath he proceeds. "Oh ho, there's many a straying sheep and many a wolf lurking around your none too pleasant pastures, but there must be a good woman somewhere that could ease your burden, what d'you say?"

"Yes, I had thought of seeking—"

"Aha, I have a struck a golden vein as they say— quite right too, Reverend."

"I had thought of seeking your opinion."

"Seek away, man. Opinions are not what we are short of in this house," he chuckles.

"I had thought of seeking your opinion, your advice, an indication of your feeling about a proposal with regard to Miss Blumer."

"Miss Blumer! My God! Are you speaking of Laura again?"

"Miss Laura Blumer."

"You mean that you intend to propose matrimony to my daughter, Laura Blumer?"

"That was what had come to my mind."

"My daughter?"

"Yes, Miss Blumer."

Dr. Blumer puts down his pipe and rises from his chair. He strides to the door, opens it, and calls out in a loud voice, "Elizabeth! Elizabeth! Come here immediately."

Charles Girdlestone Hopkinson sits forward on the edge of his chair, nervously rubbing his hands together. It now strikes him as utter foolishness to have spoken of this matter since parental opposition to any proposal of marriage is the obvious and certain outcome. There is something about himself that parents find entirely unacceptable. Of course the thing is impossible.

Mrs. Blumer comes running to the library aware of some terrible agitation that has overcome her husband.

"What is it, Luke, what's the matter?" She takes his arm and steers him back to his chair. He sits down with a deep sigh.

"Whatever is the matter?" she repeats, looking first at her husband and then at Charles Girdlestone.

"I am afraid I have upset Dr. Blumer quite unforgiveably," he rises to his feet and takes a tentative step towards the door.

"Elizabeth," says Dr. Blumer, "Elizabeth, the Reverend here has just asked me for my opinion of his intention to propose matrimony to our daughter!" Elizabeth Blumer claps her hands to her mouth and jumps up and down twice. Charles retreats further and considers how he may withdraw from the room and the house without causing further upset, but Elizabeth Blumer throws her arms around him whilst her husband looks on in open astonishment.

"Oh how I have longed for this," she says, "my prayers have been answered. Praise the good Lord! Oh Luke, how happy we are, are we not. To see our dear Laura so honoured. To see her as the loving wife of a clergyman such as Mr. Hopkinson, Charles, what joy! Mr. Hopkinson, my husband and myself most heartily commend you to our daughter. Our hearts burst with happiness."

Dr. Blumer looks up from his chair in speechless surprise.

"We are so happy, aren't we, Luke!"

"Er, happy, yes, happy!" he says, "however I suggest that our great happiness is premature. Miss Blumer, Laura, has not yet been asked, nor has she accepted—"

"But she will" says his ecstatic wife. "I know her heart, she will. Never fear, Mr. Hopkinson, Charles. Be encouraged. It is late now and Laura has retired. Call on us tomorrow morning. I assure you your suit will be successful." She kisses him lightly on the cheek and rushes from the room. The urgent clattering of her heels on the stairs to her daughter's room can be heard from the library. Dr. Blumer clears his throat and knocks his pipe against the fender again.

"Well, it seems that the matter is settled then," he says, "as usual the women have settled the matter and that is that. Yes, well, I wish you much happiness, though how I shall manage without my assistant I do not know."

"If I am fortunate enough to be accepted by Miss Blumer—"

"Miss Blumer! Do you intend to persist in calling the woman you are to marry, Miss Blumer. Good God man! Her name is Laura, and I assume that that is what you will call her in future."

"If, er, Laura will be my wife, she will not be far away, and I am sure that she will continue to assist you as before."

"Assist me! And I suppose she is to assist you also as the wife of a Reverend. Good God! Is my daughter to become a slave to a physician and a clergyman. Is my daughter to be worn out with assisting, running hither and thither all day long and half the night. Do you intend to kill my daughter, sir? Her first duty must be to you as her husband. So be it."

"But do I have your blessing, sir?"

"Blessing! For God's sake man, it is you who are in the business of blessings. I am in the business of medicine and surgical procedures. If you are to be my son-in-law, so be it, I say. You need no other blessings than the one you have in my daughter."

Charles Girdlestone rises. "I will say goodnight to you then, sir."

"Goodnight! We have only just had supper, man. If you are to become my relation, as it now seems that you are, the women having decided, you will sit and enjoy another glass of port with me, and let us drink to a long and happy association."

At eleven o' clock on the following morning, Charles Girdlestone Hopkinson presents himself at the front door of the doctor's house. He is ushered in by the housemaid whose face, having taken a few minutes to compose itself in an expression of high seriousness, seems now about to crack open and dissolve into uncontrolled giggles.

"I have come to see Miss Blumer," he says.

"Oh sir, I dunna, that is, I do not know whether she is able to receive you," she lies, "she is writing letters. If you would be so good as to wait here, I will hascertain whether, that is, I will go and find out." The girl disappears down the hallway. In a moment she returns. "Miss Blumer will see you, sir," she says.

"Of course I will, Tilly, don't be ridiculous," says Laura Blumer stepping in front of her. "Please come in Charles."

He follows her into the drawing room, and stands awkwardly clutching his hat.

"I have come to—" he begins.

"Charles, if you have come to ask me to marry you, let us not waste time. The answer is 'yes' under certain conditions."

"Well, I — thankyou — I am honoured and—" he stammers.

"Let us not be honoured. Let us talk of practical matters."

"Indeed."

"The calamity that befalls far too many marriages in my opinion, is that the parties fail to discuss in advance those matters on which the foundation of such a partnership depends. We are too old and wise for that sort of thing."

"What matters can I offer you assurance on?" he asks.

"The first and most important. You have a child of one or two years old, I believe."

"Yes, a girl, Amy."

"Named for your wife."

"Yes, Amy."

"And where is your child now?"

"I have employed a woman to care for her in Cumberland, but recently ill health has obliged her to give up and Amy is placed temporarily with another family until I can find a more suitable person to care for her."

"And where is this suitable person to be found?"

"That I have not yet—"

"So, am I to understand that this poor child within her short two years of her life has lost her mother, and now been shuffled about, as one may say, between two women who have been employed to look after her."

"Yes, it is he best I can do until a more suitable arrangement can be found."

"Charles, let us not beat about the bush. *I* am a more suitable arrangement. There can be no question of a marriage between us if you do not agree to bring this poor child here immediately, to be looked after, cared for and brought up properly by us both, and if we are blessed with children of our own, Amy will be equal with them, their older sister. It must be our first concern to make her feel happy and warmly received into our household."

"I do not know what to say, Laura, your goodness astounds me."

"This is not goodness, Charles, it is common sense and our delight."

"Is that the condition that you referred to, if so, it is easily agreed between us."

"No, there is another. You were married to Amy's mother and she died."

"She died, yes."

"This has made you very sad and sometimes I see that you are almost overcome with sorrow and can hardly lift yourself from it."

"That is true but I will overcome it."

"No. Charles, it is not necessary for you to overcome it. You will always feel it. One does not overcome grief, it may mellow as we take it by the hand, but it does not go away. I will not be your first wife and I daresay I am not like her in any way. I am who I am. Therefore I need to know that you have enough feeling for me, as myself, not as a replacement for someone else."

"Truly, I know that you are yourself, and I love you for it. But if we are to investigate feelings, Laura, I must ask you what your feelings are for me."

"How very blind men are," she says, "Charles Girdlestone, I have loved you from the first moment that you set foot on Monkwearmouth Shore. Is that enough for you? If not, I will add that subject to the conditions I have mentioned," she smiles awkwardly, "I believe that it has been my considered intention to marry you since that moment."

"That is enough for me," he says, smiling, "I really think it is."

Outside the door, Mrs. Blumer and the Tilly, the maid, whose ears have been pressed against the panelling, straighten up and hug one another.

Laura Blumer goes to the door and opens it.

"Why, Mama, so you and Tilly just happened to be outside at that moment," she says.

"Oh, Miss Laura," Tilly throws her arms around Laura Blumer, " Oh, Hoppy! I mean Mr. Hopkinson. Wait till I tells everyone."

"Off you go, Tilly," says Mrs. Blumer, "go now and fetch Dr. Blumer."

§

I have heard a thing from Mam that must make us all glad. It is said, though not for sure that Hoppy is to be married, and who to? Why none other than our doctor's daughter, Miss Laura Blumer. Mam says that Hoppy must get over his sadness and wed with Miss Laura who nobody thought would ever wed because she is old already, and the same age as Hoppy. She is used to looking after folk and she will look after him because he neglects himself with not having a wife. Me Mam and me Ganny talked of it a lot, and me Ganny said that sooner he is wed the better, because a Reverend who is not wed is an open temptation to all the young women who'd be after him. Me Ganny says that to wed is the best thing for a widower. I asked me Ganny why she didna take another man for to be her husband, as she is a widow, and if to wed is best for Hoppy, why not for me Ganny? I dunna understand why not. If to wed is best thing why must it not even be spoken of for me Ganny? Afterwards I asked me Mam why not, an she said that Ganny Laidlaw is much older than Mr. Hopkinson, an she has lost her husband who she dearly loved an she doesna need another husband to look after her because she can do that for herself. But that isna true because it's we that looks after her now. I thinks that me Ganny has had enough of men and that is why she is right, because I will never marry, that's for sure, for I will never meet with a man like Hoppy who is far above me, an that is the only sort of man that I could wed.

When I lay in bed last night I thought of Hoppy and of what he said to me about love which is like a silver shining ribbon stretching to a Holy place and stretching back again, which I will ne'er forget. I am glad that he will marry Miss Laura because folks has said that we are all glad, but inside my heart and my head where no-one can be but me I am not glad at all, which is wickedness in me. I am not at all glad because he will live with his wife and soon enough they will have bairns and he will have no time for sitting about an eatin' apples wi' me. Hoppy will not be mine, like he was. He will be Miss Laura's, an that's it. That's what I feel inside me, and that's the truth of it, and a wicked truth it is. In me apron pocket, guess what I have? An apple core! I watched with a keen eye where his did fall when he threw it from him, and though mine fell beside it, I remembered which one was his, and after he had gone I ran and picked it up and put it in me pocket, where it now is, although brown and dry. I will always keep it, because it was Hoppy's apple that I will always have of Hoppy which no-one will ever take away.

MONKWEARMOUTH
NOVEMBER 1894

CHAPTER FOURTEEN

John Richard wakes early in the morning of November 14th 1894. In four days' time he will have been married to Marjorie for twenty two years and though life has never been easy, it has been a good marriage. What the union has lacked in passion it has made up for in companionship, each partner understanding their role, each contributing what they must in terms of support and commitment to the whole and the whole is, of course, the family, which means the wider family too, for John Richard is now largely responsible for the well-being of his mother-in-law, Ganny Laidlaw, and must keep the balance of peace between all the men in the house, too few of whom appear to take their own responsibilities seriously. Of his two brothers-in-law, Thomas, the younger one, suffered an accident two years back when he fell off the gang-plank and into the water between the ship and the dock. This is a not uncommon occurrence and a number of men have drowned, being too incapacitated by alcohol to save themselves. Thomas was hauled out badly injured and now cannot find any kind of employment which would accommodate his disability, a seriously damaged back. This injury in no way interferes with his capacity to reach the Public House or to drink himself senseless and without the discipline of regular working hours his temper is given full licence to flare and strike whenever the mood takes him.

John Richard's own boys are all at the yard now that they no longer attend school. The two eldest, John and Jim are apprentice riveters but little Tom, the youngest is his father's rivet heater and has no ambition to be more.

"I will not work in the Yard all me life," says little Tom, now nearly fourteen years of age, "I'll not do it, Dad. I wants to work in a garden and see things grow and look at the sky as is seen upwards and between the branches and leaves of a great tree. I hae no liking to see that sky through the dead tree trunks that bear up nothing but the platforms around a ship. Therefore I willna learn the riveting, for that will mak me what you are forever. I'll stay here on the ground and heat up the rivets, which is but a boy's job. If I canna be a gardener, then I wull be a boy forever, mind."

The other two boys, John and Jim must be guided to avoid the habits of their uncles who live on the floor above at 24 Hardwick Street. They must be warned to resist the temptation to spend their wages from the Yard in the Public Houses and all of these responsibilities fall heavily on John Richard. There is one further anxiety. For nearly two years now Marjorie has ailed. She has grown thin and pale and she complains of stomach pains. She eats little and when she eats she vomits soon after. Sometimes she rallies and recovers for a while and then he hears her telling Meggie, " I've got that rotten feeling again, lass," and Meggie will fill a stone bottle with hot water and wrap it round with a shawl so that her mother can hug it to her stomach. So she sits, either propped up in bed, or in a chair, doing what tasks she can, mostly the sewing and such to help Meggie. All this has brought Ganny Laidlaw downstairs again, for someone must see that there is food on the table for the large family.

Meggie is John Richard's pride. She was apprenticed to a dressmaker at twelve years old when she left school, able to read, write, calculate, sew and knit, and she took to the dressmaking with ease. Now she has set up her own modest business and many a fine lady comes from over the water to her work rooms in Marley's Buildings. Even the ship owner's wives and daughters know of Meggie Balcombe's reputation for fine work and reliability and her earnings together with those of her father maintain the family whilst at the same time she takes much of the responsibility for its day to day welfare, helped by her mother and Ganny Laidlaw, who in spite of her mourning clothes and insistence on unrelenting grief, likes a bit crack and a bit gossip.

The day, like the day of his marriage to Marjorie, will come up cold and grey once the blackness of night begins to lift but there is no fog, for the air is cut by a sharp and biting wind that makes little Tom cry out and try to hide beneath the covers of his bed. As he dresses, John Richard is aware of feeling the cold more these days than when he was younger. He cups his hands under the icy flow of water from the tap in the back kitchen and splashes his face. Marjorie is sick and still in bed but Meggie is up lighting the fire and has made strong hot tea for her father and brothers who crowd the kitchen. There is bread and dripping or meat and fish paste for the men to take to the Yard. The two older boys, groaning from the bad heads they have inherited from the night before, leave the house first to get to the Pub for the first drink of the day before the Yard gates open. Little Tom, still a child, looking small and frail with his white, pinched elfin face now almost covered by his red neckerchief and flat cap, waits for his father, as they will walk to the Yard together. John Richard puts the bread and dripping wrapped in oiled paper into his inside pocket and winds a woollen scarf around his neck against the wind. Then Meggie hands him two old glass medicine bottles filled with hot water and he puts one in each pocket of his jacket. He has been doing this for the past two winters so that he can warm his hands in his pockets as he goes to work.

"Mind now, Dad, lap up warm. There's a raw wind today. Lap up Tom." She pats the scarves to make sure that they are snug around the necks of her father and brother.

"Meggie, we'll be warm enough around the rivet fire," says Tom, " but me Dad will suffer up there in the wind."

"Lap up, Dad," says Meggie.

"Aye, lass." John Richard shouts to his wife in the back room, "We're off, Marj, take it easy lass. I'll be back at dinner time to see how ye are."
As he strides down the street towards the yard, John Richard is aware of the sound his boots make and those of Tom who keeps up with him. The cold seems to be more within his body than without and he cannot warm himself even though his hands are tightly closed around the hot glass bottles in his pocket. He stops to take out his cigarette packet and he strikes a match which flares briefly against the skin of his face and cheers him. Then he draws the smoke deeply into his lungs to experience that sense of pleasure and assurance that all will be well despite the wind and the greyness and the deafening noise of hammers against iron.

"Ye go on down, Tom," he says, "I'll just pause here for a moment an get me breath."

"Ye all right, Dad?" asks Tom.

"Right as rain, lad. I'll be wi' ye in a minute."

John Richard leans against the dirty brick wall at the end of the street. He draws again on the cigarette, inhaling deeply. This time instead of the usual satisfaction he has a slight feeling of nausea, even dizziness. It's the time o' the year, he says to himself, tis naught but colds and chills like what Marj has had. He will call at Dr. Blumer's later in the day and get something to tide him over while the chill lasts. Then unusually he pushes open the door of the Duzzy House. The air inside is already thick with smoke and he pushes his way through the crowds of men to reach the Bar counter where the tots of rum and brandy are all set up for the shipyard workers to down quickly and get to the gates before they close. He snatches a tot of whiskey and drinks it in one gulp, slaps his money down on the counter and pushes his way out through the press of men, who like a stampeding herd of cattle will suddenly leave to surge towards the gates. The whiskey acts like a fire that sears his throat and for a second takes away his breath, but with new life in him he strides through the gates to sign on. It is 6.05 am.

John Richard climbs the ladder to his position against the great black structure of the ship. The plate handlers are already there waiting to hold the steel in position for the riveter. John Richard's legs seem to lack strength today and the climb is slower. As a young man he could leap and swing his way up but the muscles have tired and it is an effort to climb. He has seen this gradual slowing down in many a shipwright as the years of heavy labour take their toll on the body. But Armstrong and Thompson and Laing and Doxford do not make money out of men whose bodies cannot lift and swing the hammer and the work must go on.

"Ye arl right, man?" shouts one of the waiting men.

"Howay! Right as rain, man," he calls back.

He picks up the hammer and swings it as the first red hot rivet is thrown to the catcher and then hammered home. The movement is one he has known for thirty years. Another rivet is caught and ready and he swings again. A sharp pain hits his chest cavity as if the hammer had struck him as it strikes the rivet. The intense pain leaves him breathless. He drops the hammer and sways for a moment, clutching his chest.

"Ye arl right, man?" shouts the man further down the line. John Richard does not answer. His face is white, his lips blue.

"Ye arl right, John?" Two others drop their hammers and come to his side. John Richard has slumped on to the wooden platform. He no longer sees the hammer, the black side of the ship, or even his own ice cold hands, but he hears the voices as if at a distance, of the men around him.

"Get him down, lads."

"Nay time, get the doctor up here."

"Tom, young Tom Balcombe, it's yer Dad, get the doctor, man."

A long way away, John Richard hears the panic, he knows he must get up, must get a grip of the hammer. His hands tighten as if to hold it firm again, he struggles against the pain which must not stop the swinging and striking of the hammer, and then he lets go and the Yard is silent.

"Too late, man, he's gone."

Marjorie has been sick for most of the night but a good dose of bicarbonate of soda has settled her stomach and she and Ganny Laidlaw lay the table with the dinner things. Meggie will come back at just before one o' clock and Tom and John Richard will be through the door soon after, followed by Jim and John who never miss an opportunity to stop off at The Duzzy House on the way back. The dinner will be on the table as they come in, mostly mashed potatoes and gravy, followed by syrup sponge. They must eat quickly and get back to the Yard where the work must go on until the day-light fails. Sometimes there is hardly enough time for the men to sit down, but the hot food keeps them going until the darkness falls. Today it is gone one o' clock and the women wait. In the Duzzy House the men leaning against the Bar are talking.

"Riveter went today."

"Riveter? Which one?"

"Balcombe."

"John Richard? He was nay more than forty two or three."

"Aye. A good age fer a riveter, mind. They dunna last much beyond forty five, so watch yerself man!"

"There's his sons over yonder. Hey, Jimmy, hey Johnny, wha' about yer Dad?"

"Wha' about him?"

"Gerraway home, lads. Ye'll be needed."

"Wha' about me Dad?" asks Jim shouldering his way over to the Bar.

"Yer Dad's had an accident, gerraway home."

"Yer dad's dead, Jimmy, did nay one tell ye?"

Jimmy lets out an ear splitting howl. "Me Dad! Me Dad! Me Dad canna be dead!"

The men take his arm and help him out followed by John, white faced and silent.

At 24 Hardwick Street, the waiting women hear a loud knocking at the door. Ganny Laidlaw does not need to be told what has happened, the only question to be answered is to which one. Then the door is pushed open by little Tom, his face is scared and his hair standing up, his cap lost and his scarf untied.

"Mam!" he calls out.

Marjorie and Meggie go into the dim hallway. A group of men stand outside, their caps in their hands, amongst them John and Jim, helpless and pinched with anguish. Behind them is a handcart with more men beside it. On the cart is the body of John Richard still carefully wrapped and tucked in against the cold in his jacket and scarf.

"It's your man, Marjorie," says the man at the front of the group, "he's gone, lass."

Marjorie's hands cover her mouth to stop the scream of panic escaping. Meggie puts her arms around her mother whose head now rests on her shoulder. Then, calmly, Margaret Laidlaw, Ganny Laidlaw, steps forward.

"Clear them dinner things off the table," she says to the boys, " get a good white cloth, there's one upstairs in my cupboard, Meggie, and when ye has it cover the table." The men wait respectfully with the handcart. Neighbours begin to gather in the doorways of the other houses.

"Now, bring him in an lay him on the table," she says.

The men lift the body that now seems so slight and frail against the white cloth, onto the table.

"Get Dr. Blumer," she says. The men, silent, caps in hand, retreat and trundle the empty cart back up the street leaving the family to stand around the table. Soon they are joined by a whispering throng of neighbours who have heard and seen the trundling cart. Marjorie leans over her husband's body and strokes his face. Meggie feels in his jacket pockets and takes out the bottles, now cold, that she had filled to warm his hands. Ganny Laidlaw loosens his scarf.

"Canny lad," she says, "never ye fear ma canny lad, ye're out of it now, the struggle an arl. Twill be better fer ye. The Lord kna's ye weel fer a guid mon. Dinna fash yersel' aboot us, now tis arl well wi' us."

Tom, Jim and John stand silent, shocked, looking at the body of their father on the table. Meggie's arms around her mother are insufficient to restrain the frantic Marjorie whose fists pound the table beside the body. She looks up and grabs Ganny Laidlaw by the shoulders. "Will ye stop, Mam. He's gone, my man is dead. He canna hear ye, Mam. He canna hear ye, he's dead! John, my John Richard is dead." Her sobs shake her body and she sinks to her knees so that her forehead rests on the table beside her husband.

"Whisht, ma girl, there's the quick and there's the dead, an I knaws more that's dead than quick. But listen ti me, arl o' ye, an tak this from an arld woman, the more I knaws that's dead, the more I knaws is more quick than some o' ye. He's dead, aye, but ne'er gone. He'll ne'er be gone, nay more than my Johnny is gone. They is not gone, ma lass. The lad's spirit is wi' us now, an he listens."

Marjorie lifts her head, "Ye're talking nonsense, Mam." She turns to face the boys and those who have gathered, caps in hands to stand respectfully in the room. Her face is white and running with tears.

"Me Mam is out o' her mind. Me Mam is mad. Look at him, look at ma John, he's dead. He's dead, I tells ya, Mam." She breaks down, shuddering with sobs and buries her head on Meggie's chest.

"There, Mam," says Meggie, tears running down her face, "let Ganny Laidlaw say whatever she will, come on, Mam, sit down, sit down, Mam." Someone calls out from the street. "Miss Blumer is here. Let Miss Blumer through."

Laura Hopkinson, still known as Miss Blumer, makes her way through the throng of people and reaches Marjorie who now stands with Meggie's arms around her by the table.

"Marjorie," she says, cupping Marjorie's face in her hands.

"He's dead, Miss Laura."

"I've been told. My father will be with you here soon, but I have come straightaway." She holds Marjorie in her arms and turns to Meggie, "Meggie, my husband, Mr. Hopkinson will be here in a minute as well, he has been sent for. He will bring comfort."

"Comfort!" Marjorie lifts her head, and stares defiantly around at the assembly. "Comfort! Nay, no-one can bring comfort to us now," she sobs. "How will we live wi'out a bread-winner. He was our comfort, and our support, our canny man." She shakes with sobbing as Laura Blumer leads her to a chair and crouches down beside her, stroking her hair. The brothers struck to silence, still stand, looking at the helpless form on the table, the lifeless body of their father who they have relied on since they were born. Their eyes move to the hunched and distraught figure of their mother, to Meggie, and to Ganny Laidlaw by the table, who still talks to the corpse.

"Meggie," says Laura Blumer, "The Gannies will be round to help with the washing and the laying-out. There will be some money from the Union."

From the doorway again comes the cry, "Dr. Blumer is here."

Luke Blumer strides through and bends over the body in silence.

"What was it, Doctor? What was it killed my man?"

"Probably syncope, Marjorie."

"Nay, she asked ye what killed him, Doctor Blumer, when the life went oot o' him, what was it took it?" says Ganny Laidlaw.

"Syncope, Ganny. It's a faint caused by heart failure. Did he know that his heart was weak, Marjorie?"

"If he did, he didna say."

Margaret Laidlaw turns from the table to face the Doctor. " He didna die of any gran' sounding name, Doctor Blumer, though if there's 'sin' in yer syncope, yea, tha's wha' he died of fer sure. Twas no his sin, neither, but the sin tha' keeps men workin' arl their poor lives in them Yards in the bitter cold, until their bodies is broken and worn out. How many arld men is there here on Monkwearmouth Shore that was riveters? Ah'll tell ye, none! They is dead in their prime."

"Sit down now, Ganny," says Meggie.

"I wull sit, but before tha' ah'll tell ye arl. Ah rue the day ah brought ma family to this place, when arl o'us was happy in the bonny Border land. We came from sweet air and fresh breeze, ti dirt an labour an sweat, an stinking air, an naught but grief and poverty. We thought we was poor in Spittal, nothin' but poor Spittal folk, but we was rich. Ah do not knaw about yeer 'syncope' Dr. Blumer. Twas JLs tha' killed him. Tha's the way o' it fer us."

She allows herself to be led to a chair and she lowers herself slowly into it, then pointing, she cries out, "An ye can tell yeer husband, Miss Laura, ti no come callin' here wi' his comfort. Tell him ti keep his canny prayers awa' from this house. If he canna raise John Richard Balcombe from the dead, tell him tha' arl tha' a clergyman has ti say is empty wind and blather."

"Ganny," whispers Meggie, "dunna talk like tha' to Miss Laura, ye'll rue it."

"No," Laura Blumer steps forward, "In her place I would say the same. Of that I have no doubt."

"Ah hae no wish ti offend ye, Miss Laura," says Margaret Laidlaw, "but twas the Yard tha' killed tha' canny man an when ye an yeer Reverend gan ti dine wi' they Thompsons ye can tell 'em tha', an tell 'em it from me."

Three houses down, Swanny Mills picks up his Smallpipes. He goes to the door and out into the street. Above the low drone, rises the Border Lament.

CHAPTER FIFTEEN

The girl stumbles, and he draws her arm through his to hold her. An onlooker would remark on the couple as being unusual as they struggle northwards against the wind on the long sandy beach. She is much younger than her companion; a girl of some twenty-two years, whilst he is into middle age. There is also a social disparity. His height and mode of dress mark him out as a professional man, whose confidence though never disproportionate to his situation is nevertheless that of one who has inherited a sense of his own worth, sometimes questioned perhaps but too ingrained by previous generations and education ever to be totally abandoned. The girl on the other hand has a woollen shawl well wrapped around her head and shoulders in the manner of the working class. Her apparel contrasts markedly with his good quality overcoat and muffler. He is too young surely, to be her grandfather, yet it is unthinkable that he could be her father or indeed any family member of hers. As they walk, despite the wind, the sea breaks gently to sweep the shore with its white frills, like the edge of a lace petticoat beneath a grey velvet gown, and then appears to hold steady, at that point when it goes neither in or out, the point of tidal change. It is almost Christmas now. As he is supporting her, the girl is aware as she has never been before, that this is no idol, no figurehead to be held in the imagination, but a man, a human being whose breath is warm and sweet on the cold air as he exhales and whose energy is released to protect her and combat the force of the wind. His voice is as she has known it always deep and coming from somewhere in the back of his throat.

"Let's make for the rocks, Meggie, and get out of this wind," he says. Gripping her hand tightly he guides her towards the shelter of the rocks and they sit side by side on a piece of timber that the receding tide has abandoned.

"What is there for us now, Hoppy? What will there ever be for me and my folk?"

He cannot answer. She continues, "what is there here but death and sorrow, and we must be always sad, and if we forget our sadness for a little time, then it seems we are only waiting to be sad again."

He puts his arm around her shoulders. His words of comfort, carefully rehearsed and used on many occasions, desert him.

"Won't you say something then, Hoppy? Can't you say anything to me?"

He turns to face her and she looks at him, her eyes filling with tears. They look at each other without speaking. She cannot know what he feels, what remembrances of the frail and urgent female body her closeness brings back.

"I do not always have ready words," he says.

"But it is your calling."

"Is it? And do you not think that a calling is a very heavy thing to bear sometimes, Meggie? And do you not think that there are times when someone with a calling wishes to cast it off and be as you are and as others are, and wishes to disown that calling and all that goes with it?"

She turns away her face and looks at the ground, "I never thought it before, but today I think it," she says, "but I know that you will never desert your calling."

"Will I not?" he says

They sit in silence, and his arm tightens around her. Then he leans back against the rock, drawing in the air through his nose and mouth as if hungry to taste and savour the fresh savagery of the wind. "Meggie, what is the central moment of the Communion Service. You have been confirmed, tell me what you think."

"It must be the receiving of the bread," she says.

"Yes, but before the receiving. What happens?"

"It is blessed by — it is blessed to change it into the Body of Christ."

"Yes, blessed, and what else?"

"What else?"

"What else happens to the Bread, the Body?"

"It is broken. He, that is, you, break the Bread."

"And that is the centre. That is the most important moment, when the Bread is broken"

They are both silent.

"And tell me, Meggie, what happens to the Christ?"

"He is crucified."

"He is, and even his spirit it seems, is broken, and all that he appeared to stand for is broken apart. So now, what happened when you were a lass and your companion did not return?"

"Why she was crushed and she died."

"Aye, she was broken, too. And your heart, Meggie, after she was gone and after your Dad was gone, what happened to your heart?"

"It was broken."

"So that's a great many breakings isn't it! And after all these breakings, did things remain the same as before?"

"No, things was changed!"

"What was changed?"

"Life. The way I sees things. The way I understands things. It's difficult to say."

"And if I offered you a way to go back and see things as you did before, would you accept my offer?"

She sits in silence.

"Would you accept that offer, Meggie?"

"I couldna."

"Why not?"

"Because I know more now. I understands more. I feel more."

"So all this breaking, after every one of them there's a change but not a change we would want to turn back from, is it?"

"We canna."

"Then lookya lass, the truth by which we live is in the Breaking. We cannot grow, we cannot learn, we cannot know the depth of sadness and of love with all that that means, we cannot truly feel inside ourselves the nature of Grace until we understand that we must bear the Breaking."

"So much of it," she says.

" Aye, so much of it. You cannot rid yourself of it. You cannot recover from it. You cannot get over it, so take it. It is part of what you wear. It is the adornment of wisdom."

"Sometimes I have the thought that all we are here for is just to learn until we die," she says.

He draws her arm through his again and they sit silently watching the expanse of grey sea and the solid shapes of ships on the horizon. Charles Hopkinson is aware of many blessings in his life and for these he is thankful, but for all his wise thoughts and words he cannot keep one disturbing question from his mind. Who is this girl who he has known since she was a child? In his Study amongst his loving family he can be alone and quiet, but silence is not the same as quiet, and there are times when silence needs to be shared, yet there are few to share that true silence with. What if the one who shares it is not the one it should be? What if the desire for that sharing becomes a constant longing? What if the one who longs has a Calling?

"Meggie you have a work room now, I think."

"In Marleys Building. It is not very grand, but I can work there well enough."

"When you are not too busy I should like to come and sit quietly and read perhaps whilst you work."

"Why, Hoppy, you would always be welcome, and if you wants to be quiet and read without interruption I will see to it that the ladies who wants dresses an that, do not come, for mostly they are ladies who do no work and can come at any time. Sometimes me Mam is there helping us, but she is a quiet body and mostly sits up wi' the pillows on the couch in the back room."

"But I do not know beforehand when I might come, it is just that if I am visiting parishioners nearby, I might be passing and might welcome a peaceful place to rest."

"And you shall have it, Hoppy. If you comes I will see to it that the door is closed and though I can still get on with the sewing no customers shall come to disturb you."

He stands and draws her arm through his and together they make their way back along the shore.

CHAPTER SIXTEEN

Now I am decided. Me Dad is gone and me Mam near dead with grief and me brothers drinking and raging and on the warpath, except for our Tom, and though me Ganny sits upstairs and talks of nought but her Johnny who left her without a word of farewell and ne'er came back, his body at the bottom of the sea or buried in some foreign land, I will look after all on 'em. I am long finished wi' me apprenticeship and me workroom is in Marley's Buildings, for which I must pay old Marley the rent. There is plenty room there, and another room at the back where Tom put a bed for me Mam so that she can sit up and be comfortable when she has her troubles. She can help me with the pin-tucks of which there is many, because the ladies likes all sorts of fancy stitching and button holes. The ladies gets their fashion books from London and then they brings 'em to the workrooms and they says, 'Meggie, I want me gown to have sleeves like this and a bit fur here' and that's how they go on. And sometimes they gives me a kiss to sweeten me up, as they think, because they knows I will do it for them, though it will be more work. They knows nothing of stuff, and they think I can do miracles with any sort of stuff they bring in, which mostly, it's true, I can.

Since me Mam and me are down at Marley's, me Ganny, Ganny Laidlaw, helps with the dinner at number 24, which is good because it makes her stop thinking about those who have gone. Her sons, me uncles, is worse and worse, so now I keeps well away from them.

If I can sew by night and day with me Mam to help, propped up on the pillows, which she does though some days she heaves and wretches and canna eat, and if the boys will help a little with the wages, though God knows tis hard to get to them wages before the Duzzy gets 'em now that me Dad is gone, then I can keep them all, though I wish that them uncles wad gan away! Them uncles sometimes brings women from the Duzzy into our house and then there is a rare commotion all night long. Them uncles is a botheration. I will ne'er marry. I will ne'er have one o' them men like me uncles pawing and slobbering over me and worse than that. In my heart I know who I would want as husband, but though I sometimes lie in bed at night and dream of what might have been if I'd been born a lady I well know it cannot be.

Mr. Hopkinson comes to Marleys to sit a while. He comes to ask about me Mam. Sometimes he will sit and watch me sew and not say a word and I am glad of that because there is too much noise in Hardwick Street, but here we can be quiet. Sometimes he will take out a book and read. I wish I had a better room for him to sit in, and I wish I could speak proper — properly, like him. When he comes to sit and rest here I closes up the place so that customers cannot enter and disturb him.

Our little Tom no longer works at JLs Yard. After me Dad died he didna want to be a rivet heater to another riveter, so he got a job as Pilots Helper and has to go out with them Pilots in the cobles which brings a great difficulty to Marleys, an no mistake. He works for Pilot Thomas Brown who has four sons who will all be pilots too when they have worked their ticket. The eldest is Bob Brown and there are two girls as well, Mary and Sarah. Our Tom must have told them about me and they have been coming to the workroom to order new outfits. Mary is very pleasant and it is said that she is being courted by Preacher Spooner over the water where they lives in Hendon, but Sarah has a hard face and is not easily pleased. Now our Tom has come to me and told me that Bob Brown would like to meet us and maybe to walk out wi' me. Tom knows I will not marry but he tells me that a Pilot is a good match. All the Brown family is pilots, the Dad and all his brothers too. Some of them has been Pilot Rulers. Bob Brown is well known. He plays the one string fiddle and sings and keeps everyone entertained at parties. He is the life and soul, says our Tom.

§

Mr. Hopkinson came today to give us some bad news. He is leaving Monkwearmouth and going to Christ Church in Bishopwearmouth. "But it is not too far, Meggie," he said, " and we will still be able to talk and you shall visit." But it will not be the same, that I know. He looked at me so strangely and he said, "I have thought about it great deal, Meggie, and it is for the best." How can it be for the best that I will not see him as I do now and who will answer my questions about God as he does, for I know that he is very close to the Lord. I love my church but how will it be when Hoppy is no longer there? I told him about Bob Brown and how it troubled me that he was pressing my brother to arrange a meeting with me. The Brown family are not church-goers so I thought that Hoppy would not be in favour of such a one and at first when I told him he went quite pale and said nothing, so I thought he had not heard me, but when I told him again he said, "Meggie, you must consider your own interests first, and maybe a Pilot would be a good match for you." I do not know why he said that because he does not believe it, that I know. At the moment he is sad, I think, so I suppose it will cheer him up to go to Bishopwearmouth which is better than Monkwearmouth. Folk are not rough as they are here. What would he think of me if he knew that in the drawer where arl the pins are kept, there's a bit pattern paper wrapped around an old brown apple core?

§

Bob Brown's family lives in a grand house over in Hendon, Salem Hill, with a maid to come out wi' a cap on her head, who I knows to be no more than

Lily Atkinson born wi' the bandy legs. Mam says that Bob Brown comes here a-courting and is a good match that would take me out of Monkwearmouth dirt and into grand society over the water. What for would I want to leave me folk here? I wadna. What for would I want to be lying in a bed wi' Bob Brown's body next to me at night and what for would I want to be smiling and pretending to be no-one at all to his Mam, who sits lofty in her chair all day with a cap and strings to it like Queen Victoria and a sour look on her face? And what for would I want to be curtseying to the portrait of Captain Ned Welton, her brother, that hangs over the fireplace as if he were someone, when there's Captains a-plenty in me own family? All this I have seen when his sisters asked me to go over wi' the patterns for the gowns but really it was so their Mam could cast an eye on me.

Bob Brown may be the life and soul of every party as they say and he may play the one string fiddle an all like an angel on the harp, an he may sing a silly ballad or a bawdy one as I've heard until the ladies swoon, but I'll ne'er swoon. He may come a-courting as often as he likes but I'll ne'er tak him. There will never be a man for me like Hoppy and though he is happy and wed to Miss Laura and is in Bishopwearmouth now, I can see him for he still visits old parishioners here in Monkwearmouth and still he comes often to sit quiet in Marleys and I can talk wi' him of things others do not dream of. Nay man will ever match Mr. Hopkinson with his wide smile and his eyes that often seem to laugh even when he talks of serious things. He is not for me nor ever would be, so I'll nay wed and that is my last word.

December 25th 1897   6.00am

The workrooms at Marleys Buildings are already occupied, even though it is Christmas Day. Meggie and her mother must work all day to get the gowns ready for the New Year's Eve Ship Owners' Ball. The ladies placed their orders at the last minute and according to whatever latest journal they study, change their minds with every turn of page and whim of fashion. Meggie works the treadle machine and Marjorie, white with stomach pains and the sickness that she has been suffering increasingly over the last year, is propped up in the narrow bed in the back room. It is quieter there and she can work at the pin tucks and buttonholes without being bothered by the customers who call to see her daughter in the workroom.

The women have been working for nearly five hours when Miss Christabel, Miss Alicia and Miss Dorothea arrive. Their carriage drew up at the door of Marleys Buildings and their driver led them to the entrance and up the steep wooden stairs to the third floor, for it is certainly not safe for ladies to venture on to these dockyard streets without an escort, even though as Owners' daughters they might expect to be respected. With folk of this vicinity, however, one can never be sure and it is a pity that little Meggie Balcombe has her business in such a place when it would be more convenient for ladies to call in Hendon or somewhere on the South side of the river. Meggie's reputation though, is such as to make it impossible to go elsewhere and the almost intolerably low streets of Monkwearmouth must be braved in order to visit her premises. From the workrooms Meggie hears the clattering of heels and the excited giggling of the young ladies who burst through the door.

"A Merry Christmas to you, ladies," she says.

"And a Merry Christmas to you, Meggie," says Miss Christabel, "and Meggie you'll never guess what we have come about, leg o' mutton sleeves, Meggie!"

"Yes," Miss Dorothea joins in, "we have just returned from School, where we have been for weeks and weeks, and you can't imagine how tedious it is, and there are no fashion books, even though we are supposed to be there to improve and learn how to be high ladies and know our etiquette and goodness, Meggie, how can we improve without fashion books, and how can we make good matches when fine gentlemen will not look at us in yesterday's fashions!"

"Yes, so we must have the very latest. Leg o' mutton sleeves as worn in Paris, Meggie!" says Miss Alicia.

"Now don't be *ennuyante*, that's French, Meggie, and we learn it to become high ladies, don't say it is too late and the sleeves are already done on our Ball Gowns," says Miss Dorothea, "for if they are done—"

"—they must be undone!" says Miss Christabel, as they burst into shrieks of laughter, "and that without delay, dearest Meg, and we must have leg o' muttons!"

"Young ladies," says Meggie, "there are just five days to go before the Ball and I have at least a dozen orders to complete. It's impossible to re-do the sleeves now."

"A dozen gowns, Meg? And pray, do tell us, are any of them with leg o' muttons?"

"Why no, they are not, for I should never be done if all the young ladies were to want them now."

"But, dearest, sweetest Meggie that is precisely the reason why we must have them. We must, we must!" cries Miss Christabel, "listen, Alicia has a little secret, yes, Alice, we will tell Meggie. Alicia has a beau and he will be at the Ball, and how is she to win his affections in a gown without the leg o' mutton sleeves?"

"Will his affections depend on such things then?" asks Meggie.

"Aye, they will. Oh Meggie ye knows very little of gentlemen! Save Alicia, save us all and let us be the belles at the Ball. See here, we have pictures cut from Mama's journal, look, see here, 'leg o' mutton sleeves, buttoned at the elbow, as worn by the ladies of Parisian Society.' "

"You will never get ye a man, Meggie, if ye do not wear the leg o' muttons yourself," giggles Miss Christabel.

"When the likes of Meggie is a-wearing them, we will be a-wearing some other Paris mode," says Miss Dorothea.

"Anyway, I hear that a good match may be made for you, Meggie," says Miss Alicia.

"That is not so," Meggie replies quickly.

"Well, that's what I heard," Miss Alicia continues, "they say that Robert Brown, eldest son of Pilot Brown comes a-calling and that he is mad for ye, Meggie."

"Do they say that, then? I know nought of it." Meggie picks up the pictures of the sleeves and studies them.

"And it would be a good match, and bring you over the water where we could visit without dread, and you'd be a Pilot's wife and maybe even Pilot Ruler's wife which is something, I'm told."

"I will try and re-work the sleeves," says Meggie, "but I have only me Mam to help us at this time, and it will be dfficult, what with the wants of other ladies too."

"Yes, but Megs, if other ladies should come asking for the leg o' muttons for the Ball, ye will say no." Miss Dorothea takes Meggie's arm beseechingly.

"I will say 'no' because I canna take on more work before the New Year."

"Do ye promise us then to do it, Meggie?"

"Wait, I must ask me Mam if she can do more of the other work. Wait while I ask me Mam."

Meggie leaves the girls, chattering and giggling, as she opens the door to the back room. Her mother sits propped up with two pillows, her head forward as if bent over the cloth between her fingers. The needle and thread lies on the cover in front of her.

"Mam," Meggie goes over to her, "Mam, you're tired out. I canna ask ye to do more, but the shipyard ladies is come — Mam?"

Meggie goes over and touches her mother's bowed head. "Mam," she says. Meggie cannot scream, cannot make any noise. Her Mam, Marjorie, is dead. The sickness that was getting so bad has done for her. Meggie stands at her side, her hand over her mouth to suppress the panic she feels. "Mam," she says again.

Outside the giggling and the chatter of the ladies rises to a crescendo. All that Meggie knows is that she must keep working for now she is all that stands between her family and destitution. She leaves the back room and closes the door turning the handle quietly.

"It's all right," she says, "Ye shall have your gowns by the day of the Ball."

"And the sleeves, Meggie?"

"And the sleeves as ye want them."

"Thankyou, Megs,"says Miss Alicia taking her hands and jumping up and down. Then they run to the stairs and clatter down like over-excited children. Meggie hears them calling to the driver. When the coach has pulled away she goes downstairs and knocks on the door of old Mr. Marley who owns the building.

"What d'ye want?" he says, coming to the door.

"Mr. Marley, will ye go and fetch a doctor, please, and will ye go and fetch one o' me brothers, whichever one ye can find, Mr. Marley, maybe in the Public House by now. Me Mam is dead, Mr. Marley. Me Mam has died."

§

Charles Girdlestone Hopkinson unfolds the piece of lined paper that John Balcombe, the eldest son of the late John Richard, has given to him. He reads:

Dear Mr.Hopkinson, Me Mam died on Christmas Day. Best Wishes, Meggie.

He folds the paper with its careful handwriting, and puts it back in the envelope. He turns to John Balcombe, who stands with head bowed, his hat in his hand at the door of the Study.

"How did this happen, John?"

"She was always sick, Mr. Hopkinson. She couldna keep anything down, but Miss Laura's father, I mean Dr. Blumer, was away and the other doctor came to Marleys Buildings where me Mam an me sister was working."

"On Christmas Day, John?"

"Well, that's the busiest time for the dress-making, Mr. Hopkinson, an me sister had many orders for the New Year Ball."

"All right, go on, John."

"The other doctor, he looked at me Mam. He said she was dead, but we knew it already. He said it was heart. Her heart stopped."

"Thankyou, John. My wife will be sad to hear this. She was very fond of your mother. What about you grandmother, Ganny Laidlaw, how is she taking it?"

"Me Ganny sits upstairs and says that life is naught but grief and why doesna the Lord tak her, since she is dead already. She says she canna grieve more fer arl the tears is out o' her."

"John, I will come back with you to Hardwick Street. Wait, I'll get the dog cart. Sit down, John, whilst I tell my wife. She will want to see Meggie too, I know. You'll take a cup of tea, John. I'll have one brought to you."

He rushes out of the Study. John Balcombe sits uneasily, his hat slowly revolving between his hands, a tingling of nerves in his throat. He could do with something stronger than a cup of tea. Within a few minutes Mr. Hopkinson returns with his wife. John Balcombe rises to his feet.

"Oh, Mrs. Hopkinson, Miss Laura that was, ye've heard the news."

"That I have, John. Will you tell Meggie that I will come and see her tomorrow. It's best that my husband goes with you now, but tell Meggie that I will come early tomorrow morning to help with the laying-out and do what I can for Ganny, and for all of you."

"Thankyou, Miss Laura. Meggie'll be glad o' that."

The maid, Clancey, who has not left the employ of Charles Hopkinson, enters with a small tray on which is a cup of tea. John Balcombe takes it but his hands shake, not so much with the distress of the last days as with the fact that he has not had a drink for several hours. Clancey bends down to whisper in his ear, "There's a good drop o' hard stuff in the tea, lad. Sup it up."

"Drink your tea, John, and I'll just go and get my coat," Charles Hopkinson and his wife withdraw into the passage outside.

"It was heart, then," says Charles.

"It was not heart, my love, or it was only heart in the sense that every heart stops beating whatever the cause of death. My father examined Marjorie many times. He said it was an ulcer of the stomach, and for that he treated her but he knew for sure that it was the ulcer that cannot be mended. A cancer. Poor Marjorie, poor body! She suffered. Go and see what you can do for the family, Charles, and be sure to tell Meggie that I will help with the laying out tomorrow. What a terrible New Year for that poor family."

"Meggie," calls John Balcombe, "Mr. Hopkinson is here. He shouts up the stairs,

"Meggie, Mr. Hopkinson is here."

The door of Ganny Laidlaw's room opens and closes quietly, and Meggie Balcombe looks down from the landing.

"Mr. Hopkinson" she says "Me Mam is laid in the back room." Her brother John turns and goes out into the street. He hesitates for a moment and then, glad to be away from a place of such sadness, he lights a cigarette and ambles off towards the Public House to re-join his brother, Jim, and his uncles, Thomas and Robert Laidlaw.

Meggie comes down the stairs to where Charles Hopkinson holds out his arms and closes them around her small, frail body. She turns her head and rests it on his shoulder.

"There is naught in this life but dying," she sobs, "naught but sadness. What is to become of us?"

He cannot reply. All his theology, all the profundity of his thinking, his faith, his belief, his certainty, his uncertainty, his resolve, everything deserts him.

"My canny lass," he says, stroking her hair.

She leads him into the kitchen which is empty and cold. The fire that had burned cheerfully on Christmas Day is out and no-one has re-lit it.

"I am sorry, Mr. Hopkinson, I have not had time to tidy and light the fire."

"Where are the boys, Meggie? Where are your brothers?"

"Our Tom is with the Pilots where he is helper."

"And the others?"

"Jim and John is, you know where they is."

"And what about Thomas and Robert Laidlaw, your Ganny's boys?"

"Since his accident me uncle Thomas canna work, an me uncle Robert, he can work, but—"

"Where are they now?"

"At the Duzzy, wi' me two brothers."

"At the Duzzy! At the Duzzy! And what is your Ganny doing?"

"She canna do—"

"So there is no-one here to help to keep the house, no-one except you, Meggie?"

"Well, I must do my best, but we have nay money coming in except for Tom, but he is only Pilot's helper, and I canna keep the house an get through all the sewing for New Year, which I must do, an must get someone to help us. I must work now, Mr. Hopkinson. There is no other. I am sorry there is nay fire to welcome ye but I have lit me Ganny's fire if you would prefer to gan upstairs."

"You misunderstand me, Meggie. I will not leave you today. I am going now to buy hot pies and peas."

"I have a bit bacon for me Ganny, but I must get back to Marleys to finish the work."

"Then we will eat our pies at Marleys. Get your Ganny's bacon ready and take it to her. I will go and get the pies."

She opens the cupboard beside the kitchen fire and takes out her purse.

"The boys has borrowed me money for today, Mr. Hopkinson, I canna buy pies an tha.'"

"Put your purse away, girl. We are having good pies today." He turns and goes towards the door, then he turns back, "Meggie," he says, " Meggie, I— never mind, wait for me at Marleys, I will be back shortly."

Charles Girdlestone Hopkinson burns with anger. He strides down the street and pushes open the door of the Public House. He hardly notices the fog of smoke, the noise, and the smell of beer as he pushes his way to the Bar. Nor is he aware of the whispers as he enters.

"It's Mr. Hopkinson, lookya. The Reverend, used to be here at St. Peter's."

"What can I get you Reverend?" asks the barman.

"Whiskey," he says.

"We haven't seen you in here before, Mr. Hopkinson," says the barman, pouring out the measure.

"No, but maybe it's time you did." He drinks the whiskey in one gulp and puts his money down on the Bar. Then he looks around. His voice, always deep and loud enough to proclaim God's word to the entire congregation of a church, now breaks through the noise.

"Where's Jim and John Balcombe? Yes, and I'll have Thomas and Rob Laidlaw too!"

John Balcombe emerges from the press of men around the Bar. He hauls Jim out with him and they stand before Charles Hopkinson.

"What are you doing? What are you doing to help your family?" His voice now fills the Bar room, as the company go silent.

"Me Mam is dead, me Dad is dead, what family?" Jim's speech is already slurred.

"Then who is to provide for the rest of ye? Who is to pay the rent and see to the victuals?"

The brothers are silent. Then Robert Laidlaw emerges from the crowd, followed by his brother Thomas.

"And when did you last work, Rob Laidlaw? And who provides a roof over your head, eh?" Charles Hopkinson confronts him.

Rob Laidlaw comes right up to Charles Hopkinson and faces him, "Very well fer ye to come pokin' your clergical nose into our business, you who live in a gran' house and was never hungry in your life and never had to lift a hammer on steel when your body was near broken wi' the pain of it, aye, an never knew the longing for some'at to tak awa the pain o' living, an the only thing to do tha' Reverend, is in a bottle, no a church! Gan awa' wi' you, Reverend. Gan awa' and sup up wi' the bosses where ye belongs."

John Balcombe puts out his arm to push his uncle back. "Leave off, Rob, leave the Reverend be."

"I suggest you go back to the house and do what you can to help Ganny Laidlaw and your sister and the four of ye, four grown men stop wasting your time and your wages and think about the welfare of your family."

Robert Laidlaw steps forward again, "Aha, now we's getting to it, lads. It's me niece, Meggie he's on about, our Meggie. You've always taken a good bit interest in her, haven't you, Reverend, ever since she was a bairn. A good bit interest. Listen, you, Reverend or whatever you be, I'm head of the household at 24 Hardwick Street now. And I'm telling ye, man, leave me niece alone. D'you hear me, man, d'you hear me?"

"I hear you well, Rob Laidlaw, and you're right. I have always respected Meggie. She's too good for you. What are you going to do, let her work for the lot of ye? Spend your days and half your nights here, all four of you, while she works like a slave to keep you, and when you come in at all hours all she gets from you is shouting and drunken fighting and yes, you know what else. Yes, I do care about Meggie, and it's a good thing I do, because no-one else does it seems."

"I'll gan back to the house," says John, "an Jim'll come wi' me."

Robert Laidlaw spits on the ground and lurches backwards into the crowd. "A man o' God, tha,'" he says to anyone that will listen, "a man o' God an a married man, that's after me niece. Tha's wha' they's like, them lot."

"Gerraway, man," says one of his mates, "He's a good man that 'un."

In Marleys Buildings Meggie waits for the hot pies, though in truth she has hardly eaten for two days since the shock of her mother's death. Then she hears the confident sound of Charles Hopkinson's boots on the wooden uncarpeted stairs. He enters with the pies, wrapped in their greaseproof paper and Meggie spreads out some unused pattern paper on the work table, on which to put the food. He takes his pocket knife and cuts the pies into smaller pieces. Mr Hopkinson, Meggie notes again, eats enthusiastically and talks with his mouth full when he has something urgent to say.

"Meggie, listen. It's no good for you here. You've got to get away, lass."

"I canna Hoppy. I canna leave me Ganny an me brothers now."

"You can. Whatever chance you have, take it and get away."

"I have no chance."

"Listen, as long as you stay in Hardwick Street, those brothers will not work. They'll waste their time and their money, what little they have, in drink and women, you know that, Meggie."

"They's not bad boys, really."

"No, they're not, but as long as you are there to provide and work and keep house, they will never pull themselves together."

"What about me Ganny, then?"

"Ganny Laidlaw has two sons. If you're not there, Meggie, they will have to support their mother."

"Thomas canna. His back is bad since the accident, when he near died."

"His back is nay bad enough to stop him getting to the Duzzy and carrying on there."

They sit in silence, crunching on the hot pastry and enjoying the pork jelly that drips from the side between the pastry and the pork.

"I have no-where to go. All my folk are here, you know that."

"I hear that you have somewhere to go."

"Where's that?"

"I hear that Robert Brown comes a-courting here."

"You mean I should accept Bob Brown, you mean that, Hoppy?"

"He can offer you a decent life and a better home than you have here."

"But I feel nothing for him."

"No, maybe not, but marriage is not always about feeling. It is usually about living."

How can she tell him what she feels, then? How can she tell him of her whole body stiffening and recoiling from Bob Brown's touch? How the sweet smell on Bob Brown's breath is sour and not at all like the sweetness of his own breath.

"But we has nothing to talk about, he and me. He does not understand me thoughts, Hoppy. He doesna listen to me thoughts. He doesna know me mind at arl."

"Maybe that is not as important as the chance to get a better life. Many people take that chance, make that choice."

"Maybe many people do. I am sure that's true, but I canna. "

"It is for the best, lass."

"You dunna believe that, Hoppy. Why do you tell me things that you dunna believe?"

"I truly believe that you deserve a better life, and that life here will bring you to the same untimely end as your Mam and Dad. I cannot bear to think of that, Meggie. If there are other things that I believe, you know that I cannot say them."

They sit in silence again. She wipes her fingers slowly on her handkerchief for she must be careful not to get any of the grease from the pie onto the stuff.

"We both know of things that we must not say," he continues, "but Meggie, wherever you are, in whatever circumstances, I shall be your friend, always. I will find you, whatever happens."

The long silence that follows in which each of them considers what has been said, is shattered by the loud noises on the stairs, as Robert Laidlaw bursts through the door.

"So," he shouts, staggering in the doorway, "so, there you are, Reverend, just as I thought, wi' ma niece. Can't leave ma niece alone can ye? I telled ye ti keep awa' from Meggie." He lurches forward and raises his fist, "Ye'll do wha' I tells ye now, Meggie, ye'll no' hae more ti do wi' this clergyman. We'll hae less o' church, an God, an Reverends tha' come sniffing aroon. Ye'll do wha' I tells you, woman!"

"You're drunk, Rob Laidlaw," Charles Hopkinson stands up and faces him, "you're drunk and if you lay a hand on your niece, I'll have you up before the magistrate, never fear."

Meggie looks up at them. "Rob," she says, "Gan home now. Gan awa' home, man. Tell me Ganny ah'll no be long, an then ah'll make up the fire an see to some victuals. Gan awa home now, Rob."

He looks at her and without a word, turns and moves to the door unsteadily, then he clatters down the stairs.

"I will not tolerate the thought of you living like this, Meggie," says Charles Hopkinson, "promise me that you will consider what I have said, promise me."

"I will think about it."

"These lads will never pull themselves together until you go."

" I will think about it, but I wish you had not said it."

"It has been said to you before, I'm sure, by others. Maybe by your Mam."

"It has been said to me many times by others, Hoppy, but I wish that you had not said it."

She clears the work table and takes up the sewing. They sit quietly together until at four o' clock the darkness begins to fall.

HENDON 1899

CHAPTER SEVENTEEN

Number 3 Salem Hill in Hendon, on the South side of the River Wear is a substantial terraced house of four storeys and a basement seen through an iron grill below the pavement. The front door, solid symbol of a growing respectability, is approached by five stone steps with a cast iron hand-rail. The colour of the house itself has been determined by the amount of soot in the air, so that the brickwork is blackened and the whole terrace has a rather gloomy appearance but the steps are white and scrubbed. Every morning at about seven o' clock and mostly before it gets light they are scoured to whiteness by a little woman whose skirts are hitched up for ease of movement revealing a pair of bandy legs with which she was not born, but which became deformed as a result of poor feeding in infancy and dire poverty. She has large reddened hands and strong arms. This same little woman has lit the fires and prepared the ewers of hot water to take to the rooms of the family. Having scrubbed the steps and fed the parrot in the basement, she prepares the tea, lays out the bread and the marmalade and awaits the various breakfast orders. After this there is the general dusting and cleaning, all to be accomplished before noon when she changes into a black dress with a white apron and cap and becomes a maid. She opens the door to callers, takes their coats, brings refreshments and conveys messages from the mistress of the house to the woman below stairs who without much skill in culinary matters, is called 'cook'. Cook does not live in, but arrives in the morning to prepare 'dinner' which is at one o' clock and leaves after 'tea' or 'high tea'. This bandy legged maid of all work has a room in the attic beneath the low sloping ceilings where in winter she is allowed some coals for a small fire but which in summer is stuffy and air-less.

A person of such a humble, one might almost say exploited position in the household, is nevertheless expected to perform her duties in all their diversity whilst remaining deaf, mute and blind when it comes to witnessing the goings-on of the family she serves. The abject poverty of her own family who live in Barrington Street, running parallel with Hardwick Street in Monkwearmouth and the rickets which have caused the deformity in her legs give her the background and appearance of a somewhat handicapped person, and therefore the mistress of the house, who was Mary Welton before she married Thomas Brown, takes inadequate legs for an inadequate head. In this she is mistaken, for Lily Atkinson is, as they say, 'all there'. She sees, she hears, but on the whole she does not talk of the family's business for she considers herself fortunate to have a position that allows her to wear the uniform of a ladies' maid, given her lack of height and ungainly side to side gait. However, she listens with particular interest to conversations that concern her childhood friend, Meggie Balcombe.

"Thomas," she hears the mistress say to her Pilot husband, "I want you to speak seriously to Bob. Are you listening, Thomas?"

He puts down his newspaper and sighs, "Aye," he says wearily.

"That girl o'er the water is making a fool o' him. Dilly dallying, keeping him on a string. People'll be talking."

"Aye."

"It's high time they wed, people are talking."

"Aye, so you said." Thomas Brown's gentle eyes and good-natured face turn to his wife, "so what folks is these, then, that's talking?"

"Everyone."

"Everyone?"

"Yes, Thomas. That girl makes a fool out of our Bob. He's been courting her for two years, maybe more, and everyone knows, yet it seems she's in no hurry to be wed. They must be wed by the New Year, or folk will talk."

"I thought you said that folk was talking now. D'you mean tha' they will talk more than they is talking now?"

"You know what I means. Our family is a credit to Captain Welton, any slur on our name is a slur on his, and I willna have it!"

"Ned Welton is on the other side o' the world, Mary. He has business in the China seas, I canna believe he is a-sitting aboard ship, in his cabin, biting his nails wi' anxiety about our Bob."

"His good name and reputation is in our hands when he is away."

"And it is heartily to be wished that he would make a speedy return to these shores, and tak wi' him his cursed parrot when he departs again. If Ned Welton is such a damn fine fellow wi' a spotless reputation, where did his parrot learn all them words? It screeches them words from morn 'til night. Tis a bird without shame, I tell ye."

"Tis a sea-going parrot. It cannot be helped."

"It is nay a sea-going parrot. It's a land-lubber parrot! It's a parrot that's lived in our below stairs for nigh on two years, disturbing the peace. It's no' a God-fearing bird, that one."

"We will look after Ned's parrot as long as he wishes, Thomas, and Meggie Balcombe is either Mrs. Robert Brown by the turn of the century, or she is left to herself to be no-one at all in a household of disreputable men."

"Bob is his own man." Thomas Brown opens up his newspaper again and begins to read.

"Aye," his wife pulls down the newspaper and peers over the top. "Therefore speak to him firmly." She sits back down in her seat, then rises again and addresses her husband over the top of the paper, "and when the marriage is arranged, the girl is to come before me."

"Why?"

"Because she is from a poorer class and must be instructed how to enter a respected family, a family connected by blood to Captain Welton."

"Aye, and his confounded parrot."

"A family with a daughter who is just married to Preacher Spooner as well. Tell our Bob that he is to bring the girl to me as soon as he has spoken."

That evening the bandy legged servant hurries across the bridge to Monkwearmouth. She calls at 24 Hardwick Street, but not finding her friend there she runs with as much speed as possible to Marleys Buildings where she finds Meggie still at the treadle machine.

"Come in Lily," says Meggie, "sit you down, lass."

"Give me some o' that, Meggie, I'll help ye with that bit sewing. I'm no happy when I'm idle."

"Gerraway, lass, ye dunna ken what idle is." Meggie passes over the piece that is to be hemmed by hand.

"Meggie, has ye seen Bob Brown today?"

"Nay, I havena, an me heart doesna bleed for that! Far as I knows he is gone on a clipper, Southampton bound, and God willing and an unfavourable wind it will be three weeks before I sees him again."

"The wind is a following one, I hears, an he will be here in no time, an Missis is kickin' up an' sayin' ye must be wed, an that before the New Year."

"An if I willna wed?"

"Then he is to leave off comin.'"

"I dunna care."

"Well, mak sure ye dunna care, mind, Meggy, for it's a good chance, an your brothers an your uncles is going down fast."

Meggie Balcombe puts down her work after the visit of her friend, Lily Atkinson. She calls for the apprentice she has taken on to put the kettle onto the little fire in the back room that used to warm her mother as she sat up in the narrow bed.

"Mak us some tea, Ellen," she says.

Bob Brown has been visiting since before her mother died and though Meggie has given little encouragement she has not discouraged him either and now she must face up to the fact that an understanding has arisen between them. She realises that she must make a firm decision, one way or another. She is twenty six years old, an age when she could be said to be a spinster and 'on the shelf.' Without marriage, a future of toil, a life-time of supporting her brothers and living in a household of noise, dirt and increasing depravity appears to stretch out before her. Bob Brown, after all, comes from a long established family of Pilots. At the beginning of the Century his forebears risked their lives in a storm the violence of which had never been known before, to save a shipwrecked crew and they have done this many times since. His great grandfather Thomas Brown, after whom his father is named, served under the command of Admiral Nelson in the Battle of Trafalgar. His ship was The Minotaur and his great uncle, Benjamin Brown was under the same command aboard The Revenge. These seamen were heroes whose courage and loyalty were beyond doubt and his father is well known for his kindness, fairness and gentle manner in spite of the dangerous nature of his calling. Life as Bob Brown's wife would certainly be quieter and easier. Later that day she goes upstairs to see Ganny Laidlaw.

"What shall us do, Ganny?" she asks.

"Tak the lad, hinny. Tak yeer chance whilst ye has it."

"But, Ganny, what will become of me brothers without me?"

"As long as ye is here, hinny, yeer brothers will rest on ye. When ye is gone twill be the making o' them arl."

"But what about – ye knows – the ways of men an tha.'"

"Men is arl the same, from the highest to the lowest, arl beasts and animals, tha' is except ma Johnny Laidlaw. But he was awa' at sea an when he wasna his mind an his heart was. He had his mind on nay pleasure but the sea, but when he took it wi' me it was mine too. But arl men is the same, lass, ye canna choose between them."

"But I may no be able ti bear it, Ganny."

"Hwha'! No be able ti bear wha' arl other women bears! Di ye think tha' arl the women in this street is waitin' wi' joy ti be used by their men and hae more bairns. Nay, a woman must suffer. It's the way of arl life, tis the Curse of Eve, tis the punishment fer wha' she did in the Garden o' Eden. Ye'll get used wi'it, like us arl."

"Not arl men is like tha', Ganny."

"Arl! Arl is!"

"Wha' about the Queen?"

"Ach! Poor body! Her sufferin' in tha' is over now, but lookya at arl her bairns! Poor body! Tak yeer chance, hinny, ye'll no get a better one."

So now there's me and me three brothers downstairs, me Ganny and me uncles upstairs, and on the top floor there's Stephensons, our lodgers with five children. That's fourteen of us in this house. The men drinks and shouts by day and night, the bairns is shrieking and running in and out wi' no shoes, the stairs stink and mostly I would rather burst me bladder than go to the earth closet down the yard.

In Hendon I would but a bare mile from Christ Church, Bishopwearmouth.

I will marry wi' Bob Brown.

§

The first floor drawing room at 3 Salem Hill is shielded from the daylight by heavy lace curtains once white but which have now taken on a brownish colour in keeping with the general mood of the room which is sombre. A child pressing his or her nose to the curtains as little Mary Brown used to do or gathering the folds to drape around her head in an imaginary wedding veil, would smell the accumulated odours of stale tobacco and age. This is the room where her mother, also Mary Brown, formerly Mary Welton, spends most of the day. She has modelled herself closely on the appearance, as she has studied it in drawings and even seen in a photograph, of Queen Victoria, a lady whose face in repose takes on a dour and down-turned look of some severity particularly around the mouth. It is of course well recorded, though few have seen it, that the Queen has moments of great hilarity, even gaiety, and that her face when lit by the spontaneity of her smile reminds of the sun breaking through an obscuring cloud taking everyone by surprise, but this interruption in the gravity of Her Majesty's expression and demeanour does not occur as far as Mary Brown, formerly Welton, is concerned. For her, life has too many possibilities of descent into an uncontrolled loss of dignity and rather like the passenger on board ship who feels that he must stay awake to keep the vessel afloat, so Mrs. Brown must keep herself and her features under control if the family is to retain and indeed gain in respectability. This concept of respectability is not to be set aside lightly. Before Industrialisation, families did not live under the strain of being closely packed together with all the tensions and temptations that such living brings. The family made a living from the land, or from the sea, dwelling in small communities. Above them were the Gentry, and there was no such thing as a Middle Class, except perhaps in terms of the doctor or the clergyman, or the lawyer, educated people who were respected as such. Now Mary Brown is aware of the fact that though her husband and sons still brave the perils of the sea daily, they have risen, and not without the help of her determination, to a status that is located above the labouring class and below the Gentry. In other words they are in the Middle and what the new Middle must strive for above all other things is the recognition conferred by Respectability. Respectability of course, is not the same as respect. Respectability means that whatever is going on in the bosom of the family, no sign of it will be given on the façade that faces the world. The brass that covers the top step will be polished and the other steps scrubbed every day and thus with clean veiled windows and whitened steps no-one will be able to speak ill of the household within. It is true that with a husband whose interests in life are more or less bounded by the sea and the stars, particularly the stars, for he is building a modest observatory at the top of the house, and moreover, with four thick-set and pugnacious sons, it is necessary to be vigilant if the coveted respectability is to be maintained and it is for this reason that she is determined to put an end to the speculation about her eldest son's interest in women and their interest in him, by marrying him off to a quiet girl who can be trained to become a wife in her own image.

Meggie Balcombe is led up the stairs of 3 Salem Hill by Lily Atkinson. As it is mid noon Lily is wearing her black dress, white pinafore and cap. The dress was in fact made for her by Meggie, since the uniform of a previous maid could not be modified to fit Lily's size and shape. Before knocking on the door Lily presses Meggie's hand and whispers a word of encouragement in her ear, then she opens the door to announce the arrival to Mrs. Brown, who sits in her upright chair, hair tightly drawn back under a long ribboned cap, as true a copy of the Queen herself as one could wish to find anywhere.

"Miss Balcombe is here, ma-am," she says. She nudges Meggie to go forward, and then hovers in the doorway.

"Thankyou, Lily. Go on, girl, you may leave. Sit down, Miss Balcombe." She gestures to a similar straight backed chair opposite her own.

"I shall call you Meggie, though I believe your name is Margaret."

"Yes, ma-am, after me Grandmother, Ganny Laidlaw."

"Well, yes, never mind that. You are to marry my eldest son."

"Yes, ma-am."

"He tells me, as do my daughters, that you are employed as a dress-maker."

"I am not employed, ma-am, I has me own business and an apprentice."

"You are in business?"

"Yes, ma-am."

"And why does not your Mama keep you at home to help with the running of the household?"

"Me Mam is dead, ma-am."

"I'm sorry to hear that, but surely your Pa needs you all the more to take your mother's place."

"Me Dad is dead too, ma-am."

"Ah. You have brothers I believe, one of whom helps my husband, a pilot's helper."

"Yes, ma-am."

"And your brothers are undisciplined, I hear."

"At times, ma-am, but they is good boys, really, and I am sorry for the trouble they causes."

"Do not be, girl. I am the mother of boys and I knows the ways of men. That is why I must talk to you."

"Yes, ma-am."

"When you are married to Bob, you will call me Mam."

A shadow passes over Meggie's face, "but me Mam, me own Mam—"

"In this house you will call me Mam, is that understood?"

"Yes."

"Firstly then, men is all the same. Start as you mean to go on. When you are married you will not work. You will give up your business, you will make no more dresses. If you work, my son will let you do it. He will not labour whilst he has you to keep him. Men is like that. You will live here in this house, and help my daughters. In time you may be able to rent a small house nearby. You will be with my daughter Sarah, and my elder daughter, Mary, who as you may know is married to Preacher Spooner. By the way, what religion are you?"

"I goes to the Church, ma-am."

"We are not Church of England. We follow the Methodist line. In particular we adhere to the message of Preacher who tells us of the evils of drink, and reminds of the hell-fire that awaits the fornicator. I do not suppose, however that my son-in-law will make any objection to your attendance at St. Ignatius. Now lift your eyes, Meggie and look above the mantelpiece. What do you see?"

"I see a picture of a gentleman in Captain's uniform."

"That is Captain Ned Welton, my brother. When he is ashore he makes his home with us."

"We has Captains in my family too, ma-am."

"Your captains are nought but Master Mariners in the Merchant Service. Captain Welton is a naval man. He is a Captain in the Queen's Navy. He is respected and honoured, both in this house and throughout the world. As my son's wife I don't doubt that you will meet Captain Welton, and that you will be sensible of the honour."

"Yes, ma-am."

Mrs. Brown leans forward and pulls the bell rope by the fireplace. The door opens rather too quickly and Lily enters, for in truth she has never wandered far from it.

"Lily, Miss Balcombe can be shown out now. Tak a bit fruit cake, Meggie, when ye goes. Lily will gie ye some." Mary Brown's style of speech sometimes lapses after a prolonged period of the exertion required to keep it apart from the accent of common folks.

"How d'ye get on?" whispers Lily as Meggie descends the stairs in front of her.

"I dunno, Lily." A tear forms in Meggie's left eye. Lily puts a hand on her so that she turns. Then Lily gently wipes the eye with the edge of her apron.

"Come on, lass. I'll be here arl the time. We'll have a bit laugh and some tark together, lookya."

"Ah canna like her, Lily."

"Ye dinna have to. Yeer no marryin' wi' his Mam."

She opens the front door. "I'll no gie ye the cake, Meggie. It's no good cake, not like yeer Mam and yeer Ganny made. They did a real fruit cake."

She puts her arms around her friend, "It'll be arl right, lookya."

§

Laura Blumer Hopkinson notes that her husband has eaten little all day, and that his Study door has remained closed since early morning. She took a tray to him at lunch-time, but the food was largely untouched, although he denied that he was unwell or out of sorts. "I have a difficult discourse to prepare, a knotty theological problem to unravel," he said, and she understands that it is wisdom to leave him undisturbed.

Behind the closed doors, safe from the hustle and bustle of the household and the noise of his growing young family, Charles Hopkinson sits at his desk, his head in his hands. He knows himself to be lucky. Undoubtedly he is happy. Now Vicar of Christ Church, his progress within the Church is certainly more assured. In all probability he will be made a Canon in due course. Like his Bishop, he has a reputation for good debate and openness on theological matters without being controversial and amongst his new Parishioners he is highly respected. Certainly he still takes the dog-cart to Monkwearmouth to revisit old friends but after all, his wife's family are still there and they cannot be neglected. He has a wife he deeply respects and who cares for him and understands his needs in every way. She runs his household, brings up his children and manages his finances with admirable common sense. Charles Hopkinson knows himself to be fortunate, secure in Faith, a contented man. It seems, however, that he can never quite escape that mist of gloom, even at times, despair, that descended after the loss of his first wife, and now returns, in spite of everything, for no good reason. Laura Blumer (she is still known by this name in Monkwearmouth) has tried to penetrate the shadow that from time to time surrounds her husband but without success.

"It's little Meggie Balcombe, isn't it," she says. Her husband feels a surge of illogical anger. How dare she try to pin down the profundity of his feelings in such a way.

"It is not. It is not Meggie Balcombe. Please, Laura, do not speak of that. I have much work to do."

"It's for the best, Charles. She cannot continue to live in that house with those men. Let me assure you that within months of Meggie leaving them, those boys will be married and away."

"It's a great pity then, that they do not get themselves away now."

"That will not happen whilst Meggie is there to look after them. It's for the best. The family she will be going to will be able to provide a much more satisfactory life for her."

"Satisfactory!"

"Indeed."

"So that is what we must all aim for is it? A satisfactory life! That is it, that is what it is all about, a satisfactory life!"

"You know what I mean. What else can she hope for, a girl of her background?"

Charles Hopkinson rises to his feet. "Why should not a girl of her background as you call it, have more than 'a satisfactory life' I ask you? Why should she not have joy and fulfilment and true happiness? Uhm! Why not, Laura?"

"I am sure she will have those things. Certainly her father-in-law to be has worked hard. Though he lacks much formal education I hear that he is a thoughtful and scholarly man, who provides well for his family. Meggie will have many more material comforts."

"Material comforts! Ah, so that's the answer? Material comforts! Is that what I must preach, then?"

"Of course not, Charles, but I have lived amongst those Monkwearmouth folk long enough to know that all the spiritual comfort in the world cannot make up for Bread!"

He stands in silence, his eyes blazing with an unaccustomed fury.

"I'm sorry, Charles," she says, "I should not have said that."

He sits down.

"It is for the best," she says.

"I know it is, and I have told her so. Please do not speak of it again. I have very much work to do."

"Well, I will leave you, dear," she says, lightly patting his shoulder. He shrugs her hand away and waits for her to go out of the room shutting the door gently behind her. Then, pushing his papers aside on his desk so that there is a clear space for his elbows, he lowers his head between his hands and stares blankly ahead.

CHAPTER EIGHTEEN

Little Mary Brown can hardly conceal her delight at the prospect of a new sister, for that is how she thinks of Meggie who is to marry her eldest brother. It was Meggie who made the dress in which nearly a year ago she was married to Preacher Spooner. The fact that Preacher chose her as his wife when he had so many ardent admirers amongst the women of his Evangelical Mission was a joy and a surprise for Preacher was tall with thick fair hair that fell over his face in a disconcertingly appealing way when he was moved by the Spirit. Both in his attire and in his person Preacher gave the impression of being newly washed. This strong-limbed man had impeccable manners and an apparent concern for every other living creature. When he spoke the Word of the Lord none could resist his message of repentance and forgiveness, even though it was a hard message with many 'do nots' and prohibitions and many warnings of eternal damnation and hell-fire. On their wedding night little Mary was surprised by Preacher's ardour and apparent experience for chastity and preservation of virginity, resistance to fornication and even thoughts of such things were the very foundations of his teaching. Mary regarded herself as small and slight in build and not very pretty so that when Preacher Spooner began to favour her with his special attention she was utterly won over. Before long all her thoughts centred on him and her wedding day was the most joyful of her life. Preacher explained that he had been, in the past, a Sinner, which accounted for his knowledge of women and the ways of the Flesh. He had felt the very lick of the flames, but that there had been wild rejoicing in Heaven when he had seen the Light and become Saved. The general approval and delight of the family at this union was not entirely shared by her father Thomas Brown for though he wanted only his daughter's happiness he had had to shoulder the financial burden of housing and feeding the couple, since Preacher, being a Man of God, had practically no money and certainly no prospects except in Heaven. Moreover, Mary was now expecting her first child and there was no sign that her husband would be able to offer practical support for his family. Indeed, there was no sign of Preacher. Seven months after the wedding, as Mary's pregnancy was showing, Preacher left to spread the Word in another part of England. He explained that the Lord had called him, and that he had to obey, that nothing except the command of the Lord would part him from his darling little girl, and that before long he would return joyfully having saved many more souls.

Mary's sister, Sarah, was a hard woman, stubborn like her brothers, but Meggie would be different. Meggie would rejoice when the baby was born and they would become best companions. Meggie would look forward, with her, to Preacher's return.

§

Robert Brown stands with his hands behind his back against the small fireplace in Marleys Building, having returned from Southampton rather unexpectedly with a following wind in three days. To tell the truth he and his shipmates have not been too pleased to leave, for congenial and affordable company well away from their own doorstep so to speak, was readily available in that Port but Bob Brown will not allow passing pleasures of that nature to divert him from the achievement of his ambition. A Pilot's life as he knows only too well, is one of unrelieved stress for not only must he be prepared to brave the mountainous black seas, the churning, mysterious infinite deeps, but he must do so in a coble and race against his fellow pilots to reach a ship to bring it into Port. If he fails to reach it first he fails to bring it in and there is no money. Some of the cobles stay out all night or all day in fearful seas and winds as far Northwards as Holy Island in order to be first to approach an incoming vessel. Many men are lost at sea under these conditions and there is something else. Bob Brown is known for his pugnacious temperament. His mouth is firm beneath his proud moustache, his eyes look straight ahead fearlessly. His strong, stocky frame stands upright with resolution. He will not be wrong; he will not give in. At the same time no party is complete without him. He sings, he plays any musical instrument handed to him, he laughs and he knows how to interest the ladies whilst remaining a man's man. But there is this other thing, a demon that is not known about him. Above all things he hates the sea. He detests the heaving waters and he fears them. He is seasick on every trip and he cannot swim. He has never doubted that he would follow his father and grandfather and great grandfather and all the generations before that, even back to the time of Elizabeth the Queen of England, for not to do so would be a betrayal of his family's calling but every trip out to meet that appalling black enemy and its unknown depths calls for strengths that go well beyond the physical, demanding levels of mental resolution that often leave him drained, and secretly exhausted.

Bob Brown has a dark and sometimes violent temper; he bears grudges and makes enemies, but every day and on many nights he knows again his loathing of the sea by the churning of his stomach and he forces himself to confront it. Above all other things he is a man of considerable courage for it does not take courage to do brave things, no, it is only courage when one does them in full knowledge of the cost and in the face of fear.

Now he has a plan. Ships are built in the many Yards on the Wear. They are taken to Middlesborough or Newcastle for engine fitting and without an engine a ship is light in the water and must be guided by Tugs and a Pilot after launching. If he can make himself agreeable to the Ship Yard bosses for he is already known to them, he believes that he can become contracted to at least one or two, exclusively, as their Pilot. In this way he will not have to join the scramble to find ships at sea but will have assured work. He has considered very carefully how to achieve his aim. Firstly, he needs a quiet and respectable wife; secondly he must study the politics of his prospective employers and like them, be seen to be a committed Tory. Thirdly, and probably most important of all he must become a freemason. From time to time he will need to align himself with the Temperance movement or even the Band of Hope, whilst being ready to take a drink in the convivial company of one or two of those with influence. Once he has made his plan clear he does not doubt that he will arouse the indignation of his brothers and his fellow pilots. Their aim is to organise themselves into shifts whereby everyone will take their turn at sea and the stressful, even dangerous competition between them will end. This may be all very well but it is not enough. Bob Brown does not fear their disapproval. He is sure of the direction in which his future lies.

The pose that he has taken up with his back to the fireplace is one that he has noted in the houses of the prosperous middle class. There, men warm the seat of their pants with their hands clasped behind them, whilst they consider matters of weight and substance. This stance completely blocks the heat of the fire from reaching others in the room confirming the importance of the one who has taken it up.

Meggie has heard the heavy footsteps of her husband-to-be on the stairs some minutes earlier and she feels her stomach tighten as she bends over the machine with greater concentration.

"I'm back, then, Meggie."

"I sees that."

"And is ye pleased to see me then?"

"Aye."

"Ye dunna seem pleased."

"I am."

Meggie continues to sit at the machine, concentrating on the work in front of her.

"Then where's a kiss?"

She gets up, re-arranging the weight of the cloth in front of her and goes over to kiss him on the left cheek. As she fears his arm tightens around her in a fierce and unyielding grip.

"Wha' kind of a kiss d'ye call that, girl? The parleyvoos gives kisses like tha' to them's they don't even know. Wha' kind of a kiss is tha' to give to a husband?"

"Ye're no my husband, Bob."

"As good as, an ye may as well learn now wha' kind of a kiss a husband expects, especially when he's been awa' at sea."

So this is the price to be paid then. This is the stark reality of the choice; not something to push away into the recesses of the mind, not to be thought about until later. This is the content of the ticket to a cleaner more secure world of respectability, the world that her deceased parents had striven, against the odds to maintain, the world that had disintegrated since their deaths. This is what it takes to escape from brawling drunks and barefoot bairns and damp rooms and endless toil with the needle and fear of sickness and not being able to get the work done for the demanding gentry and bosses' wives, and most beloved mothers killed with the anxiety that eventually gnaws the stomach away as they labour. At this moment if she struggles to release herself from the grip that fills her with terror and repugnance, she could lose the chance of escape forever.

"Come on, Meggie," he murmurs in her ear, "we can do anything we wants now we're to be wed."

"We're no married yet. It's wrong."

"It's no wrong for them that's to be wed very soon. It maks nay difference."

He pulls her down onto the sofa covered in a shawl where the lady customers sit to look through the pattern books. Above the sofa, on the wall there is a framed black and white picture of kittens playing with a ball of wool that her Mam had cut out of a paper and little Tom had framed to make the workrooms look canny.

"Nay, Bob, stop! What if the apprentice comes in?"

"She willna come in, an if she does she'll learn something that'll do her good."

"Nay, please, Bob!"

"Gerraway girl. Dinna tell me ye never saw a man's organ before, or ye never saw wha' is done wi' it, when ye comes from Monkwearmouth and lives wi' brothers an uncles, an arl yeer beds together an yeer bodies laying side ti side at night ever since ye wuz a babby. Ye knows how ti perform as well as any."

His hands are lifting and pulling on her clothing and at the same time holding her down on the sofa so that she is helpless to prevent what is happening to her. She can hear and feel the wrenching of the delicate stitching at the seams, the workmanship that is her pride being torn by the roughness of his hands, and the shawl that covers the sofa, the best shawl that she and Mam and Ganny have made between them to be good enough for the ladies is tugged this way and that like any old bit cloth. All this as much as the invasion of her body causes her to clench up inside and resist in the only way she can, inside her mind. His breathing comes with heavy groaning noises and the smell on his breath is sweet with that edge of sour that signifies a life lived with repressed fear. His weight crushes down upon her and then suddenly he collapses with a sighing moan.

"It'll be better next time, Meggie. Tis always like that at first. There you are, lass, now it wasn't too bad was it! Dinna vex yoursel' my girl, we'll soon be man an wife. Nay harm's been done."

She puts her hands up to her dishevelled hair and feels for the hairpins that have become tangled and dislocated. Her fingers, trained over the years in a refined dexterity with threads of silk and the most delicate of needles, flutter now in agitation and between her legs she feels a shameful trickle of something wet and warm. He stands up buttoning his trousers and tucking in his shirt. He pulls his braces back up over his shoulders.

"No harm's done," he repeats, "it'll get better ye'll see. Ye'll get used ti it. Arl the women gets used with it. No harm done. I'll leave ye now an be on my way."

She sits up and waits to hear his footsteps heavy on the stairs and then the closing of the street door as he goes. She looks around the room, the workroom that she and her Mam set up together with the sofa and the best shawl and the picture of the kittens that no longer seem so innocent and playful. The room that was hers and no-one else's, where Hoppy came quite often to sit and read or talk a little, her own room which is no longer her own, no longer a place of safety and refuge, and where the shawl lies tangled and scuffed on the floor.

§

Laura Blumer Hopkinson answers the Vicarage door herself and is surprised to see Meggie Balcombe standing in the porch looking a little dishevelled.

"Why, Meggie, come in, lass. Come in out of the rain. You're wet."

"Nay, Miss Laura, it's nothing."

"Well, come in, you look tired."

"Is Hoppy – I mean is Mr. Hopkinson in, please?"

"He's at work in his Study. He's asked not to be disturbed this morning."

"Oh, then I'm sorry, Miss Laura, I'll not trouble him. I'll be on my way."

"No, you will not, my dear. You will sit and have some tea. Perhaps there is some way in which I can help."

"No, it's nothing at all, I'll not trouble you."

"Meggie, are you all right? What about Ganny Laidlaw and your brothers, are they all right? Has something happened?"

"Nay, they are arl well. Everything is all right."

"Well, I do not believe it. Let us go together to see if my husband is still busy. I am sure he would not want you to leave without his seeing you."

Meggie follows Mrs Hopkinson, as she now is, though still called Miss Laura by those who knew her as the doctor's daughter, down the passageway to the door of the Study.

"Charles," his wife calls softly as she knocks gently. There is no response from within.

"He has not been quite himself lately," says Mrs. Hopkinson, "a little out of sorts. He works hard here amongst the Parishioners and it tires him sometimes, but wait, I'll tell him you are here." She knocks again and opens the door very slightly, then almost whispering so as not to disturb him too much she says, "Charles, Meggie Balcombe is here, will you see her?"

Inside the room Charles Girdlestone reaches the door in three great strides and throws it open. "Meggie!" he cries, "Laura, why did you not tell me that

Meggie was here?"

"I did tell you, Charles, I have just told you, my love." She gestures to Meggie to wait outside for a moment and she reaches up to murmur in her husband's ear, "I think Meggie is distressed. She will not tell me, but perhaps she will tell you."

He pushes past her and reaches out his hand to take Meggie's arm and bring her into the room.

"I'll leave you with my husband, Meggie, but you'll take some tea before you go. The weather is rough for walking."

"Walk!" Charles Hopkinson's voice booms out, "walking in this weather! What nonsense is this? I will take Meggie back in the dog cart."

Laura Hopkinson closes the door quietly and retreats down the passageway. Inside the Study, Charles Girdlestone leads Meggie to a chair beside the fire.

"You are not well, Mr Hopkinson?"

"Well enough, Meggie, and the better for seeing you. How are you? How are you, canny lass?"

"I canna marry."

"You are not to be married! But I thought that the matter was decided and that it is for the best."

"Nay, I canna marry."

"Has he told you that he will not marry you then, after all?"

"Nay, he wants ti wed us, but tis me. I canna marry him."

"What has he done? Has he hurt you?"

"Nay." She looks down at her hands lying in her lap. How can she tell this good man who has been her friend and guide, her support and strength since she was a little girl though she is nothing compared with him, how can she tell him of her shame, of what happened in the workroom when the man she is to marry came to call on her? How can she talk to him of her disgust and the soiling that she feels, when in this good man's company she has never felt anything but clean and respected? How can she speak of it, when what she suffered is no more than what she must suffer many times as a wife? He knows of the brutality of life in Monkwearmouth but how could he ever imagine that she would allow any of it to touch her. Surely he would have expected her to resist with all her strength.

"Meggie, I beg you to tell me what has happened. Look at me, lass. Now, what has happened?" She lifts her face.

"Its just that I canna wed wi' him."

"Why not? Why not? It is surely for the best."

"I dinna care for him."

He is silent and sinks back into his chair.

"I hears that you are not so well. Your face is pale," she says.

"Oh Meggie, what is to be done with us, you and I!"

"It will be all right, Mr. Hopkinson. I can work an I can take on another girl to help us, an maybe me brothers will wed soon."

He holds both her hands in his and looks at her down turned face. "Whatever is best for you. I can only say that I want the best, the very best, Meggie, for you."

The front door of 24 Hardwick Street is opened suddenly from the street side and swings out of the control of Robert Laidlaw's hand as he lurches in from the darkness outside.

"Meggie!" he shouts, "Meggie where is ye?"

Meggie Balcombe, in her white flannel nightdress, a shawl around her shoulders opens the door of the downstairs room.

"I'm going to bed, Rob, it's late. Dunna shout like that. It's late, man."

"Late or no late I wants ti know why the whole street was seein' you three days ago wi' the clergyman in his dog cart? Tha' clergyman tha' is no the clergyman fer us now, tha' is gone ti' folks like them at Bishopwearmouth, an yet, as arl is sayin' comes a-ridin' here wi' me niece sittin'up beside him, tha' is ti marry wi' Bob Brown. Is tha' a man o' God, or wha'? Man o' God, tha's bin after me niece since she was a bairn. Wait ye until ah tells Bob Brown, he'll give him man o'God!"

"Haway, man. Ye knows nothin' of Mr. Hopkinson. Gan ye ti yer bed. Yeer Mam is waitin' up fer ye."

Robert staggers towards the stairs and leans heavily against the newel post. Then he begins to climb, muttering as he does so. "Ye'll bring shame on this house, niece, wi' yeer ridin' in them dog carts wi' them Reverends."

"I canna bring more shame than is here already, man. Gan ti bed."

Meggie closes the door and goes back to her narrow bed around which she has managed to fix up a curtain partition affording her a little privacy. She climbs back under the covers and looks up at the cracks in the ceiling. The cracks have been there ever since the house was built when her mother was a young girl and as a child she could form pictures, faces and shapes of animals from them and they were friendly lines, but now they are getting deeper and longer under the trampling weight of her uncle's feet as he lurches around overhead. She stares at the familiar patterns that seem to shudder with the moving light from her candle flame. Her uncle's return from the Duzzy House means that soon her brothers will be back, perhaps with women. Tom will go quietly to his bed in the corner but the others will be rowdy until the drink and the women cause them to fall into a groaning and snoring slumber.

Meggie's eyes fill with tears. She has tried to put a great anxiety out of her mind. She did not think of it when she went to Bishopwearmouth as if the comfort of Mr. Hopkinson's care for her would dissolve it. But now, in the brief moments of calm before the return of the men-folk, it returns and cannot be ignored. It is more than six weeks since Bob Brown's visit to Marleys Building, and the bleeding has not come.

§

On the first day of the Twentieth Century Margaret Ann Balcombe, Dressmaker, of Monkwearmouth, married Robert Brown, Pilot, of Hendon, Sunderland. The young couple moved into a room upstairs at 3 Salem Hill, and under the supervision of his mother and with the connivance of a discreet midwife, a baby was born sometime around August, whose birth was registered on both the 1st and the 3rd of September, there being some confusion as to the actual date. About one thing, however, the young mother was adamant. Although there was no precedent for it in either family, she insisted that the child be named after someone she believed to be most honoured, most worthy of honour, and most fortunate. Meggie's baby was christened Laura.

CHAPTER NINETEEN

A natural order of living soon establishes itself within the house on Salem Hill. The basement kitchen and scullery are largely occupied by Lily Atkinson and the woman who comes in daily to cook. This territory is never visited by the Head of the family or his sons and only rarely by his wife. The attic with its low ceiling is Lily's bedroom and though cramped has the advantage of being extremely warm and comfortable in winter when she has a fire in the small grate. In fact Mary and Meggie often join her there for a pleasant gossip, ignoring the disapproval of the mistress of the house. Mary Welton, now Brown, tries in vain to impress on her daughter and daughter-in- law the folly of mixing on equal and familiar terms with servants. This uncalled-for intimacy she suggests, is likely to impede the family's progress upon the social ladder. Thomas Brown himself for the most part occupies a small room on the ground floor, variously named the Study, the Office, the Library, or the Smoking Room, depending on who is naming it. It contains two large revolving globes on heavy brass and mahogany stands, one of the world and the other of the starry heavens. The various telescopes of awe-inspiring magnificence have been taken up to the little glass Observatory which he has had erected at roof level, but it is this room on the ground floor to which he gratefully retires, sometimes wearing his plum velvet smoking jacket and flat embroidered hat with its silk tassel. Here he contemplates the Universe about which he is an acknowledged authority and when old ship-mates call it is here that vessels and voyages are discussed, and tales told of those fathers and grandfathers who served with Nelson at Trafalgar and whose fingers trace the old shipping lanes on the revolving globe. Here they share their knowledge of the stars, ocean currents, winds and land masses. The eldest son, Bob and his wife, Meggie, occupy two rooms on the second floor where there is also a room for Sarah whose lot in life it seems is to remain unmarried and act as unpaid servant overseeing the activities of Cook and Lily. Sarah's temperament is somewhat dour and certainly cynical. She has heard things about Preacher, and she is not surprised. She does not see why her sister Mary, by virtue of being a married woman, albeit one whose husband is never sighted should have a better and larger room than herself on the first floor, next to the drawing room which is presided over with such dignity by the oil portrait of her uncle, Captain Ned Welton, about whom she has also heard things. The conclusions that she has come to are that most men are not to be trusted and that by and large what you see is not what you get and this is equally true of her brother Bob, whose pugnacious temperament matches her own, and with whom she does not speak for extensive periods of time which makes sharing a floor with him and his new little wife who is friendly with the servant, very difficult.

One year after the birth of Mary Spooner's baby, little Flo has still not been introduced to her father, and in fact it is true to say that no-one has heard of Preacher or his whereabouts, though Mary's faith in him never wavers. Therefore his sudden return to his faithful little wife and baby daughter appears to justify that faith, filling the house at 3 Salem Terrace with Mary's joy. As he explains, the work of a Saver of Souls means that no matter how grievously one feels the separation from one's loved ones, one must obey the command and forsaking wealth, as well as father, mother, wife and children offer up everything in the service of the Lord which is never ending and life-long and it is for this reason and this reason only that after three blissful months of his radiant company resulting in a second pregnancy, Preacher announces that once again he is Called and with much regret leaves within five minutes' of the announcement. Mary's father, a man of generous heart and warm sympathies nevertheless makes an ironic enquiry as to the whereabouts of Preacher's wealth so unselfishly abandoned, since it appears to him that it is he who is now required to house and feed his daughter, her child and inevitably, the child that will be born in six months' time. He goes so far as to suggest that it is no difficult matter to sacrifice something one never had, and it is now growingly apparent that the family of his eldest son Bob will have to move out of 3 Salem Hill. It is fortunate that one-storey cottages are being built in Guildford Street nearby, and number 7 is vacant and ready for occupation.

"It's just round the corner, Meggie," whispers her sister-in-law, "and we shall see each other every day."

"Aye, and Lily will be coming round too and willna be a servant in my house."

§

Number 7 Guildford Street might have been all that Meggie had ever dreamed of. Although only a one-storey terrace house it has a vestibule with a solid front door painted and grained to look like oak leading into a dark hall which gives it an air of gravitas. The first door on the left goes into a front parlour with lace curtains at the bay window, and a large slate fireplace of imitation marble. This room is also dark to preserve the furnishings from too much sunlight, even though too much sunlight is never really a possibility in Guildford Street. This parlour has a peculiar sweet-sour smell because it is hardly ever used, and consequently never heated, in spite of the fact that a brass handled fire-screen with a lead backed mirror decorated with oil painted roses stands in readiness in front of the fireplace. Above the fireplace hangs a black and white picture of kittens unravelling a ball of wool. A second door on the left leads into a cosy kitchen living room, where there is always a good fire in the black-leaded kitchen range. Partitioned off from this room is a small single bedroom on the right, which is not much more than a large cupboard, and beyond it, an extension into the back yard on the left, which is divided into another bedroom and a washhouse. This is ample room for a little family of three, and best of all it is theirs, and the accommodation does not have to be shared with anyone. Meggie has escaped Monkwearmouth and Hardwick Street. She has freed herself from a household of rowdy drunken men, and even from a stern mother-in-law who must be called 'Mam'. She may sit nursing her baby in front of her fire and she even has a girl, Ellen May, aged twelve years who comes in daily to help with the washing and the baby. This is what life is when it is for the better.

§

So now I am a married woman, an likely to be so until the end of me life unless I becomes a widow, which it would be wicked to think on. Here in the cottage we can have everything the way we wants and the baby, little Laura, will grow up safe. In all me life I never knew feelings like I have for this little bairn. I loves her more than anythin' in the world, an here's me machine from Marleys, where we's finished now, an we can make arl the little frocks. She has black hair that comes from Bob's family, not the pale auburn of ours, and the hair is curly, plenty black curls, mind. She's a pretty bairn, lookya. Once or twice a week I gans o'er the water ti see me Ganny an fer her ti see the babby. I goes when me uncles is not there. Me brothers is nay there neither. Arl three o' them is wed an livin' wi' their wives' Mams. They arl wed wi' canny lasses when we left, so there is strangers living where we used to be on the ground floor o' number 24 but Ganny Laidlaw is still upstairs. Her legs is bad, mind, so I unrolls her stocking an I rubs 'em wi' Sloanes Linament. Me little brother Tom wed Lizzie Mills, sister of Swanny and Smithy, and our little companion when I was a scholar. An he has a garden. It's on a piece of land not far from the Shore an there he can grow bonny flowers and vegetables which he brings to me if there's too many for him and Lizzie an arl them. Our little Tom, he's so content in his garden.

I has been many times since Laura was born ti see Miss Laura and Mr. Hopkinson. It isna very far from here to the Cloisters at Christ Church. I dunna tak little Laura ti see him, for Lily Atkinson is canny an will mind her, which she loves having no babbies of her own. Babbies makes a noise, they canna help it, an when I goes ti see Hoppy it's a time to talk, which we do, just like before. There's things I canna talk to Hoppy of, mind. I canna talk ti anybody of, except sometimes Lily, but she isna married an she canna really understand. She says arl men is beasts, an that's tha', an she is glad tha' she has the bandy legs an men dunna like her.

Bob is a good husband except for that one thing, and that one thing is wha' men must have. I canna be doing with it though, an when he comes near me I canna help but turn away, and inside there is nought but shrinking and fear. I canna bear him to put his hand on me that way. In all other ways I keeps a good home for him. His meals is good an what he likes an all, but I must keep him away from me, for I canna stand him close.
Yet I thank the Lord every day for little Laura. She is more precious to me than anything I have ever known.

§

Meggie turns away from her husband, shuddering at his touch, afraid to show the genuine affection she feels in case it encourages him. For whole days rejected and denied he does not speak to her, until his anger bursts and empties out in a fury that brings his fists down on to the table so that crockery and glass shakes and sometimes shatters. His whippet, Rippy, runs cowering under the table or the chest of drawers for safety and the little child, Laura, watches, her heart pounding with an unknown terror, not understanding why this man who often brings her an apple or an orange which he has hidden in his coat pocket, can change to become an unpredictable force that shakes the very boundaries of safety in which they are enclosed. At night when she lies in her little bed, stiff with fear, she can hear his voice rising to a crescendo of anger and then falling to an almost inaudible hiss.

"What d'ye think, Meggie! D'ye think a life at sea is easy? Is that what ye thinks? Tell me, woman, is that what ye thinks?"

"I know it is not, Bob."

"I hate the sea, d'ye hear me? There's not a day goes by when I don't curse it and the life it's forced me to."

"I know, Bob."

"What d'you think I feels, climbing from a bit boat up the dark side of a ship with the ropes swaying and and lashing against the steel in the force of a gale and the ladder itself lurching and disappearing into a black mountain of freezing water. I'll tell you what I feel woman! Fear! No! Terror, that's what I feel, though I must go through it every day and most likely every night."

"I know, Bob."

"What d'ye think it's like to steer a great iron monster into harbour against heaving waters in a gale. D'ye think I like it? I'm sick, woman, sick as a dog over the side, and I carry out me duties just the same and never fail, heaving and vomiting and cursing the sea."

"I know, Bob, I know life is hard."

"Hard! Hard she says. I know, Bob, life is hard, but get on with it so that me and the bairn can sit here by the warm fire and not be bothered."

"It's not that, Bob. I don't think that."

"And why d'ye think I does it? Uhm? Tell me that. Why d'ye think I does it? Go on tell me!"

Meggie cannot answer. She looks down and her nervous dressmaker's fingers make little rows of pleats in her apron.

He clenches his fist and raises it as if to hit this pathetic creature who does not look at him and cannot answer. Then he holds back and pounds the table as if to show the force with which he would have struck her.

"Why do I do it, uhm? It's not because me father and me grandfather and his father and God knows how many fathers before that did it and cursed it, same as me, no, it's because it's the only way I know of bringing in the wages that keep you and the bairn in safety. It's the only way I know of keeping you from what you came from, though God knows, you spend enough time going back there."

Still Meggie sits, her eyes lowered as if to concentrate on the feverish activity of her fingers. "And what does I get when I returns to me own hearth and me own bed, uhm? What does I get? Answer me, Meggie!"

In the little bedroom that adjoins the room, with the door left slightly open so that she can see the gaslight and not be frightened in the dark, little Laura hears her father's terrifying voice, and the even more terrifying silence that follows it, and she wishes that her Mam would speak and make it all right again. She cannot hear her Mam, what has happened to her? Where is she? Her father's voice again.

"I'll tell ye what I gets! A cold woman who turns her back on me and says she's tired. Tired, when are ye not tired? Ye don't know what tired is. Ye don't know what terror of the sea is and ye've never seen the pictures in yeer mind of good shipmates with their faces turned upwards in panic towards ye as they drown. What comfort can ye give as a wife, Meggie? None, nothing."

Meggie looks up. " I tries to make a good home for ye Bob. I tries to give ye good food and keep a clean house."

"An what about me rights? Me conjugal rights that are mine by law, and that ye vowed when ye married. What about them?"

"Me body is me own, Bob, and it belongs to nay body but me. When ye did what ye did to me before we was married, ye knew it was wrong an ye knew that I didna even understand what ye were about, but I know it now." She looks down and her fingers twist on the apron again. " Bob, I respect you for the man you are and the struggles and hardship you endure, and I do my best, God knows, I try, but I willna let you use my body whenever the desire takes you."

"It's my right, woman! You and your body are mine by right. Ye have no business to be telling me I have no right to your body at any time I choose. I am your husband and your master. I am head of this house, though no-one would know it by the way I am shoved aside for you and the babby. Ye can cuddle and fondle the babby all the time, but when your own husband asks for a bit of it, it's nay, too tired Bob an all that. Well let me tell you, woman, there are females out there who are willing to take your place and give their warmth to a seaman and comfort him with the solace of their bodies." He clutches the edge of the table and gasps for breath. Then there is silence.

Bob Brown turns and still breathing unevenly makes his way into the back yard, slamming the door behind him. Pulling open the door to the privy he sits down on the wooden seat and latches the door. It is the only place where he can hide himself, here despite the foul air and the squares of newspaper hanging from the hook by the door he can let the tight anger on his face crumble. Women, many of them, had welcomed his advances in the past, and he had not expected to encounter resistance. This had not happened before so why should it now with this ordinary woman who was his wife? His wife! There were a score of women who would have been glad to be married to him, who accepted his sexual advances with eagerness, so why has he now found himself with a wife who rejects him, who shudders at his touch. She sits by the fire caressing the child and has not one caress for him. And the child, the little girl, Laura, does not he, her father have a right to care for her? Does not he also love her? Does not he want to show her the great ships and teach her the ways of the sea, and maybe take her to the Pilot House and aboard a great vessel that he commands as Pilot, and on the way home buy hot pies and peas to eat together, he and his daughter? Yet he is kept away, is set outside this close bonding between her and her mother. He is an outsider in his own home. Bob Brown lowers his collapsed face into his hands and sobs.

§

After little Ernie Spooner is born, a miraculous thing happens. Preacher is seen again in Newcastle and is reported to have finished with the Saving of Souls for the present time and it is said that he has stated his sincere intention of re-joining his dear wife and two babies in Sunderland as quickly as possible (for Saved Souls cannot be abandoned at a moment's notice). Mary's heart is filled with joy and anticipation, and she is not disappointed, for Preacher returns, swearing his loyal and undying love, as well as the fulfilment he feels (which she and her whole family must share) at having obeyed God's command, though it was hard enough to bear. Thomas Brown, rejoices quietly in his daughter's happiness, but knows that one more person in the house means one more mouth to feed. His wife is secretly relieved that her daughter has a visible husband once more and Meggie is happy because Mary is happy. Only Sarah stands aloof from all this delight and views Preacher with cold eyes. Preacher does not like Sarah.

"Meggie," says Mary, "ye have only the one bairn, while me and Preacher has two an Preacher says that more wad be a blessing. Do ye and Bob no want more bairns, then?"

"I dunna care for what Bob wants, Mary, I will have nay more babbies. Little Laura is me love and joy, an I wants nay more."

"But how do ye go about that, then, Meggie? I mean, babbies comes whether ye wants them or no."

"Haway, Mary lass. Do ye no ken what they can give ye at the chemist. If ye falls pregnant ye goes to see the chemist an he will give ye what ye need ti get rid of it."

"I wad never want to get rid of Preacher's babby."

"Aye, well, not all women's the same as ye, mind."

"That's true, lass. And not all men is same as my Preacher who is loved by all."

"Not by your sister."

"Sarah is vexed because she has nay man."

"She says that Preacher will be on his way again soon."

"Nay, Meggie, he wullna. He has promised me he wullna and the Calling willna come again." She puts her mouth to Meggie's ear and whispers, "he willna go, Meggie, because another babby is coming. Tis a secret, mind." Meggie hugs her dear sister-in-law.

"D'ye not mind then, what Preacher does ti ye to get them babbies?"

"Mind! Nay, I know I should mind because good women doesna like it, but

I likes it an so does Preacher."

Meggie nods her head and squeezes Mary's hand.

"Is it no the same for ye, then. Meggie?"

"Gerraway, lass. We'll no talk of such things." She turns away, "tell me what little frocks ye needs for Flo."

Nine and a half months after the rejoicing at Preacher's reunion with his wife and family, little Annie is born. Preacher is called away by the Lord just one month before her birth. Sarah gleefully reports that he has been seen in Hastings on the south coast of England, and that he has another wife and family there. Mary refuses to believe it. It is later said and dutifully repeated by Sarah that there are those who have caught a glimpse of him in Australia. Whatever the truth, Preacher has gone, never to return.

Mary continues to smile and hope whilst she struggles to bring up her fatherless bairns, but her secret heart is heavy with an aching sorrow.

BENTINCK VILLAS
NEWCASTLE-UPON-TYNE
AUGUST 1928

CHAPTER TWENTY

The Reverend Canon Charles Girdlestone Hopkinson, retired, and Mrs. Laura Hopkinson now live in Newcastle upon Tyne. Mrs. Hopkinson waits anxiously in the room nearest to the front door so that she can answer it herself, when the bell rings. In any case their faithful servant Clancey, who has been with her husband since he first came to Monkwearmouth so many years ago, is as old as they are, and it will take her a while to hobble to the door. At the time expected, the door bell rings, a little tentatively, and Mrs Hopkinson hurries to open the door. Clancey's slow and painful footsteps can be heard climbing the basement kitchen stairs.

"It's all right, Clancey," calls Mrs. Hopkinson, "I will answer it."

This reassurance from her employer does not entirely satisfy the elderly servant. It is her job to answer the door and she has always done so. In this way she not only convinces herself, the Canon and his wife of her continued usefulness despite the years that have passed but she also keeps track of what is going on in the household. By the time she reaches the top of the stairs and opens the baize door, however, Mrs. Hopkinson has opened it and beyond her, in the doorway Clancey can make out the figure of Meggie Balcombe, modestly dressed in a brown cloche shaped hat and a good cloth coat. "My!" she thinks, "she's not fat but she's put on a bit weight since she was a lass."

"Meggie, come in," says Mrs. Hopkinson, "thankyou so much for coming, dear Meggie. I hope the journey was not too difficult."

"No, Miss Laura, I took the tram and the train. It was a nice trip."

Mrs. Hopkinson takes her by the hand and draws her over the doorstep and into the hall. Meggie notices that Miss Laura is still a fine looking woman with straight strong features, despite her age. She has not been influenced by the shorter hemlines now fashionable and still wears a plain longer day dress in the Edwardian style.

"I knew you would come, Meggie. It will cheer him so much to see you."

"Is Mr. Hopkinson very poorly, Miss Laura?"

"His health has gone down a bit since you last saw him, my dear, but it is largely his spirits that have suffered. He complains a good deal, which was not his way. As I say, his spirits are rather low. He will be the better for seeing you. I am afraid I am not the right company for him just now. I am probably rather dull."

"Oh no, Miss Laura, tha' canna be true. You were always so cheerful to us folk, always there to help us, and mind, we was always needing something from your father and yourself, and we couldna' give you much."

"It was a long time ago, Meggie, it was all a very long time ago."

"But we remembers it all, mind. We remembers how good you and your father was to us."

"How long ago did Ganny die, Meggie?"

"A good ten years ago now."

"Oh, of course, but we have seen you many times at the Rectory since then. You have always been a faithful visitor, Meggie, and it has meant so much to us, to both of us."

"She was nigh on ninety years though. She was living wi' me brother John and his wife, but her legs was very bad with ulcers. It was a sadness to her, mind, because her legs was so nimble when she used to dance a reel or a hornpipe wi' me Granda. They say she was never the same, mind, after she lost him, Granda Johnny, many years back."

"I remember your Granda Johnny. He had the blue eyes. My father used to say they were strangers' eyes because he never looked at home on dry land. And your brothers, Meggie, how are they?"

"They's all in Monkwearmouth still. Arl married, wi' sons, me nephews."

"And what of you Meggie? How are you and your husband, and your little girl."

"Me girl is no little now, Miss Laura. She's a good musician, like Bob, an she works in Ferry and Foster, the piano shop and plays the piano there for the customers when they comes to buy the music."

"And Bob, how is he?"

"He is top pilot now to Doxfords. He has a motor car."

"A motor car!"

"Aye, an he is proud of it, mind. Only the bosses has motor cars, but then they has big houses and grounds. Bob must get his motor down the back lane and into our yard, but he doesna mind that. He takes us out into the country for a drive on Sundays."

"Oh Meggie. Things have changed for you since those bad old days in Hardwick Street."

"They was not bad old days, Miss Laura. Sometimes I thinks that they were the best days even though there was a lot of sadness."

"Well, every thing is good now, and I'm glad to hear your news, dear Meggie. My husband will be so cheered to see you. Clancey, I see you lurking there. Take Meggie's coat will you. Come let's go and find my husband."

Laura Hopkinson leads the way to the Study and knocks. She opens the door gently. Inside a good fire burns in the grate and Charles Hopkinson sits beside it in an armchair, his knees covered in a tartan shawl. He is considerably thinner than he used to be and his face is pale and drawn.

" I will leave you with him," says his wife, quietly closing the door behind her.

Meggie approaches the armchair in which he sits.

"How are you, Mr. Hopkinson?" she says.

He does not turn to look at her as she draws nearer but he says, "Meggie, I have been waiting for you. My wife told me you would come. Sit down, sit down, lass."

Meggie pulls up a little stool and sits beside him, taking his hand. He sighs deeply.

"You are not well," she says.

"Well enough, Meggie," he says. "Very soon I shall be taking my leave and moving onwards. I am looking forward to the great adventure."

Meggie's eyes fill with tears, "Oh no. Hoppy, no, don't go, don't leave us."

"There is no need for distress, canny lass,"

"But you have known us since I was a bairn, Hoppy, an when me Mam and me Dad died you were with us an helped us, an now — "

"Meggie, it is nearly my time to go." He leans forward urgently, his eyes bright as he takes her hands and searches her face. "It's nearly my time to leave. There is no sadness in it for us canny lass. But before I go, Meggie, there is something I must know."

She looks back at him, her eyes full of tears.

"It was for the best, Meggie, wasn't it?"

She looks down at her hands, now tightly held in his.

"Meggie, you must answer me please. It was for the best, wasn't it, Meggie."

She cannot speak and the tears roll down her cheeks. She would like to wipe them away with her hands, but he holds them tighter, and his gaze becomes more urgent.

"It was not, then! Oh my canny lass. What have you suffered?"

"No, no, Hoppy, no. I canna say what would have been the best. How can us know that? We only know what was. It was you gave us the best, that strong Faith that has been with us since you first came and we had many a talk, though I was just a bairn. That love for me Church an for God, an all. That's what ye gave us, Hoppy. There could have been no better thing than that."

His grip on her hands loosens and he searches in his pocket for a handkerchief. Then he gently wipes her eyes.

"Here, Meggie take it," he says.

"An I will wash it, Hoppy, an bring it back all ironed."

He smiles, that same wide smile with eyes full of humour that he always had. "Ach aye, Meggie, see that ye do, mind, and bring it back, but if I am not here, if I have gone on my adventuring, then keep it, Meggie. Keep it well for me. Will ye do that, canny lass?"

AUTHOR'S NOTE

Margaret Laidlaw (Ganny Laidlaw) died on the 1st of March 1914 in Barrington St. Monkwearmouth. The cause of death was 'extreme old age'. She was being cared for by her grandson and his wife.

Meggie Balcombe died in 1968, aged 95. She lived at 7 Guildford St until 1965.

Bob Brown died of a massive stroke in 1948 at 7 Guildford Street.

Laura Brown, died in 2002 aged 102. She lived in her own house and looked after herself until three weeks before her death.

Charles Girdlestone Hopkinson became a Canon and died in Newcastle in September 1928. He continued as the dear friend and Spiritual Adviser to Meggie Balcombe for over forty years.

It would not have been possible to write this book without the tireless help of very many people in Sunderland. In particular I would probably never have got started without the encouragement over the Internet, and the photographs of 7 Guildford Street that he took for me, of Peter Clark. I bothered Margaret Thynne relentlessly, and she always came up with Census records for me and shared her enthusiasm for old Monkwearmouth. Arthur Burnside chased around finding me newspaper cuttings and genealogical information. He has acted as a friend and strong link for me with St Peter's Church, Monkwearmouth and contacted my relatives still living in Monkwearmouth in particular Ella Bell, granddaughter of Meggie Balcombe's brother Tom. In Berwick-on-Tweed I have to thank Ken Brown a superb genealogist, and Ann Booker who researched the early life of Catherine Hogarth. I am of course deeply indebted to the Revd Ben Hopkinson and his brother Giles Hopkinson, grandsons of Charles Girdlestone Hopkinson, who have allowed me to see their Grandfather's letters and notes for sermons, and told me so much about his life.

I am grateful to Chris Mullin MP for inviting me to the Doxford house which Laura Brown visited as a child, and overwhelmingly I have to thank Douglas Smith of the Sunderland Antiquarian Society for the endless delving into the Archives which he did for me, his inspiring letters, advice on dialect, and massive encouragement. Jamie Strength's Toast in Chapter Two is my personal thankyou and tribute to Douglas.

Most of all of course I have to thank my grandmother, Meggie, and my mother, Laura. As an only child I was required to sit still and be quiet, and so it came about that from a very early age I absorbed their stories. In the last months of her life, my mother told me much more. I hope I have done justice to the people I have written about, all of whom without exception, lived their lives with courage.

Maeve Creber

Maeve Creber has written books for speech and language handicapped children, as well as drama and features for radio and TV. She taught 19th and 20th Century Literature at University of Exeter. She lives with her husband in Devon and France.